Boy Crazy at Barnard College: 1962-1964

Angela Weiss

I do not assume that woman is better than man.
I do assume she has a different way of looking at things.
Susan B. Anthony

Bearissa Books - Los Angeles

PREFACE

I'm dedicating this volume to:

> Dear friend Carina and true gentlemen Max, Yeats, and Jake
>
> *Boy Crazy: The Secret Life of a 1950s Girl* and *Boy Crazy 1960-1962: The High School Diary* appreciative readers whose sequel requests inspired this final diary novel.

Presuming that you have read these prior *Boy Crazy* books, this sequel refers to events and characters in those books without repeating details. The end lists can help refresh your memory.

As Sergeant Joe Friday said on the 1960s TV program, *Dragnet*, "Names have been changed to protect the innocent."

Terminology changes. This book preserves the historically accurate, respectful term, Negro. Black and African American came later.

The year was 1962. I was still boy crazy and the world continued to be crazy, too!

CONTENTS

DIARY EXCERPTS
Prologue

Tuesday, September 18, 1962: Fright

Dear Diary, my cheeks felt wet with tears of sadness and distress. Out of breath and half asleep, I felt my heart thudding as I emerged from a disturbing nightmare:

> On a rainy night in Manhattan, I was chasing my beloved Aunt Sara. Elusive, she stayed out of reach no matter how fast I ran. I became aware of being pursued by my obnoxious parents, the bane of my existence since Sara left our home and became estranged from our entire family three years ago. I awoke as Sara seemed to disappear ahead and my parents, more like ogres, were gaining on me.

This dream confuses me. I'm happy about imminent escape from a jealous, hostile mother and angry, controlling father, who ruined my social life until senior year.

Having survived frustrations, I'm baffled about what submerged feelings have produced this upsetting nightmare. Why now when I'm grateful to be high school valedictorian with necessary scholarships and acceptance at an elite college?

Conversations with Sara while she wrote her family mental health book introduced me to fascinating psychology. Our kind family social worker has inspired me to alter my lawyer career goal to psychologist.

Eager to resume my wonderful close relationship with Sara, I'll be only forty-three blocks from her apartment. The fading dream left uneasiness, as I finished packing. I barely fit in the back of our five-year-old Oldsmobile sedan, packed with my linens and clothes, for the 150-mile NY State Thruway drive to college.

Musician Aunt Sara playing piano 1940s

1962 NYC Freshman

Sapere aude (Dare to know)

Roman poet **Horace**

<u>Wednesday, September 19, 1962: Liberty</u>
After years living like a caged bird eager for unrestricted flight, I've escaped from Albany. What could be better than living in NYC where I've always had a fabulous time? I'm excited and thankful to be at Barnard College, across Broadway from hordes of cute Columbia guys!

I'm lucky to be matched with roommate Carina, about five foot seven with long, straight, light brown hair; fair, freckled skin; enviable blue eyes; a curvier figure than mine; and a jolly smile! I'm five-five with dark brown hair and eyes.

Built in 1907, our traditional Brooks Hall dorm links new Reid with utilitarian, brown-brick Hewitt Hall in a U-shape. The bathroom with seven stall showers for ten girls in our wing is near our spacious, baby blue room. The large bookcase should suffice for tons of required reading. Brass andirons for our non-working, red-brick fireplace add charm.

On the mantel, Carina placed a photo of her good-looking, blue-eyed family. "Angela, I already miss my younger sister and three younger brothers. Last year, we moved to Indiana from Dayton, Ohio. We lived in Israel before that."

"Did your father's job change?

"As a World War II American naval officer, he helped Israel develop its navy before becoming a corporate executive."

"He sounds remarkable! I couldn't wait to get away from my parents, whose Jews-only dating rules forced me to turn down great gentile guys I adored."

"My parents, though active members of Sinai Temple, have let us decide whom to date, not that I've been asked much." I appreciated her good-natured grin.

"Angela, we can watch good-night kissing from our window looking down at the main dorm entrance." I laughed.

After a delicious roast-chicken dinner, all 200 dorm frosh went to a pajama party with skits and folk singing put on by student sponsors. I asked my senior sponsor from Brooklyn, "What if we return from a date after curfew?"

I giggled hearing, "The electric chair is out. They probably won't chain you to your bed after the first offense. Multiple violations might mean life imprisonment. Subway train delays require starting back in plenty of time to prevent latenesses."

Despite fatigue and a cold, I'm glorying in new freedom. Dorm fun reminds me of 1957 Girl Scout overnight camp, but sans campfires. My bed even has the same ancient brown and mint-green wool blankets over blue-flannel sheets.

Thursday, September 20, 1962: Orientation
In the mundane dorm cafeteria, a tasty tuna salad preceded the placement test for Barnard's mandatory hygiene class. Two Columbia freshmen guided a few of us Barnard Honeybears to the busy bookstore. At Barnard, ping-pong with two prowling Columbia Lions was fun.

At the red-brick St. Paul's Chapel, under a beautiful dome, daylight came through a circle of about twenty small windows. Though Columbia is nonsectarian, did its original Anglican affiliation make us a captive audience to the university's religious counseling service?

I wrote Cousin Ron:

> How do you like Philadelphia? I wish you could have been at today's orientation! As the brother of a Columbia grad, do you already know these facts about the fifth oldest American college (oldest in NY State), founded in 1754 before the Revolution?

Five US founding fathers studied at Columbia,
including John Jay and Alexander Hamilton (who
married at Albany's Schuyler Mansion near our
Morton apartment).
Daily *Columbia Spectator* is the nation's second-
oldest student newspaper.
Both Roosevelt presidents attended Columbia's
law school.
Famous Columbia alumni include Rogers and
Hammerstein, creators of musicals I love.
Nineteen Columbians have won Nobel prizes,
including Teddy Roosevelt for peace.
Pulitzer left money to Columbia to administer
his prizes.
At a banquet including yummy turkey, Barnard's
acting president, Henry Boorse, a famous atomic
physicist who helped develop the bomb,
welcomed us 360 freshmen. I'm eager to meet
girls from thirty-one states and twelve foreign
countries. Please write soon! Love, Angela

At the wonderful Greek Games hurdling demonstration, we
learned about Honeybear athletic and artistic talents!

"Carina, I'm pleased that Barnard considers us equal to
men. Surprised that we can stay out until one-thirty on
weekends, I'm okay listing the destination for my dates. I'll
write the freshmen curfew as my return time, e.g., ten-thirty
for weeknights. Being here is magnificent!" She agreed.

Friday, September 21, 1962: Dutiful Letter to Parents

Today's Honor Board workshop was superfluous
for us non-cheaters. Afternoon building tours,
e.g., the library, were useful. At the Barnard-
Columbia lawn party, tall Marcus and jockey-
sized Udeh from AHS and their youthfully high-

spirited roommates chatted with me. All praised their Core Curriculum literature and humanities readings. Musical Udeh said, "Hootenannies are popular. A guitar player starts singing folk songs and others join in." Ping pong with three of the eight men I met was fun.

At the Columbia-Barnard freshman dance, a nice, brown-haired, heavily built junior host talked to and danced with this lowly freshman all evening! I'm exhilarated!

<u>Saturday, September 22, 1962: The Village</u>
Spike from the ping-pong room and I attended a Columbia student hootenanny. When the subway to Greenwich Village lurched slightly, I looked at him, wondering about an emergency. He just shrugged as if it were normal.

At The Bitter End nightclub, first-rate comedians and singers performed! "Why are you called Spike?" I asked.

"On my volleyball team, I couldn't resist spiking the ball." We laughed.

Later, when Carina asked about Spike, I replied, "Joking often, he's average in height and weight with a ruddy complexion, goofy smile, medium brown hair, and hazel eyes.

"At today's orientation, I didn't find the other Albany freshmen: Eileen from expensive, girls-only St. Agnes and Ellen from Milne, a state school. Barnard's government with three branches seems as complex as the state and American governments!" She chuckled. I shared Mother's letter:

> Your roommate seems very nice. We're happy that she's Jewish. Your Aunt Rhoda served a good dinner before we left. She misses Uncle Harvey as much as ever. At least, she's near Aunt Lila.
>
> Driving to Albany through the rain was miserable. Our person-to-person call to a fake

name at Lila's number signaled our safe arrival without paying for a long-distance call. Two boarders now fill our empty nest.

Sunday, September 23, 1962: Triple Fascination

Ping pong with blue-eyed, Yonkers triplets preceded dancing at their Alpha Epsilon Pi Jewish frat party. Playful extravert Zed sculpts, like his mother, but is flunking art history. Pre-med Ted offered a massage! They're identical; introvert physics major Ned is fraternal and mentally in outer space.

My former AHS steady boyfriend called from University of Rochester. His deep voice asked, "Did you get my fall weekend invitation? I can pay your expenses."

"Luke, thank you! I'm sorry that my reply hasn't arrived. With every Barnard girl a valedictorian, I'll have to study every weekend to prevent flunking out." I felt bad when he sounded disappointed. Though fond of Luke, I want to meet new men.

Monday, September 24, 1962: Posture and Beats

Having miraculously passed the freshmen posture exam, Carina and I can skip striding with books on heads in posture class. She joked, "The January posture contest prize must be a heavy tome to maintain posture."

With three years of Latin ending in mid-1961, I'm lucky that last week's placement exam put me in third semester Latin. Professor L (below) said, "A high school year equates to a college semester." Married to a Rutgers history professor, she's a fun role model for pursuing a professional career.

In the evening, affable Spike and I ping-ponged before fun with his pals at West End Café at 2911 Broadway, south of 114 Street. "Angela, this worn bar has been famous since 1940s Beat writers Allen Ginsberg and Jack Kerouac drank here." Though I'm three months younger than NY State's minimum alcohol age, age proof was skipped for my Singapore slings. Though I can take or leave alcohol, it's part of campus social life.

Tuesday, September 25, 1962: Improvisation

The dorm's traditional living room was ablaze with light. Alto chanteuse Carina and a Columbia pianist entertained a rapt group with jazz standards!

Back from a West End Café drink with humorist Spike, I admired Carina's new drawings and poems, which her mom also composes. I beamed. "Carina, at the ping-pong table, junior Hy was like honey to this Honeybear!"

"Better than Spike?" she inquired.

I nodded. She grinned knowingly before I enjoyed letters from Cousin Ron, Mother, and Luke.

Thursday, September 27, 1962: Classes

We freshmen joined 840 older Honeybears at the mandatory opening convocation in the gym. During boring speeches, I surreptitiously read today's *Barnard Bulletin* newspaper, which deemed my sweet Latin prof a *notable scholar*. A Phi Beta Kappa Barnard grad, she taught for three years at Bryn Mawr College, where she received her M.A. and Ph.D.

Though ping pong with Spike was fun, today's high point was accepting a date with lanky redhead Hy!

Friday, September 28, 1962: Ron
Craig's amusing letter from Hamilton College left me light-hearted as I signed out for an overnight at Aunt Lila's on the East side. I said, "Thank you all for helping me attend Barnard! I hope that scholarships and summer jobs enable me to finish."

Lila, dressed smartly in a burgundy jacketed dress, was reassuring. "You're welcome. Everything will be fine, dear."

Home for the Jewish New Year weekend, Cousin Ron (below left with Luke and me) confided, "Temple University is swarming with pretty Jewish girls. Though older guys monopolize freshmen, I'm holding my own. Dating in Philly is fun! Thanks for your letter!"

I summarized recent dates before Ron mentioned Luke. "Ron, I had to decline a Rochester weekend to keep up academically. In NYC, I'd date Luke, along with exciting Lions, without going steady. I wrote thanks for the cute University of Rochester night shirt he sent!"

<u>Saturday, September 29, 1962: Synagogue and Marienbad</u>
Negroes aren't the only segregated citizens. Preferring co-ed seating at Albany's Conservative temple, I put up with Orthodox gender separation on the Kehilath Jeshurun women's balcony. At Aunt Lila's birthday lunch, I diplomatically stayed silent before Ron dropped me at Barnard.

Ping pong with pleasant Spike preceded my best date. Attractive Hy and I were exuberant, watching Columbia's football team beat Brown, 22-20!

After subwaying to West 56 Street, we entered under the dark Orsini's Cafe awning. In the cozy room at a table with a starched, white cloth, we downed pastries and drinks under flattering lighting. Hy grinned. "Angela, you may spot famous faces here." His warm, booming voice uttered perceptive remarks about *Last Year at Marienbad*, the sophisticated, stylish French film we saw. Snuggling during the mysterious movie and good-night kissing were dreamy!

<u>Sunday, September 30, 1962: Replies</u>
While my laundry finished in the dorm basement washers, I answered close AHS friend Doreen in Buffalo, in part:

> Barnard is perfect! I've yearned to be in an anonymous, cosmopolitan city. Staying on campus and on Broadway during the day, we can walk alone without fearing crime. Outside Barnard gates after dark, we need escorts. We avoid Morningside Park east of Columbia and Harlem north of 125 Street. Even in safer Riverside Park, we need companions.

I wrote Cousin Lydia (photo below), who also misses Aunt Sara:

> What's new at Gloversville High School?
> About two miles north of Sara, I long to see her and hope to get up my nerve soon. Has

she forgiven me for being dumbstruck when my parents were meanly skeptical about the rape attempt she escaped?

Our freshman orientation package lists Barnard as a Seven Sisters women's liberal arts college. Others, affiliated since 1927, are Bryn Mawr in Pennsylvania, Radcliffe at Harvard, Vassar in Poughkeepsie, and Wellesley, Smith, and Mount Holyoke in Massachusetts towns.

The Ivy League colleges educate our counterparts: Columbia, Harvard, Yale, Brown, Princeton, University of Pennsylvania, Cornell, and Dartmouth.

<u>Monday, October 1, 1962: Homework</u>
On my gray Smith-Corona portable typewriter, I typed the assigned English essay *Who I Am*:

Who am I? Like many Honeybears and other young people of my generation and like many individuals in every country, I am a seeker. Some of my needs are common to much of humanity. Few may share my occupational aims. To know my motives and aspirations is to know who I am to a considerable extent.

For the past seventeen years, I have been fortunate. My mother and father wisely forced me to choose the more difficult road to make me a better person. Although I am an only child, my parents avoided indulging me, expecting proficiency and independence. Academic success and social gratification were the fruits harvested from seeds they planted.

Having received many tangible and spiritual gifts from various sources, I want to give of myself to help others enjoy happiness. Careful consideration of my abilities and inadequacies helped me conclude that I may do the most good as a psychologist.

In addition to professional training, I seek classes in new and diverse areas, information to enjoy, to contribute to greater awareness and tolerance, and to help me cope successfully with the vicissitudes of Twentieth-Century life.

Outside of class, Barnard enriches through socializing with intelligent men and women from different backgrounds.

Emancipation from parents has boosted my confidence. Conducting one's own affairs

with relatively little supervision is a pleasure.
Four years at Barnard should unchain my mind
and motivate a lifelong search for knowledge
and freedom from ignorance.

Perhaps the most important need is a
yearning for love and security. Eventually, I hope
to find a man to love who loves me. I want a
close relationship of giving and receiving and
sharing, a husband to respect and trust, as well
as love and admire.

Raising offspring who mature into
secure, happy adults seems complicated when
contemplating today's spoiled and lazy children,
insecure and defiant adolescents, and immature
and discontented adults.

In addition to a close family life, I desire
a few true friends and acquaintances with
common interests for enjoyable companionship.

What I seek is challenging. Complete
success may elude me. As an incurable idealist
and a perfectionist at times, I will be a seeker all
my life. I hope that Robert Louis Stevenson was
right: *To travel hopefully is a better thing than to
arrive, and the true success is to labor.*

Tuesday, October 2, 1962: Dominic

Following a mandatory freshman assembly, I found pink phone
message forms taped to our door. Until the switchboard closes
at 10:30 PM, whoever's on phone duty promptly answers the
incoming house phone down the hall in case guys call. Who left
my first MCNM mystery message (Man Called, No Message)?
Returning the second message at the downstairs pay phone
resulted in a West End Café dinner with manly Dominic
(below), a favorite AHS classmate, taller than I with hazel eyes.

Bursting with excitement, Dominic showed cheek dimples, as he reported this progress:

> James Meredith became the first Negro student at the University of Mississippi! Can you imagine that Southern bigots blocked an Air Force veteran who served our country for nine years from entering college last month? Because of rioting, 500 US marshals, military police,

Mississippi National Guard troops, and U.S. Border Patrol officials had to ensure his admission. Thank God for JFK and Bobby Kennedy!

"Carina, I'm thankful to be here on scholarships when smart, informed friends like Dominic live at home and go to Albany State Teachers' College. At the AHS orchestra concert, his Tchaikovsky's Piano Concerto in B Flat Minor solo was a hit."

Visualizing his masculine hands, I imagined caresses before Carina inquired about last night's date with red-haired Hy.

"He rewarded library hours with ice cream and two date invites, including Homecoming! I can't wait!"

<u>Wednesday, October 3, 1962: Henrietta</u>
"Carina, my AHS friend (above), kindly sent a Jewish holiday card and article: *Albany State College News, President Greets New Students*:

Appropriate Attire
Men attending the reception are requested to wear dark suits. Women should wear dark dresses with hats and gloves.

"Luckless Henrietta in the reception line, inching along in uncomfortable heels to greet uninteresting big wigs, was part of the herd of 750 dressed-up freshmen."

<u>Thursday, October 4, 1962: Survival</u>
Carina commented, "I love French literature and my small English seminar. I already regret taking physical and cultural anthropology simultaneously to finish science requirements. How are you?"

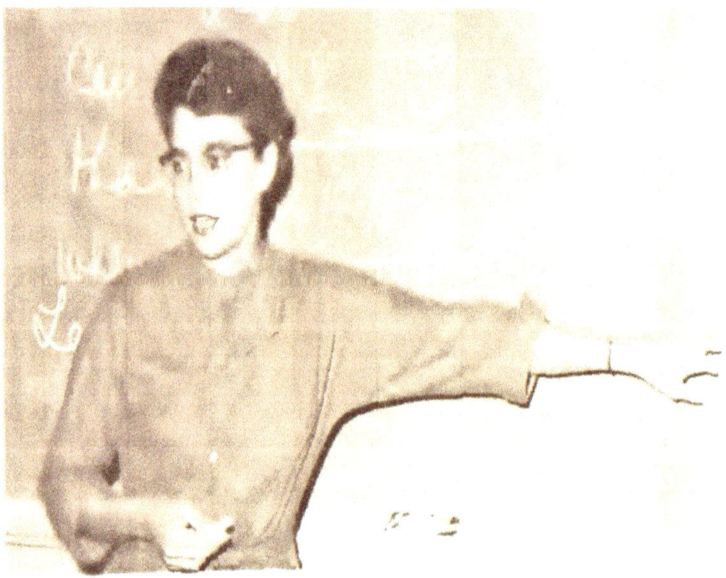

Professor Janette Eliott

"Struggling with 8 AM differential calculus in a huge lecture hall, I learned many of the brains had calculus in NYC high schools. My homework problems are often wrong. I must work up nerve and stop shirking a visit to scary Associate Professor E (above). Always stern, she cracks no jokes."

Carina smiled. "Math has never been my forte. At lunch, we missed watching you down the usual mint-chocolate-chip ice cream."

I grinned. "I ate the only library vending machine candy bar I like: Chunky with Brazil nuts and raisins in thick milk chocolate. Hy's one-hour call was my reward for non-stop library study without cafeteria lunch!"

<u>Friday, October 5, 1962: Sweet Letter</u>
My widowed aunt would disapprove of Chunky superseding fasting:

My dear Angela, I hope you're in a routine which isn't too consuming. Sorry your tummy is still upset. It must be the food or the tenseness. Last night, dear old Kaopectate helped me.

Nothing much here except hard bookkeeping work at the office.

Making meals, etc. for boarders must bog down your mother.

Well, my darling, just wanted you to know I do think of you. The phone tempts me, but I understand it takes away from your study time and others who share it.

I'll be eager to hear of your social life first chance you have. I wish you could spend Yom Kippur with us. It's easier to fast together. If you can join us, come Sunday for Kol Nidre services and stay over for Yom Kippur services. Uncle Bert will surely take you back Monday night. All my love, Aunt Rhoda

<u>Saturday, October 6, 1962: Dress Code</u>
Lean, brown-eyed, attractive Hy and I shopped on Broadway before joining Carina and Dave, a tall junior. At his apartment off Broadway north of campus, Dave asked, "Are you following the Barnard dress code?" Puzzled trying to recall Dorm Guide and Student Handbook rules, I looked at Carina.

Chortling, Dave said, "In 1960, Columbia President Kirk disliked how Honeybears looked in *inappropriate* slacks and Bermuda shorts."

Trying to look serious, Hy warned, "Studying at Butler Library wearing Bermudas, especially if tight or more than two inches above the knee, even under a long coat, will land you in Columbia jail for life." We girls giggled.

Dave added, "Even on Barnard's campus, slacks can't be brightly colored or tight."

Carina joked, "Angela is still free, though her red-plaid slacks wake me when she leaves for calculus." Her blue plaid skirt and twin sweater set resembled my pink one.

Mentally vowing to memorize dress rules, I inquired, "Are there still panty raids?"

Affable Dave replied, "Our generals are planning one." Carina and I laughed.

Hy and I subwayed to 1678 Broadway near 52 Street. Birdland is named for brilliant saxophonist and heroin addict

Charlie Parker, who died young in 1955. Appreciating the racially-mixed audience, we tried to be the epitome of cool at the long basement bar against one wall. Fine jazz played as we subtly searched for stars through the low-lit, hazy air.

Sunday, October 7, 1962: Imposing Butler
I looked up at Hy who pointed out famous writers' names inscribed above the row of majestic Ionic columns fronting Columbia's library. "Hy, maybe by graduation, I'll be familiar with Plato and Aristotle." Studying with super-smart Hy was elating.

Answering Mother's letter, I included:

In Latin, I'm appreciating *Selections from Cicero*!
More petite than I, my fun professor wears low
heels, wool skirts, and turtle-neck or cowl-neck
sweaters. Without makeup and with straight
brown hair in a bun, she resembles the classic
educated, intellectual bluestocking. I admire her
lack of pretentiousness, approachability, and
delightful wit about Latin and Roman antiquity.

Monday, October 8, 1962: Hy's Poem
Nocturnal Ode to a Damsel in Constant Threat of Being Devoured by a Dragon, presented at Butler, touched my heart.

Mine heart riseth up with passion at the thought
of your approach,
Beating madly, wildly, it courses blood, hot and
red with longing, through mine veins.
Oh, to have you, hold you here beside me, in
this, the hour of my need!
Empty are these arms that caress not your body.
Empty are these hands that hold not yours.
Empty is this heart that has not you!

Oh, my love, these moments when I'm without
you are torturously many;
The times when I'm with you painfully few.
Eager is my love, my heart, my flesh to possess
you.
Empty is my life when we are apart.
Oh, but to tell you of the heights to which your
love makes me aspire,
This poem, dearest one, is the only outlet for my
burning soul.
Forever may be our happiness,
Or on the morrow, with golden dawn breaking
more than day, it might all end…
Still, I could find solace; for in all Life's
uncertainties, this I would know: we loved.

"Carina, appreciating that Hy expresses his urges in a
gentlemanly way, I hope that he's self-controlled. We've dated
only two weeks. I'm determined to stay a virgin until marriage.
I'm relieved that Hy's serious about school. Struggling to keep
up with assignments leaves me in a perpetual state of terror.

"Carina, though I love literature, intimidating full Professor John Kouwenhoven (above), an illustrious author, expects us twenty Honeybears to critically analyze fiction. For an *A*, must I be a sycophant, quoting in a paper from his non-fiction books: *Adventures of America, 1857-1900* (1938), *Made in America: The Arts in Modern Civilization* (1948), or *The Beer Can by the Highway* (1961)?" Carina laughed.

Tuesday, October 9, 1962: Dreaded Code
Hy and I studied at Barnard's modern library before a wonderful parting kiss.

"Carina, my sponsor confirmed that the dress code in both handbooks is real."

Carina snickered. "How many Honeybears are in jail?"

I giggled. "The guys made that up. Can you believe that tight pants and short shorts are forbidden everywhere? Caught on Columbia's campus without a long coat over even loose slacks and long Bermudas means trouble." A laughing fit relieved tension from studying.

Wednesday, October 10, 1962: Double Fun
Around 9 PM, our sweet neighbor knocked on our door. "Angela, men on different lines want to speak to you." I enjoyed chatting for the allotted five minutes each with sensitive, intellectual Hy and somewhat athletic, jokester Spike.

Thursday, October 11, 1962: From Home
"Carina, thanks for reading me your wonderful poem and the interesting letter from your family!"

Asked about my doings, I replied, "Hy and I saw Columbia lose a debate with Oxford University. AHS National Forensic League debates were engrossing.

"I had to turn down a Cornell weekend invite from Jerry, my 1961 AHS senior prom date. I'd get too far behind."

She nodded enthusiastically when I offered to read Mother's letter:

Receiving your two letters was nice. Birdland sounds like fun. When I gave your love to Tumba (below), he chirped, "Angela." He likes boarder Karen, who talks to him.

Cuba worries everyone. We hope and pray that the UN will prevent war. Kennedy is doing the right thing.

We learned more in art class Monday than all of last year. At speech class, the teacher said I did pretty well.

For Saturday's Mr. and Mrs. Club synagogue show, I'm in charge of hospitality, name tags, and introductions.

Everyone asks about you. I'm sure you passed that worrisome math test. It's very cold here. I hope that you find a warm coat.

This Saturday, save afternoon time when I'll ride there with the Levines.

"Uh oh! Carina, Saturday, I'll be with Hy at Homecoming."

<u>Friday, October 12, 1962: Holiday</u>
"Carina, how was Barnard's 4 PM coffee hour?"

"Enjoyable! Upper classmen discussed creative writing and art activities, like *Focus* literary magazine, *Barnard Bulletin* newspaper, and *Mortarboard* yearbook. Though I'm concentrating on passing courses, volunteering tempts me."

"Despite terror of flunking out, I can't resist special Lions in my little free time. I'm compensating for parents making me turn down invites until senior year with Jewish Luke."

"Did Hy take you to Brooklyn today?"

"Yes! I met his quiet father, lively redhead mother, outgoing older brother, and brother's nice-looking fiancée."

"He must be serious to bring you home!"

"Even though exceptional companion Hy is smart, fun, and cute, I'm too young to be serious about anyone. Hy and I enjoyed the Yale-Columbia glee club concert and ZBT Jewish frat party! The cap to a perfect day: drinks at the beat-up, but cool Gold Rail on Broadway near 111 Street!"

<u>Saturday, October 13, 1962: Columbia</u>
Carina asked about Homecoming. "Hy and I loved beating Yale 14-10 at football! A soaring bird escorted our meander through Riverside Park. Dinner was a tasty cheeseburger in a Gold Rail booth carved with student initials. In Greenwich Village after a subway ride, running into an AHS former date disoriented me! Hy and I saw an interesting musical comedy, *The Premise*, before Gold Rail cocktails ended another extraordinary date!"

"Angela, at a Midwest college, we'd drink soda pop until age twenty-one." Chuckling, I appreciated her fun, upbeat personality.

<u>Sunday, October 14, 1962: Open House</u>
Hy and I studied in my room. Back from the library, Carina asked, "Did you follow the three-feet-on-the-floor rule?"

I giggled. "I'm grateful that Hy is a gentleman. With the door open as required, we kissed, but mainly studied."

"Since everything is possible with four feet on the floor, I'm chuckling."

I chortled. "I'm amazed that men may be here up to three hours every other Sunday!"

Tuesday, October 16, 1962: From Rochester
Another Honeybear's call ended my five minutes with Luke. "Carina, Luke sounded lonely. Dating's harder for male freshmen. Being female is ideal!"

"How did going steady end? Do you miss him?" Her voiced conveyed warmth and interest.

"Luke understood my need for freedom to date at college. We dated this summer, but not exclusively. Charming Hy keeps me too excited to pine for anyone else."

Wednesday, October 17, 1962: Baseball
Studying at the library, dear Hy, dressed in tan chinos and tweedy jacket, asked why I was smiling. "Hy, cute Mickey Mantle and other Yankees won their twentieth World Series, beating San Francisco in the seventh game!"

"I was a Brooklyn Dodgers' fan until they defected to Los Angeles." We exchanged grins.

Friday, October 19, 1962: Hy
Around midnight, Carina asked, "Did you have fun?"

"Hy and I played ping pong before drinks at the reddish gold Gold Rail. You would have enjoyed the music group, Trade Winds, at the Israeli Café!"

Carina and I chortled about Mother's unsexy description of Hy after introductions last weekend:

We like your *nice Jewish boyfriend* with attractive red hair. Dad said, "Columbia men have more class than Angela's high school dates." After only a month at Barnard, you look more sophisticated.

My effective speaking class includes learning parliamentary procedure with a class club. Our creative teacher is writing a play for us to perform! I must redo my pantomime about how to paint in oils as a speech.

Dad declined to join the class. "Fern, I'm too tired to go out every night like you."

"Herm, being on your feet all day makes your job harder."

Saturday, October 20, 1962: Impulse

Hy and I felt let down, seeing Columbia lose, 36-14, to Harvard with a 6-3 football record. The Italian movie *Boccaccio 70* with four separate short stories had three famous directors: Fellini, Visconti, and De Sica. Did this movie somehow cause me to impulsively send thanks to Mr. R, my speedreading teacher? It's not his fault that I stupidly allowed his awful partner to take advantage of me on that appalling 1961 evening.

Tuesday, October 23, 1962: Music

"Carina, has anything interesting happened during my burial in the library stacks?"

"I enjoyed *Music Forum* at 4 PM in the college parlor!"

"I love your jazz singing! Was today's music classical?"

She nodded yes. "Thank you! What's new?"

"Last night before curfew, I gladly chatted with Hy. I regret that previous plans made me decline a date with Gary from my aunts' synagogue... I feel nostalgic about my *alma mater* after enjoying the latest AHS newspaper from a current senior, who may have seen me crying continually on graduation day." We exchanged smiles.

<u>Wednesday, October 24, 1962: New Man</u>
Tons of brainy Columbia men nearby thrill me! At a Columbia coffee hour, a pleasant pre-med student chatted with me before I met humorous Barry, who took me to dinner at the Lion's Den. Both were typical Lions: tenor voices with NYC accents, around five-nine, unathletic medium builds, brown hair and eyes. Ping pong and pool games were fun, including a bit of flirting with the triplets.

I regretted again having to tell Gary, "I'd like to see you but I already have Saturday plans. I hope you'll ask again."

Hy phoned for a short conversation before another call cut us off. I resumed interesting English reading about D. H. Lawrence, the British author assigned to me for the year.

<u>Saturday, October 27, 1962: Sad</u>
Luke and I subwayed to his brother's college, NYU.

"Luke, Udeh from AHS called yesterday. He and Marcus see each other often and still enjoy Columbia College's literature classics course, despite stiff academic competition."

Over pizza, Luke said that he wants us to go steady and eventually end up together. "Luke, I care about you, but need years of experience getting to know various people to know whom to marry." This caused Luke to end our relationship. I was sorry to hurt him, but more excited about Lions, like Hy.

Being with Luke, I missed seeing cute quarterback Archie Roberts lead Columbia to victory over Lehigh, 22-15.

<u>Sunday, October 28, 1962: Prison Open</u>
With Carina kindly studying in the library and our door ajar, Hy and I did schoolwork and kissed with all feet on the floor until 5 PM. Hy's mandatory coat (navy blazer) and tie (burgundy stripes) looked good with his gray dress slacks and red hair.

"Carina, am I the only Honeybear who likes rules which prevent going too far? This compulsory skirt (pink wool plaid with pleats) seems riskier than forbidden slacks, more of a barrier to male advances." Grinning, she agreed.

Monday, October 29, 1962: Presentable
Gary treated me to ice cream before we played ping-pong. Like most Columbia guys I've met, he's a smart, sophisticated brunette of average size with a sense of humor. When he invited me out for Saturday and Monday, I replied, "Gary, I had fun and hope to see you again! I'm sorry those dates are scheduled." My AHS dating famine leaves me overjoyed about more invites from attractive men than I can accept!

Wednesday, October 31, 1962: Halloween
Though we were too busy to plan costumes, Hy took me to a coffee hour. His long-legged body, an inch or two under six feet, looked appealing in navy casual trousers and a blue pullover sweater.

      Barry called before curfew. "Angela, Happy Spooks Day!" Sadly, I was unavailable on the date he requested.

      Carina said, "Barnard makes it easy to hear live classical music, like yesterday's captivating 5 PM *Music for an Hour* in the James Room."

      "I admire your taking advantage of what's offered! I'd have to reduce my precious dating to fit in events." I grinned.

Saturday, November 3, 1962: Sorry, Cornell
Library study made me miss the game. Later, Hy and I were alone at the apartment of his friend. "Angela, our man Archie led the Lions to victory: 25-21 over Cornell." Enjoying kissing him while sniffing his manly after-shave, I appreciated the lack of pressure for more, despite his wanting a serious relationship in all ways. I'm only seventeen!

Tuesday, November 6, 1962: Election
I can't wait to vote in four years! Liberal Republican incumbents, like Senator Jacob Javits, are expected to win this low-key election.

      In the dining hall wearing the required skirt (navy) and blouse (white), Carina asked if I received Hy's message.

"Yes, thanks! Pleasant Barry and I strolled around the elegant East side before a funny movie, *Divorce Italian Style*. What's new?"

"Our hygiene class book, Maslow's *Motivation and Personality* about the hierarchy of needs, helps me understand people. Once the lower physiological and safety needs are satisfied, we can fulfill the higher needs for love and belonging, esteem, and my favorite, self-actualization."

"I like that he studied the top one percent of outstanding Americans, like Einstein and Eleanor Roosevelt, rather than those with psychological difficulties... How do you like basketball for your physical-ed requirement?"

"Better now that girls move farther with three-bounce dribbles, instead of two. Two players per team can roam the court and snatch the ball."

"As a junior high guard, I chafed at the half-court rule. Do you play guard?" She nodded as we unloaded our used dishes and utensils in gray bins and stacked our beige trays.

Wednesday, November 7, 1962: Home
Wearing her navy plaid robe over light-blue pajamas, Carina alertly listened as I read Mother's letter:

> With Edith out as leader, I can't avoid the synagogue choir.
> We liked Audrey Hepburn revivals, *Roman Holiday* and *Sabrina*, and *Lolita* with talented James Mason and hilarious Peter Sellers as a psychologist with a German accent.
> Dad said, "Angela may be the first female who can balance her checkbook."
> I retorted that my mistakes don't make all women bad at math.

"Angela, keep my check register errors a secret!" We tittered before Carina left me speechless with shock, "Only yesterday was slavery abolished in Saudi Arabia!" My jaw dropped open.

Thursday, November 8, 1962: Current Events

Hy called. "Angela, did you hear that we lost Eleanor Roosevelt at age seventy-eight in Manhattan?"

"No! How sad! I admired her!"

"Me, too. Better news: Teddy Kennedy won the Massachusetts Senate seat. Nixon lost in California!"

"I'm doing cheerleading jumps." I tried not to drop the phone.

"Nixon's comment to reporters cracked me up. 'You don't have Nixon to kick around anymore. Gentlemen, this is my last press conference.'"

I giggled while wishing for female reporters.

Hy's sexy rich voice continued. "Power-greedy, morally bankrupt politicians, like Nixon, often play phoenix, rising from the ashes. Did you see the cartoon of the college counselor who says to a student, "Make another choice. Ethics classes are off-limits to political science majors." I grinned. "Angela, good news: The UN condemned South African apartheid. At least, our re-elected Governor Rockefeller's one of the better Republicans." I nodded, glad we agreed about politics.

Saturday, November 10, 1962: Shopping

Alexander's was crammed with women, aggressively grabbing fashionable, high-quality, discounted clothing from crowded racks. "Aunt Lila, thanks for finding this elegant, white-wool designer coat with real leopard collar! I can't wait to wear this bargain with black leather gloves. You could write a book: *Dressing Impeccably on a Budget*." I complimented her charcoal wool sheath with matching jacket, pearls, and silver antique pin, which contrasted with her medium-length, strawberry blond coiffure. Looking pleased, she hugged me.

Smiling, she asked, "How's Gary?"

"Happy about Russian missiles leaving Cuba, he called, saying, 'I hope to graduate without being called up. We're fortunate Kennedy is in charge!' Thank you for introducing us!"

<u>Sunday, November 11, 1962: *Cheyah*</u>
Studying for terrifying mid-year exams, Carina and I let off steam by aping (pun unintended) the arm-swinging, bent-over, bipedal gait of our extinct australopithecine (below) ancestors, whom Carina studies in anthropology class.

"Angela, did you have an imaginary playmate?" After I shook my head no, she said, "Neither did I. Let's compensate for such childhood deprivation by electing Pithy as our imaginary room mascot with the australopithecine exclamation *Cheyah* as our visitor entry password." The vote was 2 yes, 0 no!

A giggle fit ensued. "Carina, though we may miss academic awards, do we take the cake for the silliest Honeybears?" Inanely squawking *Cheyah* while modeling Pithy's pacing cuts exam jitters. Classes with over twelve hundred gifted Honeybears are humbling.

<u>Wednesday, November 14, 1962: Birthday</u>
After alerting the dining room staff, I was relieved when they brought out a blue-frosted cake with eighteen candles for Carina to blow out. She wore a lavender bowed blouse and black straight skirt.

Later, Carina was touched by my silver Barnard charm gift and card. I'm glad my saved allowance sufficed!

She and Columbia stuffed lion Blondie (below) kindly endured my tuneless, but mercifully brief rendition of *Happy Birthday*. We took goofy photos with her parents' Polaroid camera gift (below).

<u>Thursday, November 15, 1962: Letter</u>
I'm joyfully surprised to hear from the tall, sandy-haired, handsome boy in my AHS advanced algebra and solid geometry classes. A member of Student Council, the yearbook staff, and Philalogia literary society, he has a dazzling smile. Parental bigotry meant dating a Protestant was out, not that he asked. After copying his touching yearbook note in my early July diary, I read it enough times to memorize it:

> I'm getting misty when I recall how sweet you were to me. You were and still are a <u>DOLL</u>. You were always so lovable. You made my days at AHS a pleasure. You did more for everyone's morale than anyone else. You're my people. I will always love you! Love, Love, Love!

With more time at frat parties and poker than at the library, he may be enjoying Cornell too much. I wrote back before answering Craig, happy at Hamilton, a small, liberal arts college near Utica, NY.

When Mother called for news, I reported:

Gary took me to the wonderful Limelighters'
Carnegie Hall folk music concert! After sitting in
ideal box seats, we went backstage for
autographs. At Orsini's, a cool coffeehouse, I
liked the red velvet walls, crystal chandeliers,
and wrought iron decor. The tuxedoed waiters
serve movie stars, not that we spotted any.

Friday, November 16, 1962: Campus Play

Fascinating Hy, in a yellow, V-neck pullover under a neat dark
gray jacket, took me to cozy V and T Pizzeria on Amsterdam
Avenue. "Hy, my first pizza here was with Cousin Hal, who
encouraged me to apply when he was at Columbia in 1960."

"I'll have to thank him! Angela, did you know that
Giraudoux's *Tiger at the Gates* was written before the Nazis
started World War II? Its French title means *The Trojan War
Will Not Take Place.* Despite experienced Trojan military
commander Hector's war opposition, idealistic poet Demokos,
who has never fought, exaggerates war's glory to drum up
support among gullible males. Our recent near-debacle in Cuba
makes the anti-war message timely."

"Hy, I wish that Hector's peace agreement with Greek
commander Ulysses had averted war. The play was absorbing."

Saturday, November 17, 1962: Brooklyn

With good-looking Hy, dressed in khaki slacks and brown
bomber jacket, I subwayed to tour his high school. Visiting his
family and best friend was fun before a Chinese restaurant
dinner. He asked about new Barnard president Park's welcome
assembly Thursday.

"Hy, Miss Park (below) supports female achievement
and equality."

He grinned. "But?"

"We need a better role model for women combining
family and careers, like my married Latin prof."

"Will you teach Latin?"

I sniggered. "My mother would cheer. Sadly, Columbia psychology emphasizes rats more than people."

Hy looked alert. "Are you a future psychologist?"

I nodded. "Too squeamish for rat experiment courses, I'll take other psych classes, like developmental, abnormal, and social and major in something else." What did his eyebrow lift express?

Sunday, November 18, 1962: Boarders
Sitting up in bed and sketching on her drawing pad, Carina perked up while hearing Mother's letter:

> The house seems empty. Unhappy with kosher food and Dad's tantrum about their bad attitudes and shallow values, the boarders left. I said, "Herm, you'd rather be right than collect forty-five dollars a week rent."
>
> "Fern, I'm glad they aren't our daughters." Though I cook less, we can't afford a cleaning woman, repair of my ancient Persian

lamb coat and turban hat for another winter, a planned Broadway play, and exterior painting of our house (below).

Fortunately, the synagogue choir and Mr. and Mrs. Club; TV, including the game show *Password*; and the *Password* board game are free.

Why didn't I see the office file drawer sticking out? Though my leg hurts from tripping, I'll return to work tomorrow. Dr. Blair, head of Psychological Services, appreciates my efforts.

Regards to Carina and Hy!

I couldn't stop a titter. "Angela, do you laugh about looking better now to your critical folks?" I nodded before Carina added, "Comic relief and poetic justice are welcome here."

"Carina, I'm sorry about Mother's leg and income loss."

"I heard that seven-foot Wilt, the Stilt, Chamberlain's 73 points defeated our NYC Knicks Friday! I'm lucky to guard Honeybears under six feet tall." We giggled.

<u>Wednesday, November 21, 1962: Vacation</u>
At the 72 Street subway stop, I felt like exiting to Aunt Sara's nearby building. On 41 Street at Port Authority Bus Terminal, I thanked Hy. "I felt safer with you protecting me on the IRT subway!"

On the Trailways bus to Albany, staring at rural views, I felt sad that Sara has good reason to shun all relatives since August 1959. Dad cruelly expressed skepticism about the rape she had escaped. Though I miss her, my September nightmare deters me from phoning. Will my visit make her more forgiving?

After less than three hours on the Thruway, the bus reached dreary Albany around 2 PM. I'm thankful for NYC.

At the Boulevard, our AHS hangout, talking to Craig and others back from college was mood-boosting, including hearing that my favorite, Mickey Mantle, won most valuable American League baseball player for the third time.

Noticing handsome Schuyler High School grad Ric's white bandage and downcast look, I expressed sympathy.

"Angela, on November 8, I broke my collarbone playing soccer in freshman PE at Beverwyck Park. I'm stuck with this soft cast until it heals. On October 22, JFK's Cuba missile speech inspired me to join the Navy Reserves. Paul, who persuaded me to sign up, drives us to Wednesday drills." A mental image of my charismatic ex, Paul, caused a frisson before Ric talked about going to Albany State.

A red-haired guy with icy blue eyes appeared. "Ric, who's this glamorous brunette?" Wowed by deep voices like his, I felt distracted by internal flutters.

"Angela, meet my neighbor Kevin, a senior BMOC (Big Man on Campus) at CBA (Christian Brothers Academy). Kevin, Angela was a 1962 AHS grad, maybe valedictorian."

Ignoring the latter, sure to squelch any guy's interest in me, I smiled and held out my hand. "Good to meet you, Kevin." Instead of a handshake, I felt Kevin's lips gently kissing my hand while he gazed into my eyes. I felt quivers down there.

Outgoing Kevin's and Ric's witty quips about their schools and Albany politics kept us laughing.

Thursday, November 22, 1962: Thanksgiving
Dad drove Mother and me to Gloversville for a jolly meal with Aunt Myrna and Uncle Abner (below), Ella in junior high, and Lydia, a high school junior.

"Aunt Myrna, thank you for this delicious turkey with stuffing, candied yams, green beans almondine, and green apple pie!"

"You're welcome! Lydia and Ella helped."

Now taller than I, my pretty cousins were eager to hear about Columbia men and NYC! Details about dates with Hy made Lydia exclaim, "What a great boyfriend!"

At home, I wrote a detailed answer, mainly about Barnard, to this heartwarming letter from our lovable, modest Norwegian exchange student (below), who enriched senior year at AHS! Her Norwegian English charms me.

When I remember the year in Albany, some persons are much clearer than others. You are one of them, Angela. I thank God I had the chance to meet you. Maybe you feel strange when I keep on telling you that, but I admire you very much. How are you really? So many things have happened since we said goodbye. Remember that you and Luke came to my house and we were pacing back and forth? I had much to say, yet did not know how to say it.

It is good to be home, sleep in my own bed, talk Norwegian, and other things. I had a wonderful time with you, and I want to travel back to you someday…. My mother says I am kinder now (yes, good influence), but my friends say, "You're just the same." Some even look rather disappointed. I haven't heard anything from Pete. I had some letters from the Belgian boy. He is fine. How is Luke? Are you still going strong?

To skip a year in school, I must take some examinations in October (math, oh!). So now I study math besides regular homework. It is hard to fail but worse never to have tried to succeed!! Did Roosevelt say those true wisdom-words? My senior gymnasium (high school) class (about 120 pupils) elected me secretary. That's fun! Angela, take care of yourself and be good. If you have time, I would be very happy to hear from you. I don't have your college address. Say hello to your family, please! Love, Mista

Friday, November 23, 1962: Goy

My dating Jewish Gary and Hy pleases Mother, off work to accompany me to the bank and to stores for holiday gifts; I skip labeling Hy a possible agnostic or atheist.

After dinner, adorable Kevin, handsome Ric, his blond date, and I bowled at the Playdium near my house and had pizza at the Moon Restaurant. Ric joked, "Last year, Kevin got sent to prison, his all-male school, to fulfill his potential without panting females diverting him."

"My folks, who think that I'm with only Ric tonight, won't let me date until I get all *As*. Since my dad drives a bus and my mom works as a library clerk, I need a scholarship for an Ivy League college."

Looking up at Kevin, I grinned. "I relate to circumventing dating restrictions and needing scholarships."

Affable Ric remarked, "Now that Angela's away at college, her parents no longer force her to reject us *goyim*."

"What's a *goyim*?" Kevin asked, widening his blue eyes.

Light-heartedly, Ric answered, "The singular, *goy*, is Yiddish or Hebrew for a non-Jew. As a Catholic, I define *goy* as *good boy*." We chortled.

When Kevin questioned how Ric knew those languages, Ric shared, "Jewish before converting to marry my father, my mother taught me a few words. A mother born Jewish makes me officially Jewish. I could have a belated Bar Mitzvah to rake in lots of *gelt*."

"*Gelt* is money." I commented, as Kevin's twinkling pale eyes met mine.

Ric asked Kevin, "Can you wangle an athletic scholarship?"

Looking at me, Kevin joked, "Harvard doesn't give money to back-up quarterbacks. To win the starting spot, I should have gotten the Russians to kidnap our superstar quarterback and exile him to Siberian salt mines. Not only have I had the misfortune of being outshone by the CBA superstar, but *Bs* in religion classes have resulted in a monk's existence, worthy of the pity of a college beauty like you, Angela."

Though my rational brain deemed this blarney, the rest of me was charmed. With the same March birthday as Ric, Kevin is less than two months my junior. A pushover for clever guys who make me laugh, I noticed that Kevin resembled the ginger-haired flirt at the 1961 Albany Tulip Ball.

Saturday, November 24, 1962: Mr. B and Kevin
<u>Saturday, November 24, 1962: Mr. B and Kevin</u>
Shopping downtown, Mother and I ran into lecherous Mr. B. "Angela, are you using your speedreading?"

I nodded. "Though slower than JFK's 1200 words per minute, I'm faster than before." I moved on, leery of Mother's inferring the disgusting history with Mr. B. It's a wonder that scandal hasn't ousted a predator from Hackett teaching.

At dimly-lit Mike's Log Cabin, reminiscent of President Lincoln's childhood home with exterior and inner horizontal log walls, Kevin explained that Ric had to be with his family tonight. After heavenly slow dances, Kevin beamed. "Angela, if can't earn an *A* in religion by studying, I'll pray for a miracle, so we can date openly and you can meet my family. My parents and brother Patrick will go for you."

"Was he at the 1961 Tulip Ball?"

"It must have been 1961 when he escorted his girlfriend, who made the queen's court, to the ball... How did you know?"

"An older version of you winked at me when he danced by with a tulip princess in a yellow gown."

Chuckling, Kevin said, "Sounds like Patrick! What a coincidence!" Kevin's strong embrace and goodnight kiss were blissful. At just under six feet, he is the perfect size for me.

<u>Sunday, November 25, 1962: Goodbye</u>
Kevin dropped by. "Angela, here's Ric's address to answer my letters without my family seeing them. I'll write soon!"

At the bus station, Mother haltingly said, "Angela, it seems like you just arrived." Her voice was less shrill than usual. I felt sorry for the forlorn-looking parents.

"Mother, thanks for taking off work to help me. Thanksgiving in Gloversville was fun! I'll be back soon." We hugged goodbye.

On the bus with eyes closed, I reexperienced Kevin's bass voice and irresistible departing clinch.

In the dorm's downstairs living room, Hy, whose red locks are darker than Kevin's, shared about his Thanksgiving.

<u>Tuesday, November 27, 1962: Attention</u>
Carina bounced into our room in high spirits. "*Music for an Hour* in the James Room featured a first-rate chamber music group! What's new with you?"

"Hy visited and Gary invited me on a date! Ric sent this flattering note:

> Kevin is besotted. If I didn't belong to your fan
> club, I'd bean him for raving about you. It's like
> *déjà vu*. At Schuyler, Xavier talked about his
> crush on you for over a year.

"Carina, I can't resist answering Kevin's fun letter tonight."

<u>Thursday, November 29, 1962: On the Town</u>
In NYC on business, Carina's handsome, sophisticated dad had an air of prosperous distinction. Younger and more charming than my father, he treated us, including taxis, to a belated birthday outing for her! Wearing my black wool sheath and cultured pearls, I admired her dad's beautifully cut navy business suit, pastel blue shirt, and red and navy paisley silk tie, which brought out his blue eyes, pale like Carina's.

Mamma Leone's Restaurant, 261 West 44 Street, was crowded with diners at tables adorned with red-and-white-checked tablecloths. We had delicious antipasto, lasagna, and Carina's birthday cake with eighteen candles. The menu said that Louisa Leone opened the eatery in 1906!

At the ornate, old-fashioned Billy Rose Theater at 208 West 41 Street near Broadway, we sat on comfortable maroon velvet seats only a few rows from the stage in the privileged orchestra section!

Edward Albee's brilliant new play mesmerized us! *Who's Afraid of Virginia Woolf?* portrays the vicious husband-wife interactions of an older university couple, Uta Hagen (Martha) and Arthur Hill (George), who invite a younger university couple, Melinda Dillon (Honey) and George Grizzard (Nick) for drinks. The first act is *Fun and Games*. Intermissions preceded the second act, *Walpurgisnacht*, and the final act, *The Exorcism*.

Reading the Playbill later, Carina and I laughed about the Northern European *Walpurgisnacht* on April 30 being a satanic holiday, like Halloween with pranks and costumes. "Angela, Martha and George were certainly devilish characters."

I chuckled. "Compared to their spiteful, smoldering hostility, my father's infantile outbursts seem tame! I'm writing your generous, charismatic father a thank-you note for an unforgettable evening!"

"Here's the address. In the 1930s, a local doctor built our woodsy country house near Lake Michigan. My dad drives to Chicago from Michigan City in only an hour."

Friday, November 30, 1962: Wardrobe
I applauded my roomie, modeling her Dad's birthday gift: classic navy Brooks Brothers separates plus a trench coat with zip-in lining. "Angela, these well-made clothes should last until I graduate!" Seeing her excited made me happy.

<u>Sunday, December 2, 1962: Empire State</u>
Carina asked about my weekend. "Hy and I kissed at the top of the Empire State Building! In Greenwich Village, a Spanish guitarist accompanied a flamenco dancer at dark, cave-like El Gitano, smelling smoky and appearing misty from patrons' cigarettes. As a tap dancer, I appreciated the staccato rhythm of the dancer's heels. Wishing for a similar black dress with red ruffles, I imagined joining the dancer onstage. Today, always shunning caffeine, I drank my usual water at the Columbia College coffee hour."

"Angela, who's number one?"

"I'm crazy about both redheads."

<u>Monday, December 3, 1962: Tea and Excitement</u>
Amongst wool sheaths and pearl necklaces, Carina, wearing her new A-line skirt suit over blue silk blouse, and I, attired in dark-gray wool suit, mingled at the 4 PM alumnae-undergraduate tea. The deanery (dean's parlor) is full of dark antique furniture on a priceless, ugly Persian carpet.

At night, a commotion in the dorm halls distracted us from studying. At the dorm rooms facing Claremont Avenue and 116 Street, normally sallow Honeybear bookworms were flushed with pleasure. Giggle fits ensued. Disgruntled about joy-killing police dispersing throngs of dashing Columbia raiders, I'll save torn underwear for future rascals.

Lacking concentration for more Latin translation, I scrawled this to answer Mother's letter:

> Thanks again for Thanksgiving weekend! Our impregnable room facing the quad made us miss even a glimpse of tonight's fun panty raid. On city streets, a crowd of Columbia Lions below the Barnard dorms clamored for lingerie. Girls threw old things no longer needed out of windows before the police stopped the merriment. Otherwise, studying occupies us.

Tuesday, December 4, 1962: Raid

Hearing about *NY Times* raid coverage, I laughed at the *Columbia Spectator* article before sending it to Kevin. My summary:

> Around 11 PM, over five hundred Lions produced a disorganized panty raid, hampered by swathes of dense fog. Students marching in front towards College Walk lost contact with those still in Van Am Quad. Traditional cries about "Barnard meat" moved the horde towards the green iron fence. Police in squad cars overreacted, using night sticks. A third of the raiders tried to enter Barnard the back way. Squad cars splintered the mass into clumps. About forty brave warriors broke through; on Claremont Avenue, they hailed Honeybears. Some threw down panties and bras. A sensible sergeant admitted that the event was harmless. "The boys were getting the girls excited and the girls were getting the boys excited." By 1:30 AM, the raid ended without arrests.

Wednesday, December 5, 1962: Second-Class

I wrote to Doreen:

> Dear excellent ping-ponger, how are you? You're lucky to freely use all facilities at a coed state school. Columbia wants us second-class Barnard citizens only for money. See the enclosed article. Love and smiles, Angela

My summary of the *Columbia Spectator* article:

> Lack of business and greed for money, rather
> than equal treatment, made Columbia's Board
> of Managers vote to allow unescorted
> Honeybears to use Ferris Booth Hall (student
> union) ping-pong tables and bowling alleys.
> Former rules excluded them from game rooms.
> To attract female bowlers, the Board lowered
> the price per alley from two dollars per hour.
> Fully used pool tables and piano practice rooms
> are still not open to Barnard students.

Sunday, December 9, 1962: Dance

Carina inquired, "How was the Dean's Drag last night?"

"Hy, handsome in a navy suit, gave me this lovely yellow carnation corsage! I had an absolute blast dancing to live music and joking with him. Red fruit punch from the gigantic crystal bowl left us tipsy!"

"You deserve fun! Do you have time for the Hewitt Hall holiday dinner tomorrow?"

"I must martyr myself in the library. Yesterday's compulsory Class of 1966 program planning meeting put me behind. My English paper will require all of Christmas vacation. Authentically mediocre or worse here, I'm past hiding high grades to fit in and have dates." We chortled.

Wednesday, December 12, 1962: Talks

I must catch up even more after today's mandatory vocational conference. This week's socializing has been phone talks with Hy on Tuesday (two hours) and Gary for a half hour each on Monday and today. Intelligent and interesting, Gary talks about himself without delving to deepen our connection.

Handing me a program, Carina said, "Yesterday's monthly *Music Forum* in the college parlor soothed me!"

"Thanks for providing vicarious culture, Roomie!" Emulating imaginary mascot Pithy, we bent over, swung arms, lumbered around the room, squealed *Cheyah*, and laughed hysterically to unwind.

Friday, December 14, 1962: Trouble in Paradise

Last week, Hy dropped by the dorm, saw me playing ping pong with brunette Pete, and looked a little jealous, even though Hy has yet to ask me to go steady, not that I would. I'm sorry if he felt hurt. I really like him.

Tonight, Pete and I stayed warm by subwaying south, east, and north to the Trans-Lux Theater on East 85 Street. His supply of tokens got us through turnstiles quickly enough to catch all trains. In the movie *Two for the Seesaw*, charming Shirley MacLaine plays a bohemian NYC dancer. Less likeable Robert Mitchum is her romantic interest. Though tweedily-attired Pete seems nice, the movie provided little opportunity to get better acquainted.

Saturday, December 15, 1962: Gary

I was surprised to have such an enjoyable time with Gary, intriguing because he breaks the stereotype of uncool Orthodox Jewish guys. No one would guess that Gary is religious. Tonight, the subway was our chariot to the upper East Side, scene of most foreign films with subtitles. Tears stung my eyes at the end of *Sundays and Cybele,* a touching French movie about an innocent, loving friendship between a young girl and a psychologically damaged war veteran.

Serendipity is an exciting East 60 Street dessert place. Tons of antiques, decorations, and oddities for sale hang from the ceiling and walls. Gary was attractive in navy blazer, red tie, white button-down shirt, and gray slacks. Downing one huge, elaborate hot fudge sundae, we looked for famous people without recognizing any.

<u>Thursday, December 20, 1962: Boy Crazy</u>
The last week before vacation has been exhilarating socially! At an eggnog party Sunday, I met Spanky, a cute, curly-haired, half-Negro artist and musician.

Yesterday, in the downstairs dorm living room, I had a blast bantering with Pete and three new guys, including one from Amherst College.

At a Columbia's Ferris Booth Hall gathering, talking to Gary was fun, though he has yet to ask, beyond superficially, about my experiences and thoughts.

While Carina and I packed luggage, I said, "Flirting elates me too much to want to settle down with one, even perfect, guy for life. Since Hy is the kind of guy I might eventually love, I'm sad that he has disappeared." She nodded empathetically before humming excerpts from Tuesday's *Music for an Hour*. We're delighted to be on vacation!

<u>Friday, December 21, 1962: Homecoming</u>
When the subway train stopped at 72 Street, I imagined exiting to surprise Sara with a visit. Paralyzed by fear of rejection, I eschew trying.

Kevin picked me up around 3 PM at the Albany bus depot. I closed my eyes during his firm embrace and delicious kiss. "My Honeybear is here for two weeks! Have you suffered from the two-week NYC newspaper strike?"

Mesmerized by his deep voice, I was challenged to speak. "No time for the *NY Times*! I glance at the *Barnard Bulletin* and *Columbia Spectator* every few days."

"Are you up for the AHS basketball game? My parents are unlikely to hear that I escorted a stunning, big-city lady." Beaming, I nodded.

At home, calls from wonderful Dominic and Jake and a warm letter from handsome Lee at college left me overjoyed.

With Kevin's muscular arm around me at the game, I felt sky-high waving to loads of former classmates. At the Boulevard, they asked whether Chubby Checker's *Limbo Rock* is a big hit in NYC. "Tonight's the first I've heard of the limbo. Columbia students, if not classical music fans, would applaud those protesting when folk singers Peter, Paul, and Mary gave their final San Francisco *hungry i* night club performance."

Kevin asked, "What does *i* mean?"

"Maybe the Freudian *id*." I giggled, thinking: *the id wants sex*.

Overhearing us, Marcus added, "Owner Banducci, a Beatnik fan, revealed that the *i* signifies *intellectual*."

Two people held the ends of a limbo pole parallel to the ground at waist level while dancers took turns bending backwards and strutting under the pole without touching it. My eyes almost popped out watching Kevin and other strong guys cleanly dance under a lowered pole! My crooked back is too inflexible. Catching up with AHS classmates elated me!

Saturday, December 22, 1962: Dominic

Mother and less-than-meticulous I cleaned house while our *West Side Story* album played, including favorites: *Maria, Tonight*, and *Somewhere*. Dressing in a warm black sweater and pink plaid wool skirt, I softly sang *Tonight*.

Holding my hand, Dominic, whose other manly hand caressed my shoulder, was so beguiling that I forgot the movie we saw. At Mike's Log Cabin, slow dancing with my eyes closed while feeling his broad shoulders was dreamy.

Until bedtime, *Somewhere* lyrics ran through my head: *There's a place for us…. Hold my hand and I'll take you there. Somehow, someday, somewhere.*

Sunday, December 23, 1962: Plans

Jake's call revealed that he's excelling at RPI. No surprise! Receiving two invites for New Year's Eve, I was relieved to have already accepted Kevin. Will his parents stay in the dark so we can keep dating? Listening to our Frank Sinatra *Come Swing with Me* album made the song *It's Almost Like Being in Love* play in my mind.

My parents and I exchanged practical Hanukkah gifts, e.g., sox, while lighting the third candle. Dad said, "Angela, your arrival ended Albany's longest 1962 spell of temperatures below freezing: December 10 to 19!"

Monday, December 24, 1962: Eve

I adored Christmas Eve with Dominic's fun family, including church with Greek Orthodox pageantry: lavish gold robes and crowns and ornate gold and silver decorative objects. His confident, attractive older brother and sweet younger sister, an AHS student, were welcoming.

Over a roast lamb dinner at their duplex flat, his tall, feisty mom joked, "Angela, must I send your parents one of our five kids for them to let us keep you as a daughter?"

Laughing, I answered, "They'll be glad to get rid of me without expecting a replacement."

Dominic's short, genial Dad kidded, "You needn't become Greek Orthodox when we adopt you. But if you want to convert, celebrating Christmas Eve here has qualified you!"

I grinned. "Thanks for making it easy. Tonight has been more fun than studying for months with a priest."

When Dominic drove me home, he whipped out and held over my head a sprig of mistletoe before giving me a long, tender kiss.

In my room, a package wrapped in blue-and-silver Hanukkah paper surprised me. In a Christmas card, I wrote Kevin a thank you note for a loving card and delicate silver necklace and bracelet, perfect for me! On Cloud Nine, I drifted off to sleep, entranced by both Dominic and Kevin.

<u>Tuesday, December 25, 1962: Family</u>
Christmas with Gloversville relatives was ideal! Lydia asked about college. "Despite my studying most of the time, the report Barnard sent parents of all freshmen rated my work fair or C in English, formerly one of my best subjects. Differential calculus problems are often incorrect. Latin was the only very good or A in the report. I got good or B in psychology."

Lydia looked worried. "I'd better choose an easier college, like Russell Sage."

"Female college pluses: skip make-up, wear slacks, and not turn off guys wanting dumber dates!" We laughed.

<u>Saturday, December 29, 1962: Wonderful Week</u>
Despite many hours on my D. H. Lawrence paper about *Sons and Lovers*, my head is in the clouds. Laughing at Kevin's jokes, listening to his flattering remarks, and discussing topics like race discrimination, psychology, and values have fascinated me. Kevin calls himself a cynical realist, but we tend to agree.

The last two evenings, Kevin, Ric (cheery with collarbone healing), and I enjoyed the Cardinal McCloskey High School basketball tournament. Noticing his jewelry adorning me, Kevin pulled me close. His kisses were heavenly!

<u>Monday, December 31, 1962: New Year's Eve</u>!
In his quiet, blond date's dark basement rec room, Ric said, "Wednesday evening Navy Reserve drills are fun, even though Paul switched to Monday after transferring to Siena College." My eyebrows lifted in surprise.

Bantering and dancing to sentimental records, like *Moon River*, Ray Charles' *I Can't Stop Loving You*, and Elvis' *I Can't Help Falling in Love*, I couldn't resist touching Kevin's fuzzy blue pullover sweater, which made his matching eyes more tantalizing.

At midnight, both couples kissed. If Kevin isn't the best, he has made me forget who is. Hearing him whisper, "My darling Honeybear," I sighed happily.

Kevin's lean, athletic build reminds me of Myles, my junior high crush, who also has entrancing, light azure eyes. As a dancer, Kevin's up there with Luke and Craig, also known as Fred Astaire!

As more of a listener, I appreciate that Kevin talks openly and expresses feelings, unlike the many cagey guys I've known. My school grades don't make super-smart Kevin insecure. His personality seems ideal. I feel closer to him after almost daily time together.

1963 NYC College Freshman

Good fortune and a good disposition are rarely given to the same man.

Roman historian **Livy**, *Histories*

Thursday, January 3, 1963: Twenty-Sixth Anniversary
As Frank Sinatra's baritone-tenor smoothly crooned *Just in Time* and *Something's Gotta Give* in the background, Dad applauded my steak/baked-potato dinner. "Angela, thanks for this delicious anniversary meal and great Sinatra album, *Come Dance with Me!* How was your day?"

"My morning AHS visit with former teachers and current seniors was fun! Downtown, I bought your gift before seeing Sinatra's suspense movie *Manchurian Candidate* and Elvis' musical about a boxer, *Kid Galahad*."

After Sinatra sang *Dancing in the Dark, I Could Have Danced All Night,* and *Cheek to Cheek,* Dad said, "Fern, let's dance soon!" Making their anniversary happy felt good.

Friday, January 4, 1963: Overheard
Heartwarming chats with former classmates enlivened AHS's basketball game.

Kevin, who seems to appreciate my idealism, made post-game remarks about philosophy and human nature. His voracious reading and intellectual maturity astonish me.

When he jested about becoming an astronaut, I answered, "Your history, English, science, and math talents help me visualize you as a winning courtroom lawyer or life-saving doctor." Hypnotized by his ginger locks, manly voice, and blue eyes, I'd agree, as a juror, with anything he says. I grinned, picturing him as a charismatic doctor with nurses fainting at his feet.

At home, Mother's abrasive voice behind the closed door of the parents' room arrested my progress towards the bathroom. "Herm, she hasn't dated one Jew!" Unaware that I was home, Mother spoke up because of Dad's hearing loss.

"Hon, we can't control college dating. I hope she's better than our shallow boarders. If we've raised her right with good values, she'll marry a nice Jewish Columbia man."

I suppressed a giggle hearing, "Jewish Marcus is ideal."

Why would anyone turn down charming, bright leader Kevin, who entertains and adores me, for dull guys, like TV fan Jed or unamusing Jerry? If someone like Hy lived here, I'd accept his date invites.

Saturday, January 5, 1963: Barnard
Marcello Mastroianni's movie *Divorce Italian Style*, a repeat for me, made Kevin and me chortle. He later asked how Ivy League classes differ from high school.

"Barnard's intimidate! Almost everyone's a valedictorian. Differential calculus problems baffle me in a class where half of a hundred classmates had calculus at Bronx High School of Science or similar NYC schools. Required hygiene class is huge, but less scary."

"Any smaller classes?"

"Popular psychology has about fifty students and our interesting English seminars, around twenty. Latin's unpopularity means small classes!" We laughed.

"What English books do you read?"

"At the end alphabetically, I'm happy to be assigned the most modern author. D. H. Lawrence, also from a working-class background, shares my interests in psychology, family, nature, and love. Critically analyzing fiction is challenging."

"How about sports?"

I smiled. "For required physical education, volleyball and basketball risk catching cold while rushing to class with wet hair."

"How about knitting to exercise fingers?"

I giggled. "That would keep wild arrows from my roof-top archery class from endangering passersby below."

"On November 21, your Cupid arrows entered my heart, changing me forever!"

I blushed in his embrace. Good-night kisses produced alluring frissons in private regions.

Sunday, January 6, 1963: *Cheyah*
Grateful for an ideal vacation without the usual winter doldrums, I'm sorry it's ending! At Trailways' small bus depot, Kevin's masculine scent and goodbye kiss enticed me.

At Barnard, wonderful birthday gifts waited. Kevin's big card with hearts was signed love! Carina's brilliant, hilarious poem *There's No Place Like Home* was on our door:

Putrid water in a vase
Decorates our fireplace.
Since they decayed and cold came on,
Where have all the flowers gone?
Our closet door sings high-pitched squeaks,
The radiator only leaks.
Our household pet, we call *The Plant*,
At first drank up this drip so scant.
But we soon became alarmed to see
His drunken little roots break free
And roam the room in search of we.

Now sizzling water, belching out,
The Times adorns beneath the spout.
To cockroach traces, mosquito-ghosts,
And crazy friends like you we're hosts.
So come right in, the candle's lit.
You'll just disturb a laughing fit.
Or if we're studying by mistake,
Please check that we are still awake.
As for this room in which we're living,
We think a damn is well worth giving.
So when the floor with dirt is spread,
We push it underneath the bed,
And dutifully replace the books
Within their cobweb-covered nooks.
You ask if outside noise offends?
Revenge is not far off, my friends!
For both awake and in our dreams,
We're busy plotting wicked schemes.

So if the H20 we spill,
But trickles from the window sill,
And flashing lights don't drive away
The booming laughter, which, by the way,
Sounds much like an ass's bray,
We may be forced to stoop, resorting

To the lowest of the low, extorting.
Those juicy tidbits, which now distort us,
May someday very soon support us.
If still into this room you'd enter,
Well knowing it's a crazy center,
We bid you do, and wish you luck,
And leave you with the password *Che yah*!!!

<u>Monday, January 7, 1963: Eighteen</u>
Running into Hy on Broadway, I felt my heartbeat quicken. After chatting, I was let down without a date invitation. Though I met his family, he never asked to go steady. If seeing me play ping-pong with someone who could be a cousin made Hy drop me without discussion, am I better off with less spiteful Lions? Did he really care, as his impressive poem suggested? Has he met someone who will have sex?

Gary's call lasted a half hour before the operator interrupted. I thanked him for his birthday card.

Cousin Hal's birthday card described the Winter Folk Music Festival with the Greenbrier Boys and Georgia Sea Island Singers, whom he and Eileen enjoyed at University of California at Berkeley.

Having never read A. A. Milne's *Winnie, the Pooh* books, I appreciated quotations Carina read aloud, e.g., "People say nothing is impossible, but I do nothing every day."

After Carina sang a jazzed-up *Happy Birthday*, I said, "Thank you again for making my birthday ideal! I can finally legally drink after starting at sixteen! Your poem is incredibly perfect!" She looked pleased.

<u>Friday, January 11, 1962: Mixer</u>
"Carina, meeting my first Japanese-American person made tonight's mixer interesting. Engineering student Den from Denver, around five-ten with black hair and an athletic build, is intelligent with a sense of humor. What keeps you away from Columbia mixers?"

"Introductions by friends are more comfortable." Her description of Barnard's annual posture contest in the gym amused me.

"Carina, I'm thankful it's optional. I'd be rated *F* from months hunched-over Wollman library carrells (below)." I called home with early birthday greetings for Mother.

Sunday, January 13, 1962: Movies
Tonight, Carina exclaimed, *"Inherit the Wind* was a great Sunday night TV movie!"

She chuckled when I said, "In 1960, a dozen cute AHS boys sitting nearby in the theater distracted me from it. Tonight, *If a Man Answers*, a comedy movie, starring cute Sandra Dee and singer Bobby Darin, amused Gary and me."

Tuesday, January 15, 1963: Exams
Already anxious, Carina and I exchanged furtive, exasperated eye-rolling yesterday at President Park's mandatory gym assembly to advise freshmen to take exams seriously.

Today, Dean of Studies Helen Bailey's required pre-exam frosh assembly exacerbated anxiety. My Latin exam is less than a week away!

Wednesday, January 16, 1963: Study Pause
Carina patiently listened to effusive descriptions of my December dates. "Angela, is Dominic losing to Kevin?"

"No, but Dom rarely communicates. Kevin made the most of vacation together with warm, romantic pursuit without possessiveness. Earth-shaking kisses made me swoon."

Saturday, January 19, 1963: Letter
Hours of exam cramming preceded unwinding with Carina, who enjoyed Mother's January 15 letter:

> Thanks for the unusual birthday earrings, showing your excellent taste. Saturday night, the crowd at the Levine house sang *Happy Birthday*. Sunday, Dad took me to Jack's Restaurant where the Levines surprised me. We ate tasty birthday cake. I appreciated cards from the office, family, and friends.
>
> Having received your two cards, we're happy that you like your birthday charm. Lydia and Ella sent cute thank-you notes for the Hanukkah sweaters.
>
> The synagogue newsletter described my Adopt a Jewish Veteran project at the VA Hospital. We volunteers will talk to forgotten World War II and Korean War veterans.
>
> With sleet, freezing rain, snow, and a blizzard forecast, driving is slippery. Our upstairs tenants reported a roof leak!
>
> In addition to synagogue choir, Dad goes to Schuyler High School's clerical refresher course for NY State job tests.

I enjoy oil painting and ceramics at Arbor Hill Community Center. When my Tuesday effective speaking class ends tonight, I'll still have speedreading.

The February 4 deadline for your Barnard scholarship forms is impossible without W-2 forms to complete tax returns.

"Angela, your mother works hard!"

"She stays out of mischief." I laughed. "If she stopped to ponder, she'd get depressed, especially during Albany winters. NYC's warmer, less snowy weather is easier!

Wednesday, January 23, 1963: Finals

Calls from men I met at a mixer and during brief ping-pong study breaks resuscitated me, almost dead after calculus and hygiene tests in one grueling day.

In our room, exclaiming *Cheyah*, Carina and I aped imaginary australopithecine mascot Pithy with arm-swinging waddles around our cheery, pale-blue quarters.

Thursday, January 24, 1963: Irresistible

Kevin's precious letter touched me:

Dear Honeybear, the extraordinary TV movie, *Inherit the Wind* about the Scopes trial inspired me! Watching Clarence Darrow and William Jennings Bryan duke it out, I pictured myself as a lawyer. Only kidding! I must finish many college courses before deciding.

Like an unnamed person I adore, idealist Bryan expects the future to be better with positive transformations. Like your rebel who needs *As* in religion, Darrow was an agnostic who doubted good can overcome evil.

Whether to take creation and other Bible stories at face value was an issue. Scientific evidence for evolution supports a symbolic view of the Bible.

Does God even exist? If God made the universe, who made him or her? Has the universe always existed without a creator?

All religions claim to be right. Whole countries of people can't all be wrong or bad for not believing in Jesus or the Pope. Was Christ influenced by Hinduism when traveling in the Far East?

Every major religion has good and damaging ideas. Religion is wrong to fight wars and kill people to force conformity! History shows that power corrupts. Different religions limit or balance power.

Religions have outstanding leaders, like Buddha, Confucius, Moses, and Mohammed. Too many Christians ignore Jesus' good ideas, like humility, and reward material success. Church leaders should be morally superior, rather than the richest members.

Brainwashing, rather than proof of existence, results in belief in God. What kind of God lets Hitler destroy millions and allows Americans to destroy most Indian tribes?

Far Eastern ideas of God as more like the world's energy seem wiser. Can God be psychologist Carl Jung's collective unconscious? Our unconscious or subconscious (what's the difference?) minds may provide access to God.

Reincarnation is kinder than mean punishment in hell. A God who prevents murders and makes most people act better is positive, even if non-existent.

God would be unnecessary if everyone were like you, wanting the best for everyone and planning to help improve the world. With an idealist like you, I feel protective. I want a fair, powerful God to help me keep bad things from happening to you and ensure life gives you the best, as you deserve. Since we can't wait passively and count on God, we must take responsibility and work hard to stamp out evil.

These topics are beyond me. I doubt heaven and hell exist, but we'll know only after death. If something good follows, I want you with me for eternity. Are our beliefs irrelevant if death is final and we end up the same, no matter how good or evil our behavior during life? I'm more of a realist: everyone can't be helped. The electric chair is too good for the evilest criminals.

Thinking fondly of you, I hope that you're right about romance and love lasting forever. We both seek the truth, but is it subjective? I fervently hope we belong together. Most people may misunderstand us.

Is a red Kodiak bear the right mate for a Honeybear? They could produce unique cubs.
No need to answer these rantings!
Love, Your Kevin

What a heart and mind! I love him! Exam prep deferred my reply.

Saturday, January 26, 1963: God
In a dream, Kevin asked my views about his letter. "I agree with everything you wrote, like the need for religions to improve. I still pray and believe in God. Faith is separate from attending temple services and following religious rules."

Wednesday, January 30, 1963: Longest

After the movie, *The Longest Day*, about D-Day in World War II, I remarked, "Gary, I'm relieved to be past ten *longest* days of exam worry and pressure!" With corners of his mouth upturned, he agreed.

Thursday, January 31, 1963: Brave

Mustering my nerve, I left the subway at 72 Street. I remembered my fun 1958 week at Sara's studio apartment, helping her (below) pack to move to Albany.

I snapped back to the present. The elderly, green-uniformed doorman in her musicians' building asked, "Can I help you?" When he called Sara on the house phone, I was disappointed that no one answered. He asked, "Was she expecting you?" I mumbled something about being nearby and wanting to surprise my aunt. I waited nervously while he checked the mail-hold list. "She's due back in a week. Would you like to leave a message?"

I smiled. "No, but thanks for your help!" Since Dad's upcoming birthday will deplete my five-dollar-a-month allowance, I resisted the impulse to tip the doorman. I can't wait to graduate and earn enough for decent tips.

<u>Sunday, February 3, 1963: Entranced and Joyful</u>
Dear Diary, don't worry! I'm still a virgin, despite three rapturous days with Kevin here in NYC. I'm under his spell!

On Friday, romantic time in his tiny, nondescript Midtown hotel room preceded laughing at Second City comedians improvising.

Saturday, he sauntered and I floated around Barnard before the absorbing movie *Freud: The Secret Passion*. Though gentile actor Montgomery Clift as Jewish Freud made me wonder, Kevin was right that Clift was convincing. Canoodling in Kevin's room left me starry-eyed.

Today, we ambled around Barnard until he left on the Albany bus. Carina commented, "Angela, you're glowing!" Even enamored, I'm still boy crazy and freedom-loving.

<u>Monday, February 4, 1963: Intersession</u>
Fluent in French, Carina asked about my fabulous date at the French bistro Larre's (menu below). "Carina, you'd love the onion soup with broiled cheese on top. Do you like frog legs?"

"They were okay the only time I ate them."

"I tasted Gary's, but preferred my veal. His family is unkosher in restaurants. Gary, dapper in a brown (my least favorite color) suit, shared his yummy dessert éclair. I related

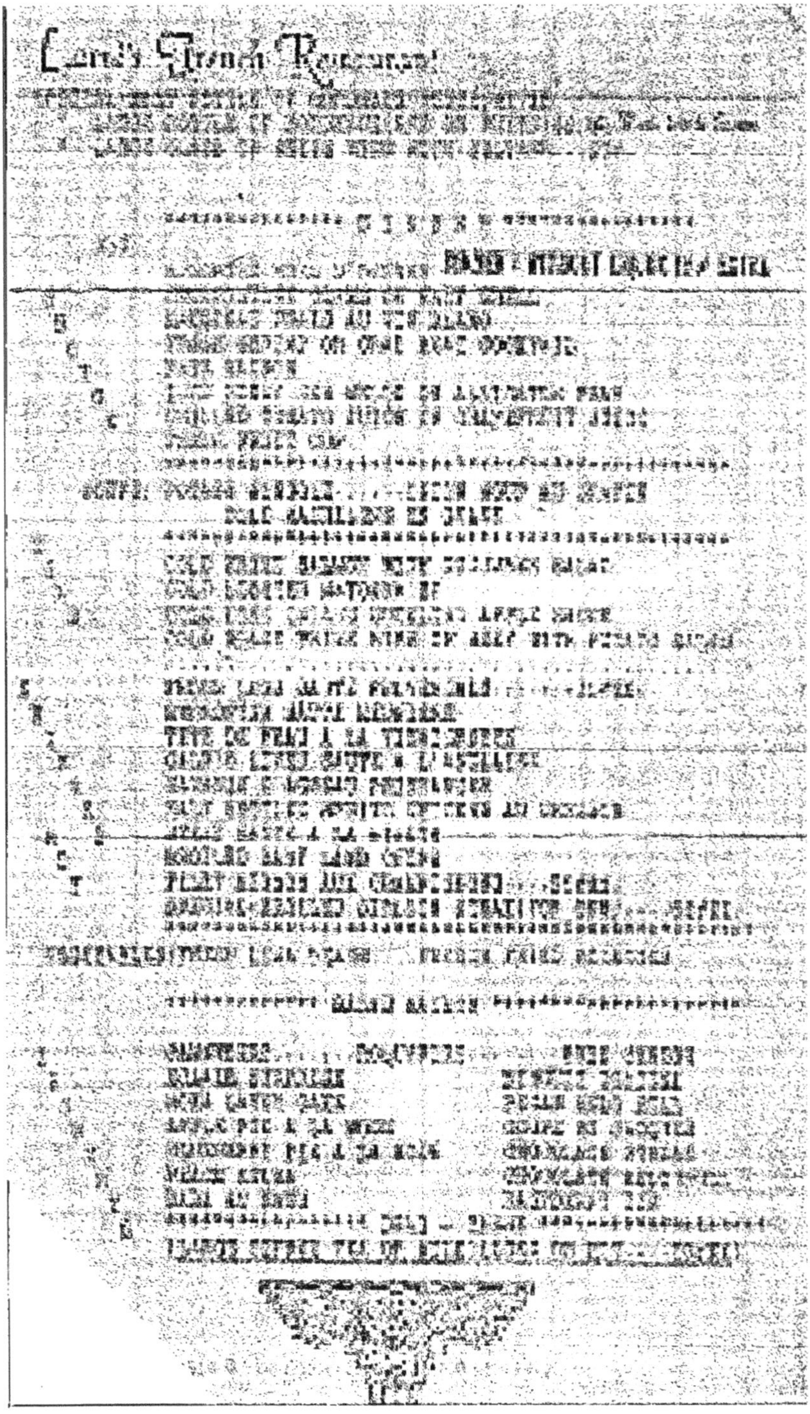

[illegible]

to the outstanding hit Broadway play, *A Thousand Clowns*. Pre-teen Nick lived with an unconventional, free-lance-writer uncle, as Aunt Sara lived with us while writing her fourth book. Actor Barry Gordon, who played Nick, belonged to our Albany temple before his family moved to NYC.

"Carina, the Tishman Building at 666 Fifth Avenue at 53 Street, features a striking lobby with abstract sculpture and waterfall by Noguchi, who went to Columbia. Through giant, forty-first-floor windows at dark, elegant Top of the Sixes restaurant, nearby skyscrapers looked otherworldly, as Gary and I sipped cocktails... Dates with Grady and Cullin will fill my last day of freedom!"

"Sounds like fun!"

<u>Wednesday, February 6, 1963: Letters</u>
This thrilled me:

> Dearest Angela, thank you for the most exciting weekend of my life! I appreciated three full days without schoolwork. May your first semester grades be tops, despite my bothering you during vacation. I couldn't resist you, but want to be a good influence to help maintain your scholarship.
>
> As I confessed on Friday, I'm in love with you. I want you to be my woman forever. I trust what you said about loving me and dating Lions for fun diversion from school pressures.
>
> Without all *As*, I could be in a monastery, annoying during senior year. This summer, we'll have a blast, especially if I can date openly and introduce you to my family. If my dream of a Columbia scholarship comes true, we can be together in NYC next fall. Love,
> Your Smitten Kevin

I replied:

> Dear Kevin, thank you for the loving letter! I'm happy about the summer and fall plans you described!
>
> Though grateful for three *As* in Hygiene, Latin, and Psychology and a *B* in Calculus, the *C Plus* in English sobered me. I can't rest on laurels with challenging second semester courses: Dr. K for English again, Vergil's *Aeneid* in Latin, introductory philosophy, scary integral calculus, and required voice and diction (can you give the weekly speeches for me?). Love, Angela

Thursday, February 7, 1963: Curfew

"*Cheyah*, Carina! Our later Sunday-through-Thursday midnight curfew will permit late dates after 10 PM library closure…. What's your opinion about President Park's speech about women's independent colleges?"

"All for our Seven Sisters and similar colleges, I wonder how many Honeybears would listen to her dry speech without compulsory presence." I sniggered.

Friday, February 8, 1963: Den

Dancing at the Lion's Den with extravert Cullin, I met his cheerful, humorous pal with tall, willowy date from NYU. At Cullin's sparsely furnished apartment, the others harmonized while singing along with favorite folk song records, like *If I Had a Hammer* on the *Peter, Paul, and Mary* album. I sang softly to keep off-key notes from bothering anyone. Music elates!

Saturday, February 9, 1963: Victorious

Gary looked professorial in a tweed sports jacket over a tan crewneck sweater. He complimented my old gray cowl neck pullover, fur-blend cardigan, and purple wool A-line skirt. With another couple from his synagogue, we happily watched our Lions defeat the Harvard Crimson basketball team!

At the bustling *Columbia Spectator* newspaper office, Gary's diminutive, sports-writer roommate said, "With victory uncommon, I can't wait to write up this game!" We kidded around with other staffers before having drinks at the Gold Rail bar. Close up, the bar resembles brass, rather than gold.

<u>Sunday, February 10, 1963: Angelina</u>
Despite yesterday's sixteen-inch NYC snowfall, my parents drove from Albany and picked me up en route to Justine's Bayside Queens apartment at 61-25 219 Street. I've loved my tall, sweet cousin since being flower girl at her 1950 wedding. A former Bloomingdale's Department Store buyer, she gave me a lovely birthday gift, a frilly white blouse for dates!

With Cousin Ron at Temple University, his parents and Aunt Rhoda helped us celebrate lovable, blue-eyed Angelina's fifth birthday.

Though happy that my love for adorable, blue-eyed Herbie, age ten, is reciprocated (his Valentine is above), I'm anxious about undone assignments without crucial Sunday library hours.

Monday, February 11, 1963: Brilliant

Mother generously treated Carina and me to *A Man for All Seasons*, Robert Bolt's superb Broadway play. Paul Scofield played Sir Thomas More, a principled idealistic, lauded in 1520 by his contemporary, Robert Whittington:

> More is a man of an angel's wit and singular learning. I know not his fellow. For where is the man of that gentleness, lowliness, and affability? And, as time requireth, a man of marvelous mirth and pastimes, and sometime of as sad gravity. A man for all seasons.

I cried when the despicable, royal egomaniac, Henry VIII, who beheaded wives, executed More, proving how power corrupts! Though I adore NYC's marvelous entertainment, another day with little studying leaves me nervously unprepared for classes.

Tuesday, February 12, 1963: Parents' Day

I was relieved that President Park, Dean Boorse, the Undergraduate Association president, freshmen advisors, and a drama presentation with refreshments kept parents occupied at 117 Milbank Hall. After classes, I caught up at the library.

Barnard dorm dinner: Dad's disparaging fury and arm-waving gestures shocked me. "We've spent years scrimping and saving for your college education. We've skipped work and spent thirty-five dollars. The least you could do is spend Parent's Day with us."

"You want me to skip classes? I spent all weekend with you! English, Latin, and philosophy were undone! I'll get an *F* without a speech for class tomorrow. I must spend almost all weekend on schoolwork. Calculus homework is often wrong."

When Mother asked, "Is that math?" I nodded yes. "Transfer to Albany State to be a good daughter!" Their excessive demands begged for an indignant rebuttal, but I bit my tongue and counted to ten to halt a public scene.

Later, I said, "Carina, I'm glad that four siblings free you from a hundred percent of parental expectations! Years of criticism and guilt trips have killed all good feelings. I want to avoid the parents."

Lumbering around like australopithecines and screeching *Cheyah* produced uncontrollable tittering. "Carina, thanks for being the ideal roomie!"

Wednesday, February 13, 1963: Marriage
Hours in the library preceded a chat with Carina. "Angela, this *Barnard Bulletin* reports that twenty-five percent of the 340 Class of 1962 grads are married, fifty before graduation."

"Could you marry without flunking out?" I asked.

"With the right guy. Otherwise, I'll join the Honeybear jazz singer at a Madrid, Spain night club, who asked, 'What else can one do with an art history major?'" I laughed.

Thursday, February 14, 1963: Valentine's Day
Still behind on schoolwork, I'm too romantic to turn down a date on my favorite holiday. Athletic male bodies running around the indoor tennis court at the Seventh Regiment Armory's men's international championships were stimulating.

This phone message pinned to our door electrified me:

I miss my Honeybear! Happy Valentine's Day!
Our formal dance is March 9. Be my date!
Love and kisses, Kevin

When AHS class president Craig (below) phoned to invite me to Hamilton College's Winter Carnival, I sadly declined. "Craig, I'd love to see you and have a wonderful time dancing, which I miss here. Even if I had the money, I'm struggling academically. My NYC aunts complain that I don't visit them on weekends, though I've explained I must be in the library. Lost in integral calculus, I'll be lucky to pass. I got a *C* in English first semester."

"Angela, though stunned about your *C*, I understand. It's tough here, too."

"I miss you and wish I could accept. Thank you for inviting me! Happy Valentine's Day!"

Saturday, February 16, 1963: Work and Reward
Until the library's 5 PM closing, I read tons of philosophy and other pages. If only my speedreading were faster....

Yojimbo was my first English-subtitled Japanese movie. At the Gold Rail, Gary, in a gray suit and burgundy tie, said perceptively, "Kurosawa's engrossing samurai story, resembling Robin Hood, the Mafia, and American Westerns, should be in Columbia's Core Curriculum." Sipping my Singapore sling, I agreed, picturing the loner hero arriving in a small town, which rival gangsters control.

<u>Sunday, February 17, 1963: Dance</u>
Answering dear Kevin's latest letter, I wrote:

> I want more than anything to attend your Friday formal dance. If I can get ahead on lessons, I can probably arrive Friday afternoon and return Saturday around noon. My parents' anniversary and birthdays gifts exhausted my meager allowance. They're too irritated (what else is new?) to advance the nine-dollar bus fare, but I'll ask and let you know. Love, Angela

<u>Monday, February 18, 1963: Herbie</u>
Carina and I enjoyed this note from my cousin Herbie:

letter I read your and I'm glad you liked my Valentine. I hope everything is okay with you. My mother is very happy that you like the blouse. And like it said on the valentine, you're my favorite. Best wishes. Love,

"Angela, he sounds like my cute brother, age eleven. I miss all three boys."

"I bet they miss the fun you invent!"

<u>Tuesday, February 19, 1963: Letter</u>
"Angela, you look upset."

"Carina, if you have time, I can read letter excerpts about Parents' Day."

"Please do. My lessons are done."

"Dad wrote, 'It was a disgrace the way you acted trying to evade us… and finally sparing an hour with us for supper. I'm at my wit's end trying to figure out why you act this way.'"

"With hours of work left for Wednesday classes, you compromised to see them!"
"Poor listeners, they ignored my need to catch up, rather than spend a third day in a row with them. Without adequate time for my speech, I got a *C*. Such mediocre grades could cancel my scholarship, especially with a D or F in incomprehensible calculus. Are your parents ever mean?"

"Not with my sister and me, assistant moms. My father has been irate with the most mischievous, impudent brother."

"Thanks for being supportive! Being here away from constant criticism has been wonderful. Unfortunately, I'm dependent on parents for money to finish college."

"How about Kevin's big dance?"

"Lacking money and time kills me. Why couldn't I fall for a Lion, like Gary?"

"I've yet to fall in love. I guess I'll know when it happens."

Wednesday, February 20, 1963: Gift
"Carina, thanks for loaning me money to buy a cute stuffed Honeybear for Kevin's March 3 birthday!"

"You're welcome. I never use all my allowance."
Omitting a gift is worse than owing money.

Thursday, February 21, 1963: Guys
"Carina, ping pong with Grady and others and two hours conversing, mainly listening, to intelligent, fun Gary dissolved hours of schoolwork tension."

"How long have you dated Gary?"

"Since October. Though he has yet to ask about me or deepen our connection as Kevin always does, I've appreciated relaxing activities without pressure to go steady or have sex. You can make his goodnight pecks more romantic by crooning jazz ballads through our open dorm window above the Brooks entrance." Carina tittered.

Friday, February 22, 1963: First
Sitting in one of four almost circular balconies, Gary and I heard his avid roommate say, "This is Columbia's first Carnegie Hall band concert in thirty years and Carnegie's first ever with combined university bands! We rehearsed with Lehigh in Pennsylvania. Proceeds from over $2000 of tickets sold will fund scholarships at both universities!"

Gary asked which pieces I preferred. "The Sousa march and Berlioz' *Grand Symphony for Band*," I replied.

Gary's tenor voice sounded buoyant. "Since that symphony has been performed rarely and recorded only twice, our version may be the best. I liked *Camino Real* by Elkus, the Lehigh band director. Both bands favor original works by American composers."

His roommate, who liked Schuman's overture *Chester* and *Tocatta Marziale* by Williams, added, "Every piece was composed for concert band. Columbia's lucky to have director Elias Dann."

Almost silently humming Beeson's *Commemoration* and Holst's *First Suite for Band*, I entered our room. From under blankets, Carina's muffled voice asked about the music. "Hearing 120 musicians in ornate Carnegie Hall uplifted me, burned out after excessive studying!"

Saturday, February 23, 1963: Gina
With two agreeable, new couples, amiable Cullin and I danced to rock and romantic records at his place after an enlivening piano recital. What fun!

When Carina asked about the concert, I read from the program. "Gina Bachauer, *the greatest female pianist of the Twentieth Century*, was born fifty years ago in Greece. Her Jewish family heritage was Austrian and German. Praised for technique, tone, and intensity, she studied with Rachmaninov in Paris and performed 600 concerts during World War II for our troops in Egypt. As a widow, she made her 1950 NYC debut at Carnegie Hall. Later, she married Alec Sherman, conductor of her Royal Albert Hall 1947 London concert."

Carina's voice sounded revitalized. "Talented, married women inspire me!"

Sunday, February 24, 1963: Sara
With nickels for the pay phone, I got up my courage. My heart leaped with anticipation when my aunt answered the phone. "Sara, this is Angela. Do you like Gina Bachauer? I loved her recent piano recital."

"I'm giving a lesson." Her gruff voice sounded impatient. The loud dial tone made my eyes fill with tears. Disheartened, I sighed deeply.

Tuesday, February 26, 1963: Apology
I reluctantly sent this:

> Dear Mother and Dad, thanks for treating Carina and me to *A Man for All Seasons*! Justine's party was fun! I'm sorry you felt hurt about Parents' Day. Please understand how challenging college is, especially math and voice and diction. Since my speech, graded only *C*, took until 3 AM and you didn't value dinner with me, I should have stayed in the library.
>
> Dad, I'll see you on your birthday Saturday. Arriving Friday for Kevin's formal dance that evening, I can sleep on the couch so your office stuff can stay in my room.

<u>Friday, March 1, 1963: Plans</u>
In case of no trip home, I mailed a silver tie clip, which used my saved allowance, and homemade card for Dad's birthday.

Despite daily letters, I miss Kevin and can't wait to wear my favorite strapless, turquoise organza gown at the dance. A song from *The King and I* musical runs through my mind: *Shall we dance? On a bright cloud of music, shall we fly?*

<u>Saturday, March 2, 1963: Tea Room</u>
Gary called thrice this week before escorting me to *David and Lisa*, a poignant movie about psychiatric hospital patients. An intelligent, sensitive boy and a girl with two personalities bonded. "Gary, this moving film makes me eager to help people with similar challenges as a psychologist."

I appreciate native New Yorker Gary, who knows and can afford the best places, like the renowned Russian Tea Room where our eyes scanned for celebrities. Gary's navy suit, white shirt, and thin, red-striped tie fit in. A few sips of a Black Russian vodka-Kahlua cocktail left me tipsy.

<u>Monday, March 4, 1963: Hostility</u>
Today's special delivery, six-page letter made me long for financial independence without accounting to parents.

> Angela, your answer to our letter of two weeks
> ago was late. You dismiss Parents' Day by saying
> you're sorry. That's not good enough. We want
> more than lip service. You thank us for the
> theater politely, but it's still lip service. Our
> daughter couldn't find time to spend with her
> parents or perhaps make a little sacrifice and
> give of herself for that day, which cost us thirty-
> five dollars. You found time to write to Kevin to
> accept the dance invitation. You don't have ten
> cents or five minutes to go to the pay phone to
> call your aunts weekly? Carina's birthday cost

twenty-six dollars for a charm and ticket to a show she'd seen. You'd spend ten dollars on Kevin's dance. There's thirty-six dollars. You ought to be ashamed of yourself. You're making a laughing stock out of us. Now you want to come home for the dance. What will you use for bus fare? Kevin asked you to come up? Suppose I asked you to come up for my birthday? Would you find time? What about all your homework? How come you have time and money for things you want but can find neither time nor money for things we or your aunts want you to do? Finally, you say not to go to any trouble. You'll sleep on the couch. Well, don't be so good to us! If you come home, you'll eat with us and sleep in your own bed or else don't come! You either act like a good daughter or there is no money for fare. I'm putting my foot down once and for all. Either you straighten yourself out or else! I expect an immediate reply. Remember, no lip service, no civil action, just consideration for others. Love, Dad

Could Dad be harsher if I were an axe murderer? I won't lower myself to his level by mentioning the cost of his gift. Working so hard in school, I feel it's unfair to miss my favorite reward: a big dance. Relentless academic pressure and studying without fun have sent Honeybears home with nervous breakdowns. If only my balanced life earned parental approval, rather than guilt infliction… Fed up with my parents, I long to escape from nastiness and will ignore them when possible.

<u>Tuesday, March 5, 1963: No Dance</u>
Without money to call long-distance, I mailed this with a broken heart:

Dear Kevin, Dad is jealous, demanding that I spend Sunday celebrating his birthday and making the Friday dance impossible. I'd fall dangerously behind on assignments. My mean parents won't lend bus money. I'm sorry and disappointed. The formal with you would be unforgettable, a dream come true! I miss you. Love, Angela

Friday, March 8, 1963: Pressures

"Carina, luckily, I was here for Kevin's call. His strict parents keep him sympathetic about my plight. Instead of escorting me to the dance, he'll visit me tomorrow for the day! I'm in love! I can't wait to see him!"

"You deserve a break!"

"Mean parental letters bother me. With mid-terms looming, I feel overwhelmed. I've got to improve in calculus, prepare weekly speeches faster, and get ahead in philosophy and Latin to squeeze in writing a long English paper about *Lady Chatterley's Lover*. How're you?"

"I'm an idiot for taking challenging physical and cultural anthropology and geology during freshman year! Even French and English are difficult here. At least, whacking golf balls in PE dissipates tension! I repeat Christopher Robin's words to Winnie, the Pooh. *You're braver than you believe, stronger than you seem, and smarter than you think.*

I nodded sympathetically before squealing *Cheyah* during an arm-swinging tramp around our spacious room.

"Pithy is excited that you'll see Kevin!" Carina grinned.

Saturday, March 9, 1963: Visit

Charming Kevin's visit was exhilarating! Cuter than ever, he put me into the usual euphoric daze as we moseyed around Greenwich Village in comfortable fifty-degree, cloudy weather.

"Angela, understanding your academic demands and shortage of funds, I used my dance savings for the bus fare here."

Beaming, I felt lost in his blue eyes. "Thank you! I'm overjoyed to see you!"

"Finally managing all *As*, I'll introduce you to my family over vacation. We can date openly!"

"Congratulations! How did you attain perfection?" I asked flirtatiously.

"Without expressing skepticism, I memorized and regurgitated back religious stuff. Despite Harvard's top status, I'd rather be at Columbia with you." Our eyes met.

"That sounds ideal! Is Yale your third choice?"

He nodded. "Sans a scholarship, I'll be at Albany State."

"I relate to everything you're experiencing."

"Thank you for the artistic birthday card and miniature Honeybear. Angelette keeps me company every night in bed." Kevin's intent gaze made my loins lurch and face hotly blush before his embrace and kiss. "At Barnard, do you feel a sense of belonging?"

Nodding, I struggled to breathe normally. "Barnard's geology department chairman supposedly said, 'Greet a Columbia boy and he nods. Say hello to a Barnard girl and she takes it down in her notebook.'" Our ensuing laugh was one of many during our fun-filled day, traipsing up Central Park's west border from 59 to 110 Street. When in love, being together without expensive entertainment is enough. At the Port Authority bus terminal, his enticing farewell kiss left me panting slightly.

"Carina, Kevin must have forgotten how I look to tactfully remark, 'No matter how good you look with makeup, it's like painting a rose. Nothing can best the rose's natural beauty.' I teased him about flattering me with a line."

"Will you reduce makeup?"

"Only slightly if he's around. At least, he turned criticism into a compliment. Men liking us without makeup is nice, but I look much better with Maybelline Turquoise Iridescent Eye Shadow, Velvet Black Magic Mascara, and Black Eyeliner Pencil. Merle Norman Beige Powder Base covers acne. Blush Rouge and Revlon Luminous Pink lipstick counteract sallowness. Does Kevin want me drabber so Columbia guys ignore me?"

"You're right! Such male remarks exercise a subtle control over us. We feel less free to express ourselves through our appearance... I've yet to try most makeup."

"Luckily, it's a bargain which lasts for ages. At least two years ago, this eyeshadow cost under a dollar."

We followed Pithy in an australopithecine trek around our quarters. "Carina, Pithy is flattered that your cute sketch of him occupies the place of honor over our mantle."

Sunday, March 10, 1963: Resentment
When I called home collect, Dad said, "Thank you for the lovely card and silver tie clip, which I wore today at our restaurant dinner with three couples. Last evening, Mother and I laughed at the comedy *Divorce Italian Style.* Didn't you see this movie?"

"Twice! I must return to the books. Happy birthday." Upset by his letters, I couldn't wait to end this duty call. I'm grateful for Kevin's visit, but angry about being deprived of dressing up for a rare dance, meeting Kevin's friends, and being led by a dance expert I love. This was the last straw; the parents made me miss too many AHS formals!

Tuesday, March 12, 1963: Opera
On the phone, Aunt Rhoda said, "A work colleague with season opera tickets can't go this Friday. Can you come with me?"

"Thank you for asking! I like opera and wish I could. Thanks for introducing me to my Friday date in 1958!"

"Joe from our anniversary party?"

"Yes! He sent his college phone number in Brooklyn. I'm eager to see him after years as pen pals."

"How romantic! Will he wear his dark red tweed sports jacket?" We chuckled before an incoming call ended our talk.

<u>Wednesday, March 13, 1963: No Five-Minute Calls</u>
I wrote to the parents:

> You know that our rooms lack phones for outgoing calls? Today, I interrupted concentration and lost my library cubicle to get coins at a machine, walk a block to the dorm, and wait in line for a pay phone. Since no one answered, I must keep repeating this disruption to reach Aunt Lila. Walking to the library, finding a quiet empty stall, and settling down resulted in an hour wasted. If she had answered, more time would have been spent talking. I need every minute and undivided attention to figure out math problems, catch up on difficult philosophy reading, start my English paper, and prepare increasingly long speeches weekly.

<u>Thursday, March 14, 1963: Letter</u>
Sitting at my desk, I chuckled at Dad's letter, which may have crossed mine in transit.

Carina looked up. "I'm dozing off. A laugh will help me finish this French chapter." I read this aloud:

> Monday, March 11: Angela, your decision to stay in NYC this weekend was wise. Thanks for your thoughtful kindness and consideration. Glad you called Aunt Rhoda. Don't leave yourself so low that you must borrow money to call at least weekly. We're fed up with winter driving over deep potholes. A broken spring and muffler and jammed door on our '57 Oldsmobile were expensive to fix. Evelyn Levine had three

weeks of hospital shock treatments for
depression. We're relieved that she's home and
back to work. We're busy with courses.
Mother's paintings and ceramics are improving.
Thursday evening reading improvement at her
office costs only five dollars for ten lessons. Take
a break from mid-terms and write.

"Angela, can jealousy of Kevin outweigh your father's desire to
see you on his birthday?"
I shrugged, baffled by old people's weird behavior. Carina,
Pithy, and I galumphed around the room, swinging arms and
shrieking *Cheyah* between silly guffaws.

Friday, March 15, 1963: Reunion
Tall, handsome, green-eyed Joe, a soph at Long Island U, is still
a perfect gentleman! During the touching movie, *Days of Wine
and Roses*, his muscular arm around me was comforting when
tears came. I shared with Joe, "This masterpiece has taught me
the dangers of becoming dependent on drinking. I'm glad that I
can take or leave alcohol."

"A social drink with friends is fun, but unneeded. Does
drinking holiday wine keep Jews from becoming alcoholics?"

"Manischewitz wine tastes bad enough to keep anyone
from craving alcohol." We chortled.

Later: "Carina, I sat on my fingers to resist running them
through business major Joe's thick, strawberry blond locks."
We giggled. "Joe's agreeable, but less thought-provoking than
intellectual Lions. Sadly, his affluent father, who bought him a
Cadillac in high school, died of a heart attack last year. I hope
Joe can afford finishing expensive LIU. The movie we saw made
me realize I'm like an alcoholic for sweets with mint-chocolate-
chip ice cream for lunch and Chunky candy bars at the library. I
never ate candy in Albany. Ice cream was only to cool off
during muggy summers."

"Is academic pressure to blame?"
"That and difficult parents."

<u>Monday, March 18, 1963: Calculus</u>
I replied to Kevin's daily missive:

> Failing integral calculus is scarier than asking my intimidating math prof for help. If only she were approachable and amusing, like my dear Latin prof. During math office hours, I waited for a student to leave. Prof E looked stern. Overcoming nervousness, I said, "I seem to understand that we are measuring the area under the curve. My answers are wrong without my knowing why."
>
> "Show me a problem you got wrong." While I searched my notes, she impatiently said, "Meanwhile, I'll help the next student." Office hours were done when the other girl left. Mentioning a class to teach, Prof E rushed off. Unfortunately, the math mid-term is this week!
>
> Seeming harassed, Prof E, whom I've never seen smile, chairs the entire math department. She's overworked with Barnard's lack of teaching assistants for large classes.

Distressed by my parents, I let timidity cause procrastination. Finding Prof E again will interfere with cramming for three exams this week. I'll pray for luck and easy math questions. In case God is busy elsewhere, I'll supplicate Pithy.

<u>Wednesday, March 20, 1963: Wobbly</u>
After my growls about calculus office hours during tooth-brushing, Carina quoted Winnie, the Pooh: *My spelling is wobbly. It's good spelling, but it wobbles, and the letters get in the wrong places.*

I snickered, spraying rinse water all over our sink. "Thanks, Carina! Will Prof E agree that my calculus is good, despite numbers in the wrong places?"

Friday, March 22, 1963: Song
Tears dropped after Carina sang:

> Words in recall and lovely sketches when remembered recreate in colors new scenes from the past.
> So with present moment, recaptured on the morrow, we will find our ties to Barnard strengthen with years.
> Strong are your gates and wide your many paths of learning where new vistas have been opened to life beyond.
> To this present moment our thoughts will be returning,
> Then we will find our ties to Barnard strengthen with years.

"Angela, how did we survive for six months without this Barnard song, an essential freshman experience?"

"To the genius of Class of 1962, including Miss Mark's lyrics and Miss Moskowitz's music! Four murderous exams this week have left me too drained for more plaudits."

Saturday, March 23, 1963: Missive
Relieved to evade disapproval, I read to Carina:

> We received your letter and heard from your aunts, who were thrilled with your calls. It takes little to make them happy and the dividends are rewarding. Buy the Merle Norman makeup near you. Parking problems keep us away from downtown. My exam is March 23 PG (Please

God). Are your exams finished? If we receive
your bus arrival time, I'll meet you at the
station. No trouble at all. My course is done.
Mother's eyes have adjusted to speedreading.
Looking forward to your vacation. Keep writing.
Love, Dad
P.S. Call Aunt Rhoda about the broken suitcases,
so she can make a claim where she bought
them. Have a shoemaker fix them or tie them
with rope. Don't lug them yourself. Get a
cabman. Be careful.
On second thought, we can take winter clothes
back in the car in May. It's too much for you on
a crowded weekend. Get a bus reservation
before they sell out.

I groaned about Dad's ludicrous orders. "Without money, how
do I pay for repairs or a taxi? Picture me, lugging large broken
suitcases down Broadway. I've yet to notice a shoemaker or
store with rope." Carina grinned.

Sunday, March 24, 1963: Tests
I studied all weekend for mid-terms without time for a bus
reservation. I can't wait to see my adored Kevin Friday and be
on vacation, though I'll have to write my paper.

Friday, March 29, 1963: Home
Gentlemanly Gary, who has also studied hard for exams,
accompanied me on the subway and carried my small suitcase.
When the train stopped at 72 Street, he said, "A penny for your
thoughts."

Did I look troubled? Rather than broach the
uncomfortable subject of missing Sara, I quipped, "Even for a
valuable penny, my exam-exhausted brain is missing thoughts.
Gary, thank you for escorting me to the Trailways bus!"

In Albany, did Dad drive me home to keep me away from Kevin? "Dad, how was your test?"

"I finished sixty-five of seventy questions in the ten-minute limit and fifty-four of sixty questions during ninety minutes allowed."

"That's good." My voice sounded flat with disinterest.

"Thank you. Mother got a perfect score on her speedreading comprehension test."

<u>Saturday, March 30, 1963: Gloversville</u>
Driving on the Thruway under metal-colored, cloudy skies to see our relatives, Dad said, "Angela, Aunt Myrna had colon difficulties when we visited on March 17. Thank God, the biopsy was negative, but she must watch her diet." Even viewing the bleak landscape of leafless trees appealed more than visualizing colon health. With top temperatures in the low forties, who would guess that it's spring? NYC feels warmer and cheerier.

Mother said, "Myrna's illness made them late for your birthday. You can choose a gift at their department store." I enjoyed hearing about Lydia's fun dance. She resembled a princess in a beautiful white gown (above).

<u>Sunday, March 31, 1963: DHL</u>
All day, I sat at my beloved blond Heywood Wakefield desk. Absent-mindedly stroking its satiny-smooth, maple top, I dredged up words for the handwritten draft of my paper:

> My report today concerns the ideas and the beauty in D. H. Lawrence's (DHL) infamous 1928 novel, *Lady Chatterley's Lover (LCL)*. I hope to provide a context for understanding and appreciating *LCL*.
>
> The earlier DHL works I read glorified nature and focused on interpersonal relationships. Last semester's report ended with *Sons and Lovers*, the 1913 autobiographical novel about DHL's youthful difficulty freeing himself from a powerful attachment to his mother.
>
> In 1912, DHL met Frieda, the older German wife of an English professor. DHL and Frieda soon were deeply in love and felt unable to live without each other. In 1914, they

officially married after Frieda's divorce. Blissful happiness and violent quarreling alternated during their decades together.

DHL's restless spirit and health issues motivated frequent travel in Europe, Asia, Australia, and North America. World events troubled DHL. His 1915 letter to a friend decries World War I as *all wrong, all foolish, all a wretched mistake.* (*The Intelligent Heart* by Harry Moore, p. 231)

This war denunciation was typical of DHL's wide correspondence. With a strong personality, he got along well with only a few of the many interesting people he met. DHL was often brutally frank, overly sensitive, and incredibly domineering. DHL modeled fictional characters closely on people he met. Unflattering portrayals produced resentment.

Do idealistic authors invent negative fictional characters to retaliate against people who have disappointed them? I'd rather honor positive people I admire.

Monday, April 1, 1963: Kevin
On a rainless, sixty-degree afternoon, Kevin and I meandered through Washington Park. His fitted blue trousers and plaid shirt accentuated his perfect body. "Angela, I missed picking you up at the terminal."

"I'm sorry that my father, probably jealous, whisked me away. Thanks to his taking tests in his NY State employment class, I'm past justifying grades less than *A*. I hardly controlled a guffaw when he responded, 'C is not a bad mark' when I mentioned fear of failing my calculus mid-term."

Kevin smiled. "I missed you all weekend." Near the calm lake, we stopped for a hug and sweet kiss, as birds flew overhead.

"I wish I could have seen you. Saturday, we were with Gloversville relatives. Sunday, I had to start my paper."

Kevin looked jaunty. "Angela, did you hear that the Russians approve of American popcorn and potato chips? Working-class cowboy origins make Russians like our blue jeans." I grinned. "With Soviets dragging feet on a nuclear weapon test ban, JFK wants to keep the four nuclear powers from mushrooming (pardon my pun) to ten by 1970."

I grinned at the pun. "If anyone can solve difficult world issues, it's our brilliant President!"

"Are you pleased that NYC again has newspapers after the 114-day strike?" His facial expression seemed mischievous.

"Is that an April Fool's joke?"
A chortle escaped his lips. "Maybe."

Later, Dad confirmed that the strike was over as we ate ground beef patties, baked potatoes, and green salad. "Angela, Aunt Rhoda mentioned your date with Joe. Did he wear his dashing red sports jacket?" Dad looked jovial.

Trying to look solemn, I couldn't resist a facetious reply. "He never showed up." I tried to grimace.

"How rude!" Dad's brow furrowed.

"April Fool's joke!" I exclaimed.

With a wry expression, Mother said, "Herm, she inherited your sense of humor!"

Dad asked, "Was Joe from Philadelphia?"

"Elkins Park, Pennsylvania. His widowed mom now lives in Vineland, New Jersey." Hearing about Joe's father's early death silenced Dad, who looked somber.

Tuesday, April 2, 1963: More DHL
A fan of *LCL*, Kevin disarmingly pestered me until I let him read my pages. "Angela, one reason I love you is that you are open-minded. Do rebels like us go for DHL?" I giggled. "Wanting to stay a virgin until marriage doesn't mean a woman is uninterested in sex. She can enjoy reading about it and imagining future joys without risking pregnancy, right?" Elated,

I felt so understood, loved, and accepted that a tear rolled down my cheek. Kevin enveloped me in a warm embrace and bussed my lips. "I love you so much, Angela! You are special! Do you love me?" Nodding, I kissed him back fervently before reluctantly leaving the park's shower-free, sixty-five-degree weather to write at home:

> DHL steadily completed poetry, essays, and plays, as well as fiction. A 1926 trip through his native English Midlands appears to have inspired *LCL*. Frequent four-letter, Anglo-Saxon words, common in real life, and detailed descriptions of sex triggered the 1928 LCL controversy. Literature seems natural and realistic when reflecting life, including everyday terms. DHL considered sex a significant part of life. His erotic act descriptions are moving and beautiful. DHL's *Fantasia of the Unconscious* expresses his disdain about objections to his writing, which is not intended for the average reader. He's right that no one is forced to read even one word of his, except for critics, needing to *scribble a dollar's worth of words.*

I laughed about unconventional DHL's contempt for critics.

> DHL's abhorrence of modern society's encroachment on nature came from an unhappy childhood in an ugly mining town. Traveling in Switzerland, DHL wrote about the *hideous rawness* of human life and the painful *desolating harshness* of increasing industrialization. (Moore, p. 204)
> DHL abhorred dominance of intellect over emotions and the consequential harm to the intimate relationships he prized. Emphasis

on the mind meant less attention to the senses
and the body. DHL lamented the sexual
experience becoming mechanical with men and
women contemplating and talking so much that
they behaved with more inhibition and less
passion. DHL deplored people scorning sex and
the body as inferior to the *superior* mind.

Agreeing with DHL, I squeeze in my Barnard social life to shun
the brainy, emotionless life DHL disparaged.

<u>Wednesday, April 3, 1963: Playing</u>
On an overcast day, upbeat Kevin and I admired the glass-brick
façade of the Playdium on Ontario Street before entering to
rent bowling shoes. Glad that the shabby interior keeps prices
affordable, we bowled. Watching graceful athlete Kevin's
perfect form achieve games of 180 and 200 was fun, despite
my terrible scores.

 Later, at my desk, I wrote:

In *LCL,* DHL celebrated men and women as
lovers, rather than platonic friends. World War I
left Sir Clifford Chatterley paralyzed from the
waist down. With a successful writing career, he
was the kind of cold intellectual DHL disdained.

Agreeing with DHL, I consider romantic attraction and love the
ultimate, though I like some men, e.g., Udeh from AHS,
platonically.

Sir Clifford's wife was a *ruddy, country-looking
girl with soft, brown hair and sturdy body, and
slow movements, full of unusual energy.* DHL
also noted her large eyes, soft voice, and rural
demeanor. (*LCL,* p. 38)

I identified with Lady Connie Chatterley's vitality, fascination with cultural and intellectual activities, and eventual boredom, confined to a country estate with social life limited to entertaining friends and relatives. Living in NYC has proven my need for variety.

> Restless wanderings in the nearby woods helped free Connie from feeling that life was empty and meaningless. She met the estate's gamekeeper, Oliver Mellors, a mouthpiece for DHL's disgust with lifeless people and mechanized modern life. Mellors, DHL's ideal natural man, preferred a solitary existence in nature.

Outdoorsy, intelligent Mellors, well-traveled as an Army officer, attracted Connie (and me). My paper's biggest challenge: discussing making love, which I've imagined, rather than experienced, as wonderful.

I sniggered about DHL's sure disapproval of analyzing his writing to death in class papers. Majoring in English would kill my love of novels.

Thursday, April 4, 1963: Pregnant
Gloomy, chilly weather facilitated cranking out more words:

> Mellors and Connie, both warm and sensitive, were disillusioned. Their capacity for a relationship in which the physical was as important as the mental was wasted with their mates. In sunshine and rain, they met in the woods, enjoying trees, flowers, birds, and other wildlife. Overcoming initial inhibitions from past unsatisfactory sexual relationships, they abandoned themselves to passion.

DHL described how love, trust, and commitment make sex wonderful. Waiting until marriage seems like the best solution to fear of being used by callow men.

> DHL portrayed his ideal, complete, romantic relationship. His tender, poetic descriptions of two strangers becoming lovers and finding happiness and fulfillment together moved e.g., *new strange thrills rippling inside her… like* me, *a flapping overlapping of soft flames, soft as feathers… like bells rippling up and up to a culmination*.
>
> The paradise Connie and Mellors created was threatened. While Connie vacationed in Italy, the gamekeeper's brutal, coarse wife suddenly returned, demanding to live with him again. Inferring that Mellors was Connie's lover, his wife spread scandalous rumors, driving Mellors away to London. When Connie returned, they joyously made plans together, eager for their coming child.

Having escaped from gossipy Albany to anonymous NYC, I relate to Mellors departing for London. I admire people who act freely without worrying about small-minded disapproval.

<u>Friday, April 5, 1963: Dream</u>
Did DHL's sex descriptions inspire last night's dream?

> At an ocean resort, like Bel Mar, New Jersey, Kevin and I viewed a romantic movie, during which his respectful caresses left me breathless. Strolling on the dark beach, we started kissing. One thing led to another. The crescendo was glorious, as DHL described.

Wind and temperatures in the thirties helped my paper grow:

> Temporarily separated, Connie and Mellors
> planned to buy a farm together after divorces
> were final. The book ends with pregnant Connie,
> reading his long letter, predicting the death and
> destruction of industrial masses. Trusting the
> *little glow* and flame between them to be
> powerful enough to survive any cataclysm,
> Mellors yearns for them to reunite soon.
> We never learn whether they
> successfully reject a cerebral existence and find
> fulfillment close to nature. Idealists like me
> prefer to picture them living happily ever after.
> I hope to have conveyed DHL's
> philosophical notions and the poetic beauty of
> the love story of Connie and Mellors. Full
> appreciation requires reading DHL books. He has
> become one of my favorite writers!

At Calsolaro's dark, worn-out bar, the amusing banter of Kevin and Ric rewarded finishing my draft paper. Spiffy in a white, V-neck pullover, handsome Ric said, "Dating for you freshman girls is a breeze. We frosh males are so unwanted that *The State University News* humorously discussed our plight." He guzzled Hedrick beer, on tap everywhere due to owner O'Connell's power as political boss.

Sipping bottled ale, Kevin, in tight, sexy blue jeans, responded, "Younger girls are thrilled to date college men."

Ric, grimaced. "Why work hard to qualify for college only to be stuck back with high schoolers? The article suggested dating college seniors, ignored when senior guys pursue freshmen." I tittered.

Kissing my cheek and massaging my shoulders, covered by a thin pink blouse, Kevin teased me. "I prefer older, sophisticated women."

I rolled my eyes. "Two months older hardly counts."

Ric asked, "How about the Peace Corps after college?"

Kevin remarked, "Building a South American school, I can perfect Spanish and learn construction skills!"

Ric added, "A 1962 Albany State graduate taught English, history, and geography at a Nigerian teacher training school. His 220 dormitory students were intelligent, diligent, and well behaved, in contrast to most Schuyler High kids!"

"Angela, would you join?" asked Kevin whose shoulder stroking caused distracting pelvic quivers.

In a trance, I managed to utter, "I'm in awe of brave Peace Corps volunteers!"

Saturday, April 6, 1963: Works Consulted

Typing bibliographical information about DHL's fascinating essays, e.g., *Psychoanalysis and the Unconscious*, I was amused by prickly DHL's comment about the misfortune of serious books being exposed in the public market, *like slaves exposed naked for sale*. Writing about psychology, especially the unconscious, carries the risk of misunderstanding by ignorant, defensive people. Admirable Freud braved ridicule to pursue his pioneering work.

Arousing, romantic couch time included feeling Kevin's hard, bulging biceps and broad, manly shoulders through his plaid shirt. Gazing into entrancing blue eyes, I imagined his red crew cut being long enough to run fingers through! Tonight, during long kisses, his back massage through my white nylon blouse generated enthralling throbs. Staying fully clothed quells anxiety about sudden parental arrival.

I appreciate his always respectful, public affection. Stroking hands and arms, he avoids intimate parts.

Tuesday, April 9, 1963: Reply

Back at Barnard since Sunday, I answered dependable Kevin's daily letter:

Thank you for driving me to the bus station and cheering me when maudlin tears brimmed. You are the only part of cold, gray Albany I miss.

Roomie Carina deserved her fun Indiana week with special parents and younger siblings. The rambunctious, brazen brother's scrapes kept her laughing.

After editing on the bus, I'm typing my paper. Fortunate to like my assigned writer, I hope my paper's final English grade tops last semester's *C Plus*.

I'm impressed that you want to read my introductory philosophy assignments, too challenging for me to speedread. Aristotle, Descartes, Locke, and Hegel address theories of knowledge and truth, epistemology. Plato and Mill enlighten about metaphysics. Kant, William James, and Russell are assigned for logic. Machiavelli, Rousseau, Hume, Nietzsche, and Marx political philosophies are eye-opening. Kevin, will Sartre and existentialism also be your favorites?

Sunday, April 14, 1963: Barbra

"Carina, what's that wonderful singing?" An LP record spun on her portable player.

"My family gave me this *Barbra Streisand Album*! Her *Cry Me a River* may be better than Julie London's. I like Barbra's *Soon It's Gonna Rain* from *The Fantasticks*. She sings the classic *Happy Days Are Here Again* sadly! Her rendition of *Keepin' Out of Mischief Now* is captivating!"

"I'd rather listen, but integral calculus beckons. With homework still wrong, I must see Prof E."

<u>Wednesday, April 17, 1963: Spot</u>
"Angela, I see a frown," said Carina, watching me read Mother's letter. "Are you in the dog house?"

"Call me Spot! They're *peeved* that schoolwork made me miss my aunts' April 8 Seder. Here's Mother's news:"

> The Levine Seder with turkey and trimmings covered the entire service, including songs.
>
> Frank Sinatra was a good Academy Awards emcee.
>
> Saturday in Latham, I paid only ninety-nine cents to dry clean three pounds of winter clothes.
>
> I bought a two-piece cotton print for work for $7.88 on sale.
>
> Friday night, Dad and I saw touching movies: *The Miracle Worker* about deaf-blind Helen Keller and *Sweet Bird of Youth* with handsome Paul Newman!

"Carina, Paul Newman's blue eyes are one of the few things Mother and I both like!" Carina's quirky grin made me smile.

<u>Friday, April 19, 1963: Cowed</u>
"Carina, on the phone, immovable Mother just demanded my presence at Aunt Lila's tomorrow. I much prefer the Greek Games with you, but Dad's nasty letters leave me too browbeaten to refuse!"

"I understand." Her tone was empathetic.

"Thanks for your support, Roomie!"

<u>Saturday, April 20, 1963: Hal</u>
This is the gist of Cousin Hal's (below) San Francisco audio tape, played during my visit to his parents' colorfully decorated apartment:

Sportscaster Ira Blue, father of Eileen's Barnard classmate, substitutes on Les Crane's midnight, call-in, KGO radio show. Well-read, nasal-voiced Ira articulately discusses any subject. Invited, we sat in the restaurant area of the *hungry i* at 599 Jackson at Kearny in the basement of the International Hotel in North Beach.

Owner Enrico Banducci, sporting his usual beret, welcomed us without minding our nursing espressos through the entertaining programs. Full meals are beyond our budget.

One recent evening, Enrico invited us into the adjacent performance space. "You must hear this!" Standing at the back of an intimate entertainment room packed with a couple of hundred people around a three-sided stage in front of a red brick wall, we laughed at comedian Woody Allen.

Thanking Enrico afterwards, we praised the spectacular young female singer. Enrico replied, "Her name is Barbra Streisand. Columbia Records just released her first album. She's going places!"

Carina and I adored learning about Barbra's success!

<u>Sunday, April 21, 1963: Games</u>
Enthusiastic Carina helped me vicariously experience the Greek Games, which the parents made me miss:

Angela, these games were dedicated to sun god Apollo. Both teams focused on his python-slaying legend. Dance and athletic skills in competitions like hoop rolling for speed and hurdling and discus throwing for form were inspiring! Artistic students designed costumes and chariots! A Greek-speaking charioteer directed four prancing Honeybears pulling each class chariot! Like Apollo after his triumph, the Barnard team leaders, imaginative artists, and winning athletes received laurel wreaths. We underdog frosh won in lyrics and properties. Entrance and music had tie scores. In athletics, the sophs won but our torch team tied. They won in dance and costumes and got overall points of 58 to our 43.

"Carina, how about the chariots?"
"I preferred our white, gold, and black chariot, but the soph black, red, and yellow chariot scored six to our three for

execution and originality of steps. Their charioteer proclaimed 'Nike!' Apparently, Nike is the winged goddess of victory in Greek mythology."

"Thanks, Roomie! We must trounce next year's frosh!" Listening to great Streisand tunes consoled us, e.g., *A Taste of Honey* from the eponymous 1962 movie I saw. I fell asleep picturing good-looking Kevin and hearing Barbra's spectacular voice sing Harold Arlen's *A Sleepin' Bee* lyrics: *he's mine for the taking. I am happy at last.*

Monday, April 22, 1963: Christian Brothers Academy
Exhilarating dream: at the CBA prom, handsome Kevin in a white dress uniform and I, wearing my turquoise strapless organza gown, mingled with other couples. I awoke with Barbra lyrics running through my head: *I will walk with my feet off the ground, when my one true love, I has* (sic) *found!*

With only a month until finals, I skipped President Park's inauguration to catch up on classwork. My preferred role model is prior president Millicent MacIntosh, mother of five and wife of a Columbia pediatrician.

Wednesday, April 24, 1963: Dread
"Carina, on my third visit, Prof E never got to me in the long line of calculus strugglers before office hours ended. Baffling homework problems fill me with an icy dread of failing the final and losing my scholarship!" I anxiously paced our room.

"My geology and physical anthropology courses help me understand. How about a tutor?"

"If asked for money, my parents would force a transfer to Albany State."

"Engineering library study might lead to free Lion help."

"You're right! Why didn't I go there and to engineering school mixers? Liberal arts majors often skip calculus."

Crying *Cheyah*, Carina and I followed Pithy (below) in an arm-swinging, lumbering traipse around our roomy quarters.

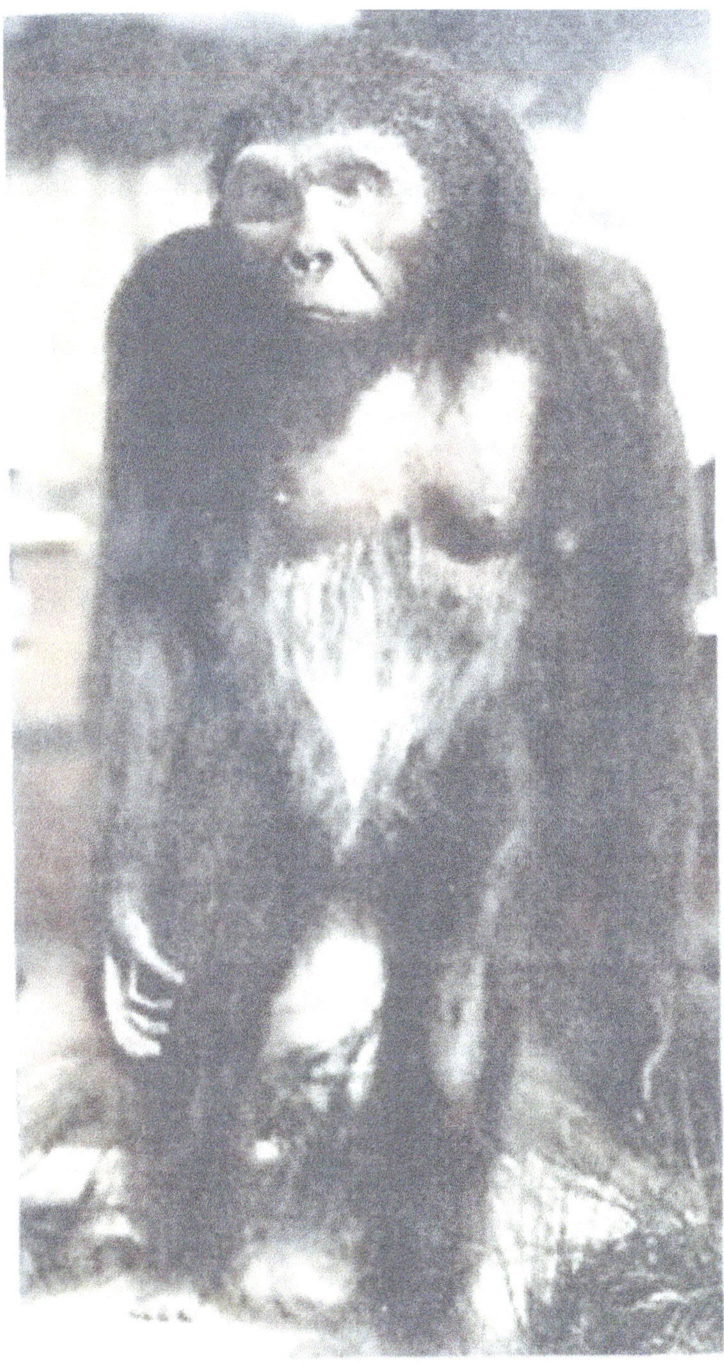

<u>Saturday, April 27, 1963: Together</u>
Enjoying Barbra Streisand singing *Keepin' Out of Mischief Now*, Carina and I caught up after days resembling two ships passing in the night.

"Carina, I love your new dramatic abstract drawings in colorful pastels!"

"Thanks! You look cheerful!"

"Kevin won a Columbia scholarship! Being together next year seems too good to be true!"

"Will you miss meeting new Lions?"

I shrugged. "Quick dates after the library closes are easier with a steady boyfriend."

<u>Sunday, April 28, 1963: Different</u>
I answered Kevin's smile-producing daily letter:

> Carina and I subwayed to Greenwich Village for an *avant-garde* performance at Judson Memorial Church on Washington Square. Six male and female modern dancers in black leotards and tights performed *Terrain*, including duets and some spoken words, by Yvonne Rainer, a choreographer-dancer. I liked that equality was one of her themes.

<u>Monday, April 29, 1963: Fatal</u>
"Carina, my beautiful, red-haired cousin Beth (below), Lydia's and Ella's half-sister, lost her adored lawyer stepfather. Only fifty-seven, he had a heart attack while talking to a jury! Fortunately, he got to know her three kids, including her son, only three. I'll send condolences."

"I'm sorry about the loss."

"Thank you. I worry about Dad's heart. Mother also mentioned that three hours of detailed Veterans' Administration volunteer training qualified her group to visit hospitalized vets. Seven women didn't show up.

Name of student _______________ Angela Weiss

Subject _______________________________

Number of this book____________________

Total number of books handed in________

Date___________________________________

B A R N A R D   C O L L E G E

Freshman Handbook reminds you that this examination is
being given under the Honor System.

FRESHMAN HANDBOOK SUGGESTIONS

For the comfort and convenience of all concerned,
Freshman Handbook suggests that:

Students sit together in friendly groups.
Joint solutions to problems are more fun.
Students talk as much as they want.

"At the temple sisterhood, Mother reported on world affairs and…" My guffaw felt uncontrollable. "She moderated a panel discussion: *Is interfaith dating as dangerous as it seems*? She probably ranted too much for the six panel members to get a word in!" Carina and I cracked up.

"Governor Rocky plans a downtown, forty-two-story NY State office building complex with shell amphitheater and reflecting pool. He should provide housing for thousands of Albany underprivileged people this Mall will unfairly displace."

Saturday, May 4, 1963: Search

"Carina, at the engineering library, I got engrossed in philosophy reading. The library closed before I could flirt with a math whiz."

Commiserating, Carina joshed. "How about the Freshman Handbook's joke suggestion (above) for calculus final exam problems: joint solutions?" Giggling, I agreed.

Monday, May 6, 1963: Presentation

My reply to Kevin's letter mentioned my relief after presenting my DHL paper and answering a few questions from twenty attentive seminar Honeybears. My final grade awaits Dr. K's scrutiny of my paper. Next: cramming for three hard exams.

Wednesday, May 8, 1963: Hunkering Down

On the phone, Gary's harried voice explained his silence. "Angela, I'm studying for finals while writing history and political science papers. My dad will disown me without more grades of *A* this year and acceptance at Harvard Law in a year." Gary sounded nervous and exhausted.

"I empathize, Gary. I need a miracle to pass calculus."

"I'm sorry. No one I know went that far in math."

If I were a son, would my parents respect my studies and demand less family time? Without time to find math help at social events, I treasure Kevin's humorous, romantic letters, which keep me sane, if I am. Haha!

Friday, May 10, 1963: Comic Relief
Summary of today's *Columbia Spectator* article:

> Columbia President Kirk threatened to cancel the Sunday women-in-the-dorms experiment if another panty raid occurs.
>
> Wednesday around midnight, Columbia raiders, imitating recent Princeton rioters, exploded firecrackers in Van Am Quad. The mob of 350 ran frantically from Ferris Booth gate, but police blocked all exits.
>
> Reid Hall Honeybears, hearing noise, flashed lights and threw down water and rolls of toilet paper from the roof. By 2 AM, the leaderless raid was over.
>
> A critical police officer referred to the students as future *advisers to the President*. Another joked about the raiders just wanting to *unsecrete pretty girls secreted in the dorm*. Only one pair of panties was acquired from Reid Hall.

Answering dear Kevin, I included the article and wrote:

> We slept through this seminal, electrifying part of dorm life. Our Brooks dorm may as well be in Siberia. We're zero out of two for panty-raid participation. The tattered garments saved since December are deeply disappointed without anticipated new owners.

Saturday, May 11, 1963: Pressure
"Any math help?" Carina looked concerned.

Noting a tremor in my hands, I said, "*A watched pot never boils.* Praying for a miracle tutor, I'm trying to get ahead in Latin and philosophy. I feel compassion for students with poor grades, despite diligence. Barnard's good for humility."

"...and nervous breakdowns. I heard about another Honeybear who went to an Adirondack rest home, rather than return after vacation." Her voice sounded sympathetic.

"Sad!" My shoulders slumped as I sighed deeply.

"Music, writing, and art keep me sane. Though my grades could be better, I'd rather graduate than go crazy trying for more grades above *B*."

Sunday, May 12, 1963: Almost Broke

I use the five-cent stamps Dad gave me during vacation to answer Kevin. Luckily, my aunts have called when I'm in our room. A nickel in the library vending machine for an ounce Chunky bar keeps me studying for hours without meal interruptions. Though raisins and nuts are nutritious, the chocolate makes my face break out.

"Happy Mothers' Day!" The parents didn't seem to mind my calling collect.

"Angela, thanks for your handmade card!" Mother sounded pleased.

Monday, May 13, 1963: Grade

Prof K's criticism of the sometimes-clumsy wording in my English paper was fair. "Carina, your ability to critically analyze French literature amazes me. My prof wanted more about DHL's interest in psychoanalysis, but *Lady Chatterley's Lover (LCL)* seemed less Freudian than *Sons and Lovers* with oedipal issues. *B Plus* is better than *C Plus* last semester! He wrote: *good job, especially in the composure and self-respect with which you handle the subject. Overall, a thoughtful and interesting essay.*"

"Congrats on close to *A Minus*!" Carina sounded upbeat.

"*Cheyah!* Let's shamble!" I snickered, imagining Pithy parading with us. Vigorous arm swings dissipated tension!

<u>Tuesday, May 14, 1963: Miami Bargain</u>
"Your mother writes well," commented Carina after reading the May 8 letter below.

"If she had written my paper, I could have lived it up more with Kevin and received an *A*." We giggled.

On the train, we conversed and played Scrabble, Password, and cards with a friendly bunch. Our breathtaking Sherry Frontenac Hotel is on the beach at 65 Street. Our beautiful room has French provincial furniture. You'd like the dressing table with a lift-up, lighted mirror. The palm trees, gorgeous shrubbery, and lovely homes are impressive. We took the bus to a restaurant on Lincoln Road. We've met various down-to-earth couples while swimming in wavy, warm, blue water and playing shuffleboard (below) and bingo. We viewed the movie *Hand in Hand* and an old-time, vaudeville show. Baritone Gus Van of Van and Schenck sang *For Me and My Gal*. The peach flamingoes (below behind Dad) at Hialeah are beautiful. Planning our Biscayne Bay tour in pool lounge chairs, we felt like millionaires!

<u>Wednesday, May 15, 1963: Voice and Diction</u>
"Carina, I wish I could've heard your long Moliere speech without missing mine. Unsure about how I'm coming across, I dislike public speaking! I'm relieved this required class is done."

"It was fun for me. Maybe I'll teach."

<u>Thursday, May 16, 1963: *I'll Tell…*</u>
Kevin loves the same music! I want to dance at his prom!

Dear Angela, I'm wearing out the wonderful Barbra Streisand album! *I'll Tell the Man in the Street* by Rodgers and Hart is a favorite. Lyrics go through my head. I feel like telling *everyone I meet that you and I are sweethearts*. I'd like to prove to the Albany *Knickerbocker News* that *we two are complete hearts*. Glad that we no longer must hide dates from my family, *I want the world to know*. Love and kisses, Kevin

<u>Saturday, May 18, 1963: Mother's Letter</u>
Sad news: my parents' friend survived the Holocaust but just succumbed to cancer…. When Mother tripped over the furnace burner in the cellar, Dad couldn't hear her shout for help. Awaiting an emergency room X-ray, she read a lot of *The Ugly American*. When I called home collect, Mother was healing.

<u>Monday, May 20, 1963: Exams</u>
"Carina, how was your anthro final?" She looked drained, the way I feel after each three-hour ordeal.

"Tough! I'm grateful my exams are spaced out."

My Latin test covered Vergil's *Aeneid*, an engaging epic about Aeneas' romantic and other adventures, wandering from Troy to Italy. If only my time-pressured translation better preserved the rhythm and meter of the original Latin dactylic hexameter, e.g., *I sing of arms and of the man who first from the shores of Troy.*

<u>Wednesday, May 22, 1963: Math</u>

"Carina, I must have held my breath in terror during the entire distressing calculus final! Then, I studied at the engineering library, wearing this required skirt (tan-and-green pleated plaid). Rising to go to the restroom, I accidentally knocked my philosophy book off the beat-up, brown wooden library table. Do men like klutzy women? Two guys I had yet to notice dove and wrestled for my book. Hardly keeping a straight face, I was pleased that the tall, well-built, ruggedly handsome guy won, bowed, and presented the book with a flourish."

"Hilarious! Is the book whole?"

I nodded. "An electrical engineering soph, Bill looked outdoorsy, like a lumberjack, in jeans and a blue plaid shirt. Though I dislike beards, his thick, wavy auburn hair beckoned to my fingers."

"Your fourth red-head?" We exchanged grins.

"Bill carried my books to Barnard where I accepted a date after finals! I forgot to ask about calculus!"

<u>Monday, May 27, 1963: Final Final</u>

Unlucky Carina! Done with geology's Manhattan shist and New England gneiss rocks, she still has French.

Though I survived challenging essay questions on today's philosophy exam, I still feel shaky. This class has made me skeptical about religions. Does God even exist? I'm thankful to be free for the summer!

National news troubled me. Brutal Birmingham police officers beat protestors whose nonviolent stance prevents fighting back, not that violence does any good against bigoted authorities!! A total coward, I admire those who have fought segregation all these years!

<u>Tuesday, May 28, 1963: Date</u>

The V and T Pizzeria wall murals reminded me of Albany's Boulevard murals. At a red Formica table, attractive Bill and I split a small, ninety-cent cheese pizza. "Angela, tomorrow, I return to Woodstock for the holiday weekend with my family before my summer road crew job starts. It pays the best! I save most earnings for college. How about you?"

"In an air-conditioned office with the nicest co-workers, I'll earn the best pay, filing NY State insurance forms, often in the bottom file drawers. Every penny goes to Barnard."

At the dorm entrance, Bill wanted my address and phone. His warm hug was ideal for a first date. Watching his sexy body depart, I realized I had again forgotten to ask for help to arrive at the right answers to math problems. Are engineering students less intellectual? Elite Columbia College students learn from eminent profs, like Lionel Trilling."

Wednesday, May 29, 1963: Leaving
I helped Carina pack before we hauled her trunk and suitcases downstairs and into a taxi on Broadway. "I'll miss you, Carina!"

"I'll write once I have the camp address! Have a wonderful summer with Kevin!" We hugged good-bye.

Aunt Rhoda, my parents, and I enjoyed Aunt Lila's cheese blintzes and cheesecake dairy meal for Jewish holiday *Shavuot* at the long mahogany table set up in her spectacular living room. I adore the emerald carpet, pale gold brocade sofa and green-and-gold-striped velvet side chairs! "Aunt Lila, your second book can be *Decorating Impeccably on a Budget*!" As bookkeeper for a famous interior decorator, who helped Jackie Kennedy renovate the White House, Lila buys elegant furnishings wholesale.

Uncle Bert said, "Ron's finishing finals at Temple University. Hal's part-time political science and international relations teaching at San Francisco State College and Eileen's English fellowship studies at Berkeley are going well." Vision: Kevin and I boarding a plane to visit them.

Thursday, May 30, 1963: Holiday
A boat trip with parents around Manhattan Island was scenic when my wind-whipped, long locks stayed out of my eyes.

Picturing a happy 1958 boat ride with Cousin Ron and Aunt Sara, I brooded about failing to connect with her. She never requested my number or showed any interest in me. Will anything alter her rejection?

<u>Friday, May 31, 1963: Art</u>
I subwayed to meet the parents and Aunt Rhoda at Frank Lloyd Wright's fabulous Guggenheim Museum building on Fifth Avenue! I love the round white exterior and the spiraling white galleries inside. I preferred the more colorful modern art to many neutral, blah, or downright ugly pieces.

Uncle Bert, Aunt Lila, Dad, Mother, Aunt Rhoda behind me

1963 Albany Summer

We are slow to believe that which if believed would hurt our feelings (translated from Latin).

Roman poet **Ovid** *Metamorphoses*

Saturday, June 1, 1963: Home

While the parents visited the Jewish Museum on Fifth Avenue, bought souvenirs in Chinatown, and meandered around Greenwich Village, I finished packing. I squeezed into the back seat of our jalopy, full of my clothes and linens. Halfway to Albany, Mother turned her head and gave me a piercing look in the eye. "We want you to see our social worker." Though three months with the parents seems grim, since I like Mr. V and can date Kevin, I'll obey.

Sunday, June 2, 1963: Finals

On a perfect warm day, Kevin and I, dressed in Bermuda shorts, moseyed around blooming Washington Park. What a pleasure to sniff his aftershave among colorful flowers! "Angela, unfortunately, our prom was May 17, when you were cramming. To keep my Columbia scholarship, I must leave to prep for differential calculus, English, French, chemistry, social studies, military history, theology, and physical education exams."

"A heavy load! As a senior, I took only English, chemistry, solid geometry/advanced algebra, and typing to allow hours on the yearbook."

"To maximize grads going to college, De La Salle Christian Brothers mandate the most rigorous academic program we poor slaves can tolerate."

"Columbia may seem easy."

"At least, religion classes will be historically factual, rather than brainwashing." Kissing goodbye was sublime after spring in the Barnard convent.

<u>Monday, June 3, 1963: Welcomed</u>
Governor Rockefeller's hiring freeze makes me grateful for my NY State Insurance Department job. After heartwarming greetings from the female clerical staff, I joked, "Have you saved the filing since last September?"

The sweet mom of an AHS grad whispered, "We file in upper drawers only." Kneeling on the beige linoleum floor to file legal-size insurance agent and broker applications in bottom drawers of long rows of gray steel file cabinets keeps me employed.

Both supervisors are nice to me. Gray-haired Mrs. R is an over-fifty grandmother with a staid wardrobe. Is Mother's fashionably dressed, under-fifty friend called by her first name because single women get less respect?

<u>Tuesday, June 4, 1963: Grades</u>
Opening Barnard's envelope with heart-racing trepidation, I was relieved about *C Minus*, my lifetime worst grade, in calculus. Latin was *A Minus*! English *B Plus* is progress. *B Plus* in voice and diction is better than expected! Without family distractions, I might have concentrated better on demanding philosophy reading and earned higher than *B*, but who knows? Competing against brilliant girls from competitive private schools and NYC top high schools makes this hick-town, public-school grad thankful to maintain her scholarship with a 3.0 or *B* average (down from 3.42).

<u>Thursday, June 6, 1963: Ric</u>
With Kevin cramming, I was happy that Ric phoned. "Angela, did you hear that Eva quit St. Rose College?" He sounded downcast. "Her parents' rent charges made practically free Albany State unaffordable."

"So sad! I'm grateful that my parents supplement my scholarships and summer earnings."

"Eva was the most brilliant Schuyler student. NY State is lucky she's now an employee."

Friday, June 7, 1963: Shock

At a small table at downtown dance venue University Club, I said, "Ric, can I treat you to a drink to express appreciation for giving my letters to Kevin?"

His smile was warm. "Thank you!" After banter about college, Ric looked serious. "I have difficult things to share." My eyebrows lifted in surprise. He gulped his beer. "Word got around our South End neighborhood that Kevin's *A* grades enabled him to date again. We young males crave intimate experience. Deprivation kept Kevin from turning away attractive girls throwing themselves at him." Ric took another swig of beer.

"I understand his dating to enjoy senior year. Kevin approved my dating Columbia guys."

"But things went farther. Kev's former girlfriend, with whom he lost his virginity at fourteen, out-competed the others. His family, friends, and classmates consider her his steady. Every weekend, they went all the way. Though he understood why you missed his March formal, he was unwilling to skip the prom, so he took her." While Ric swallowed a few sips, my heart thudded. I felt stricken with shock.

"Angela, unwilling to lose privileges, he has lacked self-control. She's an ordinary girl who's probably unaware of you. I said, 'Kevin, Angela is too sweet to deceive. You must tell her.' Though he agreed, exams are his excuse for delay. He is in love with you, wants to avoid hurting you, and fears losing you and your love. He said, 'I'm excited about the kids two weirdos like Angela and me might have.'"

Ric paused, looking concerned. "You look pale. Are you okay?" Struggling for control and not trusting myself to speak, I nodded. Ric continued. "When I objected to Kevin's procrastination, he okayed my telling you."

"If Kevin had been truthful, I would have understood." I barely held back tears.

Apologetic for bearing bad news, Ric drove me home. "Ric, thanks for telling me! Have fun during your month of Navy training as an E-1! Thanks for your picture (above)! You look devastatingly handsome!"

With the parents at religious services, I let tears engulf me. How could the open boyfriend I trusted act devious and cheat? How can I believe other guys? So much for romantic fun after a grueling schoolyear. I remain stunned.

Saturday, June 8, 1963: Oren
I sighed with relief when the parents left early for Mother's final painting class before a picnic at the teacher's Lake Luzerne cottage.

In my white pique dress (below), I accompanied the parents to Oren Levine's evening engagement party. His brown-haired fiancée, a teacher with an engaging countenance, is taller than he. Oren has always been like a nice brother. I'm glad he's happy! Pushing away Kevin thoughts, I danced with attractive Gloversville cousin Stu and tried to enjoy myself.

Monday, June 10, 1963: Carina
Carina's picture post card from camp cheered me. Missing her sympathetic ear, I answered:

> I'm shaken, dismayed, and disenchanted! Kevin carried on openly for three months with his ex, including weekend dates with full sex and his prom. I would have understood if he hadn't concealed everything. He communicated as if I was his only love. No more long-distance loves!

Friday, June 14, 1963: Obedient

Filing at work, I hoped that Cousin Ron got my card and was having a fun birthday.

This compliant daughter met the parents at Jewish Family Service for counseling with Mr. V (below). After two years, Mr. V's plain, beige office had the same anemic plant and child's woven red-and-green potholder under his white coffee mug. Glancing at his University of West Virginia social work master's degree diploma on the wall, I sat on one of three brown-upholstered chairs pulled up to his scratched wooden desk.

I endured the parents' endless rant about Barnard Parents' Day, neglect of aunts, and money *mismanagement*. With a kind smile, Mr. V turned to me for a response. I said:

> Thanks for college help, but your inconsistency confuses me. Didn't you teach me to do all my homework and attend all classes? Do good parents send weeks of shaming letters for refusal to skip classes? Didn't I skip schoolwork to spend *all* weekend with you and family? For Parents' Day, if I had received the courtesy of an advance invite, I would've declined because of classes. Monday, Honeybears with parents had finished classes. Coursework was done Saturday and Sunday. Was I thanked for further neglecting assignments to dine with you Monday? I was up until 3 AM writing Tuesday's speech to avoid an *F*. I'm unappreciated. With other parents praising my achievements and without committing a crime, I deserve an apology for your mean letters.
>
> You realize that your anniversary and two birthday gifts used up my five-dollar monthly allowance? Would you have sent more shaming letters If you got only home-made cards?

Do you remember my letter about each aunt phone call wasting an hour of study time? Losing my library place, walking to the dorm, obtaining change, waiting in line for a pay phone, conversing, returning to the library, and searching for a new place require twelve times your estimated five minutes!

Looking slightly abashed, the parents stopped quibbling about my faults. I agreed to a solo session with supportive, fair Mr. V.

<u>Saturday, June 15, 1963: Repugnance</u>
With parents at home, I led Kevin to our grassy backyard. The avenue of pink hollyhocks against the ugly concrete block wall droopingly illustrated my mood. The lilacs have died off their tall bush. Receiving a navy duffel bag of my letters, I handed Kevin a tan paper grocery sack of his letters. Apologetically, he slunk off. Disgust about his duplicity has replaced attraction. Does Kevin's girlfriend know that he said he loved me and wrote almost daily? How do I get rid of my letters, vulnerable to parental snooping in my closet, without starting a fire?

<u>Monday, June 17, 1963: Pieces</u>
Striding home from work, I stopped on a faded-brown Washington Park bench to tediously tear the initial letters to Kevin into unreadable pieces, which I sadly threw into a trash can. I wish I'd gone to Columbia mixers instead of wasting hours sharing my life with an undeserving jerk.

<u>Tuesday, June 18, 1963: Unexpected</u>
Fortunately, the parents were out. An unstoppable profusion of tears of heartbreak gushed forth while I read this:

> Dearest Angela,
> Love, faith, trust —once lost, they can never be regained. I'm sorry that I failed so badly. I'm returning my picture. I want to be remembered just a little. I'll keep the letters until someday I wake up and realize you are gone. Goodbye, my love, for you will always be my first love. Keep well and safe. Yours always, Kevin

<u>Wednesday, June 19, 1963: Bereft</u>
Longing for Sara's sympathetic ear and comforting guidance, I mailed my home-made heart birthday card to her.

Ambling home through green Washington Park was lovely until two mean little boys ran by, taunting me, "Ugly witch!" Do I need a nose job?

With the parents away, I sang along with our Judy Garland record: *the dreams you dreamed have all gone astray... No more that all time thrill... And never a new love will be the same....* Harold Arlen and Ira Gershwin could have written *The Man That Got Away* for me.

<u>Thursday, June 20, 1963: Speech</u>
How can bigoted Southerners, like Alabama Governor George Wallace, be so cruel and hateful, barring two Negros from University of Alabama?

JFK's speech to Congress about racial equality is wonderful! He's right that our nation will be fully free only if all citizens are free. Will those who need to examine consciences do so? I love his vision for America where every citizen has the *equality of treatment which we would want for ourselves* and all children have an *equal right to develop their talent and their ability and their motivation, to make something of themselves.*

I hope his warning leads to improvement:

> The events in Birmingham and elsewhere have
> so increased the cries for equality that no city or
> State or legislative body can prudently choose to
> ignore them.

<u>Friday, June 21, 1963: Mr. V</u>
I told Mr. V, "My parents' solution to my Barnard challenges is transferring to Albany State to save money. Though I can't blame them for my calculus struggles, their time demands and nasty letters contributed to my grade point average decrease from above a *B Plus* to *B*, probably the minimum for my Barnard scholarship."

"You'd like more parental support?" Behind his glasses, his brown eyes looked sympathetic. With a few strands of gray in his dark curly hair, he's probably in his early forties.

Appreciating his understanding, I nodded. "Exchanging frequent love letters with Kevin made me look forward to summer together. Kevin hid that he took his ex to the prom after weekly sex since March. I might have flunked, if I'd known before finals."

"How are you now?"

"I feel betrayed. How can a man love me and cheat?"

"Kevin's dishonesty hurts."

Nodding, I sighed. "Males seem willing to say or do anything for sex. If girls comply, guys move on to new conquests. Wanting the respect and interest of men, I must not ruin my life with unwanted, illegitimate pregnancy. Remaining a virgin until marriage will make sex a beautiful experience of love and commitment. I was okay with Luke's having sex on the side with easy girls since he was honest. I would have done likewise with Kevin, who accepted my casual dating at Barnard. Had I known Kevin was deeply involved with his ex, I would have taken his love less seriously."

"What has this disappointment taught you?"

I laughed sardonically. "To distrust men? How can I respect a pathetic, immature male without self-control? If I date again, I'll be skeptical about words of love."

"Unsure about future dating, you plan to be guarded."

I nodded. "Thankful for friendly women at work, I lick wounds as my brain rests while filing. Shedding illusions while growing up is less than fun. Philosophy class readings started to undermine my faith. Kevin's deception was the last straw. Always cynical about religion, I'm now an agnostic, uncertain whether God exists. I've been too gullible.

"You're grateful your job provides comfort? You consider yourself too credulous?" I nodded.

"Our time is almost up. How about another session?"

"Thanks for today's help! I'll return if the parents require it. They're unaware of the Kevin break-up and my agnosticism."

"You're welcome, Miss Weiss. Confidentiality rules here." Grinning, I thanked him again. On summer solstice, my favorite day of the year, I appreciated the cool breeze while strolling home under South Lake Avenue mature, leafy trees.

Saturday, June 22, 1963: Pooh
Appreciating Carina's sympathetic letter about Kevin when camp keeps her busy, I valued her Winnie, the Pooh, words: *I always get to where I'm going by walking away from where I have been.* Can Pooh explain why Kevin's cheating made me doubt God's existence?

Home alone, I sang along with Ella Fitzgerald's record, *The Harold Arlen Songbook*, especially *Blues in the Night*. I agree with Mercer's lyrics about a man as *a two-face, a worrisome thing who'll leave ya' to sing the blues in the night.*

Wednesday, June 26, 1963: Unexpected Mail
Auburn-haired, engineering student Bill, whom I met too late for calculus help, sent a Woodstock postcard:

> Are you enjoying summer? Having been paid at
> my construction job, I want to treat you to
> dinner and a show. Will July 6 around 3 PM
> work? Sincerely, Bill

Will a casual date help me move past Kevin anguish?

> Bill, I appreciate your delightful invitation and
> look forward to seeing you July 6 around 3 PM!
> Smiles, Angela

<u>Thursday, July 4, 1963: Holiday</u>
Eva was lucky to be away from home when I called. I'm too down in the dumps to cheer a friend whose parents ruined her future.

My parents and I took our Gloversville relatives for a fun swim in the giant Thacher Park pool before a holiday picnic of grilled kosher hot dogs. I made the green salad.

Sweet Lydia is excited about senior year. Sophisticated Ella seems more mature than fifteen. She ardently quoted JFK's recent American University peace speech:

> Let us not be blind to our differences, but let us
> also direct attention to our common interests
> and the means by which those differences can
> be resolved. And if we cannot end now our
> differences, at least we can help make the world
> safe for diversity. For in the final analysis, our
> most basic common link is that we all inhabit
> this small planet. We all breathe the same air.
> We all cherish our children's futures. And we are
> all mortal.

Away from parents, I talked about Barnard, omitting Kevin. Salvaging the summer requires forgetting him.

<u>Saturday, July 6, 1963: Bill</u>
Gentleman Bill respectfully arrived on time! Despite his brown rather than blue eyes, Mother, flirtatiously over-smiling at him, was in a tizzy, as with blond Marcus in 1961.

Bill and I strolled six blocks to Stewart's on New Scotland Avenue for rum raisin ice cream. "Angela, how about a music event tonight? At Tanglewood, Erich Leinsdorf conducts the Boston Symphony in a Mozart program. Lake George Opera Festival has *Tosca*! The *NY Times* praised my hometown's Turnau Opera, which offers *La Traviata*!

"Great research, Bill! I love opera!"

When I re-appeared in my silky white dress with spaghetti straps and dotted brown cummerbund, Bill's eyes widened. "White is your color!"

I felt especially feminine with a robust male helping me into his turquoise-and-white car. "I adore your Nash."

"This 1957 Metropolitan is easy to work on myself."

"Wow!" Unlike bumbling Dad, a manly engineer who fixes things is exciting!

At a rustic Woodstock restaurant, rare burgers and crisp green salad tasted yummy on the outdoor deck under maple trees.

At Bill's house, his tall parents were friendly. While he dressed up, his mom, with long red hair, pointed to a picture of a strawberry-blond young woman and infant, "Our daughter and grandson."

"You're lucky to have beautiful red hair, like my prettiest cousin!" I enthused.

My eyes popped at Bill's muscles filling out tighter attire: navy dress trousers and a short-sleeved, blue-and-tan striped dress shirt. He carried a tan sports jacket.

At Byrdcliffe Theater, Verdi's opera in English translation was touchingly romantic. I identified with Violetta's desire for both freedom and love. As my tears flowed before the end, Bill's powerful arm around me felt supportive.

In Albany, a dreamy goodnight kiss ended a lovely date! Reminder: no romantic entanglements!

Monday, July 8, 1963: Driving

Sara was attacked exiting an Albany evening bus. Driving makes solo activities safer. With lessons expensive, Dad showed me the basics. I drove our decrepit car forward, backward, and in circles in a huge empty parking lot. A nervous wreck, annoying Dad yelled, "Watch out! Slow down! Be careful!"

Wednesday, July 10, 1963: *Déjà Vu*
A call from Doreen (below) cheered me.

"Angela, I ran into my ex, J.P., who said that your ex, Yeats, enjoyed soph year at Boston University."

"Remember that attractive Yeats stopped asking me out after I nixed going steady?"

"If J.P. asks me out, I'll mention our fun doubling with you two in 1961."

"Doreen, thank you! Can we catch up in person before you leave for the country?"

"This Saturday, I'll watch a 600-pound Mills Brothers' circus lion nuzzle a clown. How about July 20?"

"The circus sounds like fun! After morning housecleaning, I can ring your bell on July 20 around 1 PM."

Unable to reach Eva, I walked the nine blocks northwest past St. Rose College to the Madison Theater. In *Hud,* sexy Paul Newman's blue eyes were like Kevin's. The second movie, *Come Fly with Me*, was not up to Sinatra's eponymous hit song.

Saturday, July 13, 1963: Barber

At noon, Dominic, handsome in a light-blue dress shirt and charcoal gray trousers, was in the driver's seat of his parent's dinged white Chevy sedan. "Angela, did fate help us cross paths yesterday downtown?" I smiled and nodded. "Do you prefer Erich Leinsdorf conducting the Boston Symphony playing Mozart at Tanglewood this afternoon, or Rossini's *The Barber of Seville* in English tonight at Lake George Opera?"

"Perfect choice! Since Lake George opera started last summer, I've longed to go!"

"Wonderbar!"

In the afternoon light, huge Lake George looked intensely blue and beautiful. Time flew by as during our marathon AHS phone talks. A year at Albany State has made Dominic eager to see the world. "If I join the Navy, I may fulfill my dream of visiting relatives in Greece."

Always up on politics, he's pleased with JFK. An Adlai Stevenson supporter, he disliked the Eisenhower years more than anyone I knew. "Angela, brave Negroes face brutality trying to win civil rights they should have had for a hundred years!"

"I agree! The treatment of Negroes is disgraceful!"

We savored a roast chicken picnic his mother packed. "Angela, the new zip postal codes should speed mail."

"How do we find the right codes?" Grinning, he shrugged.

At Diamond Point Theater north of Lake George Village, attractive, upcoming NYC singers, performing comic opera, charmed and amused us. I'm grateful to openly enjoy Dominic's company after years of parental prohibitions. Seeing him again would brighten my summer.

Thursday, July 18, 1963: Practice

I appreciated two evenings of driving until Dad got too worked up. Though I drove under the thirty-mile-per-hour speed limit, he yelled, "Slow down!" On wide streets with little traffic, he exhorted "Watch out!" I bit my tongue to stop irked retorts.

Friday, July 19, 1963: Kowtowing
When exalted superintendent of insurance, Thomas Thacher, on the way to his top-floor office, greeted us plebeians, I was already on my knees filing. Is distinguished-looking, middle-aged Thomas related to past Albany mayor John Boyd Thacher, for whom beautiful Thacher Park is named?

Saturday, July 20, 1963: Doreen
Rambling around Washington Park's placid, greenish-blue lake, we basked in upper-70s temperatures. "Doreen, I'm happy to see you!" Plaid Jamaica shorts (shorter than Bermuda shorts) and white sleeveless tops suggested that we are still on the same wave length.

"I hope Barnard was better than Buffalo State. How was your roommate?" Doreen's auburn locks shined in the sunlight.

"Carina's my favorite Barnard friend! How was yours?"

Doreen rolled her eyes. "I had a small-town gentile who had never met a Jew! In a tiny room meant for one, I had to sleep on the top bunk and listen to antisemitic remarks about Jewish money." A tear rolled down her cheek.

I hugged her. "Horrible! Your room should be a sanctuary, rather than enemy territory."

Her sweet voice sounded appreciative. "Thanks for understanding. Why didn't I visit this mainly female teachers' college before going there? I missed dating. Nice Elsie from Albany fixed me up with the handsome Jewish roommate of her State University at Buffalo boyfriend. After a fun double date, I had to turn down his invite to a Cornell weekend. Taking two buses each way in the bitter cold eventually made us give up dating." Her voice had a tinge of listlessness.

"Discouraging! All-female Barnard works only with thousands of smart, cute Columbia lions nearby."

"Last August's wonderful graduation trip motivated me to learn French. Dad's cousins, now in Paris, remembered me as a toddler in Germany after the Holocaust. I visited after they lost their daughter in an accident. Two weeks at their Paris home preceded a resort vacation at Milano Marittima, south of Venice on the Adriatic! When my basic Yiddish and their limited English failed, we pantomimed and drew pictures." We exchanged grins.

"I bet they adore you!"

"They want me to return as their substitute daughter. I need to speak French. Buffalo State, in the Dark Ages, lacked AHS' language lab. The always-late French teacher emphasized reading, rather than conversation." I nodded sympathetically.

"Biology class disappointed me. We studied only paleontology, ancient fossilized organisms. Struggling to stay awake as the prof droned on, I could imagine no use for the information."

"Only a scientist would," I replied. We grinned.

"Fundamental elementary education classes required for my major were dull."

"Almost failing calculus, I longed for something easy."

Her eyebrows lifted. "I can't imagine our valedictorian flunking anything."

"Everyone at Barnard was at the top of her class or graduated from advanced NYC high schools. *C Plus* was my first-semester English grade."

"Wow! That pressure seems worse than boredom. I transferred to more co-ed Albany State to be free of curfews and bad food at State University at Buffalo. Eating at home this past month helped me slim down after overeating bread and potatoes, rather than greasy, nauseating dorm dishes."

"Your figure still looks perfect."

"Thank you. I hope to learn more liberal arts and date RPI men." We smiled.

"Doreen, brilliant Eva from Schuyler ran out of money and quit college. If her older sisters had attended college, her parents might have supported Eva's becoming an attorney to help underprivileged people."

"Sad! We're lucky that Judaism values learning enough for some parents to help daughters finish college."

"Life should be fairer for females."

Home alone, I stopped tears about Doreen's antisemitic roommate and Kevin's duplicity by escaping into my usual refuge, a book. *The Heavenly City of the Eighteenth-Century Philosophers* is about famous Voltaire, Hume, and Locke.

<u>Wednesday, July 24, 1963: Alice</u> (below)
On lunch break leaving Harmanus Bleecker Library, I greeted my ninth-grade classmate. "Alice, how are you?"

Her soft voice sounded keen and her eyes gleamed. "As a future teacher, I'm grateful to work for Albany's Board of Education!"

"The father of an AHS student I dated works there." I mentioned Yeats' dad's name.

"He's my supportive boss, a capable administrator who has trusted me to verify all the numbers from every homeroom register in all Albany schools."

"He must value such a conscientious, organized employee!"

"Thanks! He knows the concentration and attention to detail required. His positive feedback makes work a joy."

"I consider myself fortunate to know the 1962 NY State volunteer-of-the-year award winner!"

"Thank you. St. Rose College volunteering has been satisfying. How are you?"

"Grateful for my NY State summer job, but melancholy about Eva's leaving St. Rose."

A Schuyler classmate of Eva, Alice looked downcast. "What a waste of brilliance! Eva scored at the top of the civil service test. NY State Employees' Retirement System is lucky to have a gifted worker with character."

"I hope she gets promoted to an absorbing, well-paid job. Has her phone number changed?"

Alice shook her head no. I looked at my watch. "Lunch break's over. Seeing you was fun!"

Dropping Cousin Lydia's seventeenth birthday card in the mailbox, I marveled at the coincidence of Yeats' father supervising Alice.

<u>Saturday, July 27, 1963: Dear Carina</u>
I sent a Washington Park picture postcard:

> *Cheyah*! How are you and family? Does ESP
> (extrasensory perception) explain my running
> into my ex, Yeats, on Central Avenue after
> mentioning him the preceding day? He seemed
> as agreeable, easy-going, and cool, as ever. I
> gladly accepted a date! I miss you! Love, A

<u>Wednesday, July 31, 1963: Tanglewood, Twenty-Sixth Season</u>
Handsome Yeats (below) picked me up at work and drove us to Barn Restaurant in Lenox, Massachusetts, for a tasty steak dinner.

Why does anyone pay up to six dollars to be cooped up inside the Tanglewood music shed when a lawn ticket is only two-fifty? Without a breeze, the evening temperature was perfect for lying back and gazing at the sky, while Arthur Fiedler conducted the Boston Pops.

"Yeats, thanks for bringing this Black-Watch plaid blanket. Blue, green, and black make it my favorite tartan."

"The pattern is from an 1881 Scottish infantry regiment. Black Watch was an Eighteenth-Century watch patrol company." His demeanor is still pleasantly unassuming.

"What interesting history!"

"Since Nathaniel Hawthorn's gloomy *Scarlet Letter* wasn't a favorite, I'll skip beating down library doors for *Tanglewood Tales*, which he penned while living in a cottage on this estate." I nodded agreement about Hawthorn.

Later, Yeats quiet voice sounded energetic. "My favorite piece was Rachmaninoff's *Concerto No. 1, in F-Sharp Minor* with pianist Leonard Pennario."

"Yes! *The Sweetest Sounds* from Richard Rodgers' musical *No Strings* and Maurice Jarre's theme from *Lawrence of Arabia* were also satisfying." Yeats' company delighted me, including a just-right, good-night kiss.

Thursday, August 1, 1963: Driving
We hit one of Albany's many potholes, which the entrenched Democratic Party's political machine lacks motivation to repair. Dad bellowed, "Slow down! Driving fast on residential streets is dangerous! You have a lot to learn!" Have parallel parking on my first attempt and paying for gas at thirty cents a gallon kept excitable Dad from quitting?

Friday, August 2, 1963: Counseling
The parents required today's solo session. "Mr. V, I hope overweight Dad, who hollers during driving sessions, escapes a heart attack."

"You want him to stay well?"

"Yes! Since Yeats and Dominic will be long distance next month, their silence after one fun date each is okay."

"Do dates signify progress regarding Kevin?"

"Not really. Disillusioned, I brood. How can virgins have trusting romances when men say or do anything for sex?"

"You doubt male integrity about sex?"

I nodded. "Although I can't imagine Dad cheating, others seem untrustworthy."

"You want men whose honesty about sex you can respect?"

Nodding, I snickered. "Could Dad be the only non-cheater?" I hope that Mr. V has been faithful.

Married teacher Mr. B's date invitation to Aunt Sara and his later exploitative behavior with me were repulsive. Though I like Dad's best friend, Karl (below), I wonder whether his flirtations, e.g., with Cousin Beth at my parents' anniversary party, cause his sweet wife's (below) depression.

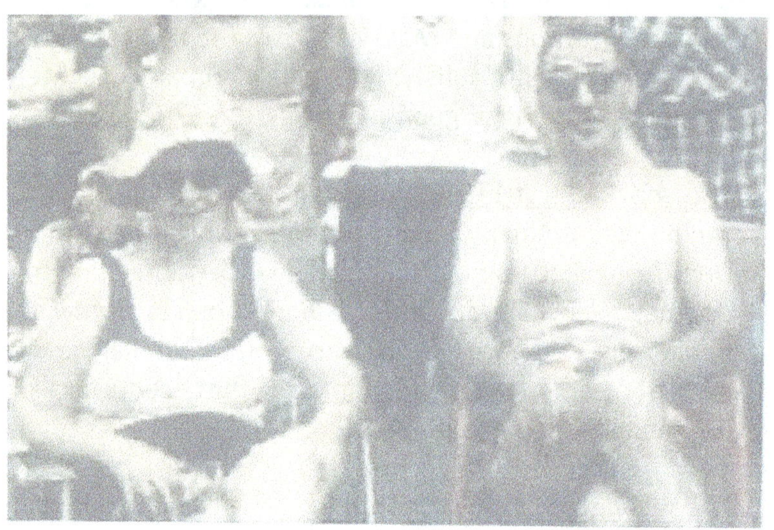

Tuesday, August 6, 1963: Marilyn
At work, no women expressed sadness about Marilyn Monroe's one-year-after-death anniversary from a sleeping-pill overdose. Unlike admirable Jackie Kennedy and Audrey Hepburn, Marilyn seemed unfriendly to women, who saw through her fake helpless act with men. Though Dad prefers brunettes, too many men made an icon of a dumb blond. Why can't men go for smart females without feeling threatened?

Wednesday, August 7, 1963: Serenity
What a relief that calm Mother, a better driver than exasperating Dad, supervised an hour of practice tonight! "When's your driving test?" she inquired.

"When I can pass."

"Sunday afternoon, you can drive us to and from Tanglewood for experience."

"Thank you!"

Sunday, August 11, 1963: Heroic *Eroica*

Leinsdorf, conducting Boston Symphony Orchestra's soothing classical music, calmed Dad's agitation from my driving to Massachusetts. Sitting on our old flowered bedspread on the lawn, we picnicked on tuna-salad-on-rye sandwiches I made.

Beethoven's *Symphony No.3* in E-flat was my favorite piece. I also liked pianist Jorge Bolet's performance of Prokofiev's *Concerto No.3*. I may have dozed off during Kodaly's Suite from the comic opera, *Hary Janos*.

Home without Dad's exploding with rage about my driving, I sighed in relief.

Tuesday, August 13, 1963: Ceramics

At the Albany Art Institute, Mother fashioned a clay ash tray to paint her favorite purple. I spiraled long, thin clay into a small plant pot to paint pink and aqua. With Dad present, I drove home sedately at thirty miles per hour, under the speed limit.

Friday, August 16, 1963: Test

After work, Mother drove me to the Department of Motor Vehicles. With only one wrong on the written test, I passed the vision test without my glasses.

The gruff, beefy road test examiner barked, "Parallel park!" Backing into the space on my first try helped me pass. I can drive alone with my interim license! Freedom!

Mother hesitantly confessed, "At eighteen, I nervously failed two tests in our 1930s Marmon car." Her usual expressionless face looked a bit uncomfortable.

"You drive better than Dad. How many tests did he need?" Silence. Imagining Dad flunking numerous times, I avoided smirking, grateful for the miracle of passing the first time. I wrote them a thank-you note for teaching me to drive.

<u>Saturday, August 17, 1963: Chekhov</u>
A scenic drive preceded seeing cute Williams College guys walk down tree-lined Williamstown, Massachusetts, streets of quaint, white-clapboard houses.

After a tasty Williams Inn baked-cod dinner, Yeats and I saw Williamstown Theater's *The Cherry Orchard*. "Yeats, with themes of loss and sorrow, why did Chekhov label the play a comedy?" Did my cynicism make me miss humor?

With a kind look, he shrugged. "Maybe the Russians are too deep for us. Chekhov studied hard to become a doctor. Supporting his large family and treating needy patients without charge left him short of money. He died young of tuberculosis."

"What a pity for someone so generous! I appreciated this interesting performance!" Yeats' educated companionship and good-night kisses elevated my mood.

<u>Saturday, August 24, 1963: Mike's Log Cabin</u>
At our dark AHS hangout in a rough-hewn log booth, I nostalgically drank a watery Singapore sling and danced with Yeats.

I was excited when Craig appeared. "Hi, Yeats! May I borrow Ginger Rogers for this dance?" Yeats graciously agreed.

Craig gallantly bowed. Smiling, I took his extended hand. "Mr. Astaire!" We fox-trotted to Tommy Edwards' *It's All in the Game* on the jukebox. Loving our whirling turns and deep final dip, I laughed at his quips about college challenges.

<u>Monday, August 26, 1963: Corresponding</u>
Trying to sound upbeat replying to Carina and Cousin Ron, I focused on recent cultural outings. To Carina, I added:

> I'm glad camp has been fun… After weak,
> juvenile Kevin, I need a self-controlled, mature
> gentleman to respect and love. Am I too
> idealistic to expect my trust and love to be more
> important than sex temptations?

<u>Friday, August 30, 1963: King</u>
Playdium bowling games, mine with abysmal scores, preceded a gleeful discussion of Wednesday's 250,000 Washington, DC, protestors, marching for jobs and freedom! On our front porch, Yeats and I read aloud inspiring quotes from Martin Luther King, Jr., speaking at the Lincoln Memorial. "Angela, King poetically described the Emancipation Proclamation."

> ...a great beacon light of hope to millions of
> Negro slaves who had been seared in the flames
> of withering injustice... a joyous daybreak to end
> the long night of their captivity.

"Yeats, we need Dr. King's brilliant, non-violent leadership!" Spellbinding quotes inspired Yeats' dynamic tone:

> We must forever conduct our struggle on the
> high plane of dignity and discipline. We must
> not allow our creative protest to degenerate
> into physical violence.... We must rise to the
> majestic heights of meeting physical force with
> soul force. The marvelous new militancy which
> has engulfed the Negro community must not
> lead us to a distrust of all white people, for
> many of our white brothers, as evidenced by
> their presence here today, have come to realize
> that their destiny is tied up with our destiny,
> and they have come to realize that their
> freedom is inextricably bound to our freedom.
> We cannot walk alone.

Choked up, I appreciated Yeats' hug. He sounded animated:

> ...even though we face the difficulties of today
> and tomorrow, I still have a dream. It is a dream
> deeply rooted in the American dream. I have a

dream that one day this nation will rise up and live out the true meaning of its creed: "We hold these truths to be self-evident, that all men are created equal." I have a dream that one day on the red hills of Georgia, the sons of former slaves and the sons of former slave owners will be able to sit down together at the table of brotherhood. I have a dream that one day even the state of Mississippi, a state sweltering with the heat of injustice, sweltering with the heat of oppression, will be transformed into an oasis of freedom and justice. I have a dream that my four little children will one day live in a nation where they will not be judged by the color of their skin but by the content of their character.

King's eloquence made my tears flow. "Angela, I'm tempted to join the protestors." Yeats energetically read the electrifying end, while his cowardly date admired King's bravery:

This is our hope… to transform the jangling discords of our nation into a beautiful symphony of brotherhood… So let freedom ring… From every mountainside, let freedom ring… When we… let it ring from every village and every hamlet, from every state and every city, we will be able to speed up that day when… black men and white men, Jews and Gentiles, Protestants and Catholics, will be able to join hands and sing in the words of the old Negro spiritual: "Free at last!"

Saturday, August 31, 1963: Opera
"Angela, you look fetching in that yellow dress." Glad I wore my full-skirted halter frock, printed with pastel flowers, I

thanked Bill. In a heavily-wooded park under a tree canopy, we ate green salad and bologna sandwiches from his house. Like me, he must be frugal to get through Columbia.

At the opera with his arm around me, he complimented my tan skin. During the performance, he lightly caressed my bare shoulder and whispered in my ear, "Smooth as velvet!"

Bewitched by his manly, outdoorsy scent, I tried to ignore quivery pleasurable sensations down there.

We laughed often at Donizetti's Italian farce in English. Elderly bachelor Don Pasquale (DP), to stop supporting nephew Ernesto, wanted him to marry a rich wife. Ernesto, loving poor young widow Norina, refuses.

To disinherit Ernesto with his own heir, DP marries his doctor's sister (Norina in disguise). After her extravagance makes his life miserable, DP wants out. Overjoyed to be legally single since the notary who married them was phony, DP lets the young lovers elope.

Adoring deep voices, I reveled in two bass singers and a robust baritone.

In Albany, Bill's muscular arms embraced and warmed me in cool night air. As we kissed, my eyes closed and my hands slipped down from his neck to his shoulders and upper arms. "Have your muscles grown?"

Blushing, he looked pleased. "Fortunately, my job ends soon. I can't afford a new wardrobe to keep seams from bursting."

I giggled. "Can I feel your biceps muscle at its peak?" Feeling it flexed, I almost swooned with delight. He caught me in his arms for more smooching and mentioned meeting in NYC!

<u>Monday, September 2, 1963: Labor Day</u>
I answered Carina about recent dates and ended with this:

> Yesterday, this good daughter used her new
> license to drive the parents on the NY State

Thruway and local roads to Sacandaga Reservoir. A soothing day included swimming with Gloversville relatives against a backdrop of dark evergreens and vast, bluish Adirondack mountains. Cousin Lydia will soon return to jail (school) after missing summer adventures while toiling in her father's department store. Ella enjoyed being an arts-and-crafts day camp counselor, as I did in 1959.

Today, in rain-free, ideal weather, I accompanied the parents and the Levines to a park in Saratoga Springs and Mother Goldsmith's Restaurant, a long-standing favorite. Shy Robin Levine, now an AHS senior, wants to help people after college as a social worker.

Roomie, I can't wait to see you in person! Love and *Cheyah*!

Sunday, September 8, 1963: Speeding

During lunch at Howard Johnson's, I said, "Yeats, your tennis skills amazed me yesterday at Washington Park." I feel safer with athletic boyfriends.

He smiled. "Thank you. You held your own! Snacking at the Boulevard was fun."

Before boarding the Boston bus to return to college, he mentioned NYC dates. Though I love and respect sophisticated Yeats, I'm not *in love* with anyone. Emotional attachments must wait until I graduate. Long-distance love is out forever!

On my drive to Thacher Park, a good-looking state trooper stopped me, making my heart thump in dread as he examined my precious license. Sternly, he said "Thirty-eight miles an hour in a thirty-five mile per hour zone! I'm warning you to observe the speed limit or risk a ticket!"

Relieved, I replied demurely. "I will. Thank you, officer!" My heart quieted. I must control my heavy right foot on the accelerator pedal and resist speeding on Albany open roads.

I cleaned the attic, full of old junk, and polished my nails pretty pink. We saved haircut expense when Mother trimmed the back of my long locks.

Monday, September 9, 1963: Science

Jim, the 1963 AHS graduate who used to flirt and accompany me home, invited me to Green Mountain Raceway between Williamstown and Bennington, Vermont. Breathtaking scenery preceded exciting horse racing! Though I lacked money for bets, Jim won big, betting on two horses I liked. "Jim, at Saratoga Race Track, Mother's boss treated his staff to two-dollar bets. A crowd gathered when shrewd Mother won all eight races and hundreds of dollars."

"Angela, let's devise a scientific way to bottle her intuitions." I chortled.

Tuesday, September 10, 1963: Lee

A loving letter from former AHS wrestler Lee (below), my three-year crush, left me astonished, but happy! Tears brimmed about his feeling as if looking in from the outside at something near, but far out of reach. My jaw dropped reading that he thinks about me constantly and imagines my smile, which makes me *beautiful* and him crazy about me. Lee described us in the third person:

> From another world, he feared venturing into
> her world or bringing her into his world. Since
> she was such a special girl, he wanted her to
> have what she was accustomed to, something
> he couldn't offer (no car, little money). Though
> he can't take her to all the nice places she

deserves, is there a happier ending for this boy? Can he see his love (Angela Weiss) before she returns to school?"

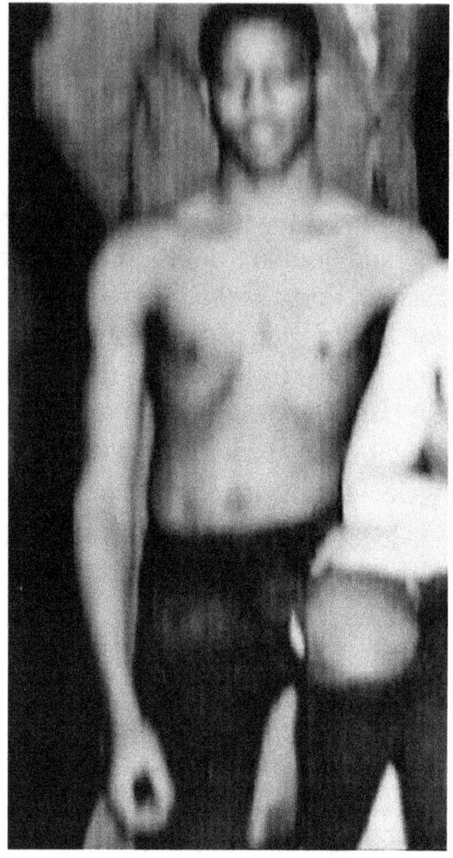

Lee called for a date! Will my AHS fantasies come true?

<u>Thursday, September 12, 1963: Freedom</u>
At a parent-mandated solo session, Mr. V's lack of disapproval about my socially unacceptable feelings impressed me. "Years of demands and criticisms have killed childhood positive feelings for the parents. Conforming to their *good daughter* definition to avert conflict, I can't wait to be financially independent to be done with their disagreeable company."

"You feel frustrated enough to want to skip seeing your family when you get past needing their support?"

"Yes! At Barnard, I feel under their thumbs, expected to drop everything to see them, instead of studying for a test or finishing an assignment on time. Rather than relieve academic pressure by cutting loose with friends in my limited free time, I must spend at least an hour phoning my aunts weekly. I relate to my parakeet's boundless joy when flying outside his cage."

"You can't wait to be free?" He looked empathetic.

I nodded. "Needing driving practice, I counted to ten and put up with Dad's continual nervous outbursts."

He grinned. "How are things with your mother?"

"I appreciated her taking me to the driving test. Mother didn't realize that datelessness made me join her at ceramics class. My infrequent dates may have decreased her jealousy. The parents are unaware that Jewish Bill and Yeats are unreligious. I earned a *Summer without a Gentile Boyfriend* award!"

Looking pleased, Mr. V wished me a good school year. "Miss Weiss, the door is open for a session when you're in Albany."

"Mr. V, I'm grateful for your help, as always!"

I exchanged DMV's punch card for my permanent license before chauffeuring the parents from work. "Mother, thanks again for summer job help! Helen and the other supervisor gave me this pretty, pink-flowered shower cap on my last day... The orthodontist said I must wear my night retainer to keep teeth from slipping back."

When asked about yesterday, I replied, "I liked the Strand's double feature. *Wall of Noise* with Suzanne Pleshette was about training racehorses. *Lafayette* conveyed the French nobleman's importance in the American Revolution."

I dropped the parents at home before treating myself to pizza and spumoni ice cream at the Moon Restaurant. I ran into AHS bass player Bob, who pursued me in 1961, and chatted with him and his friendly mom.

AHS classmate Hank called about enjoying Brandeis University near Boston. I appreciated Carina's and Cousin Ron's postcards before answering Yeats' letter.

<u>Friday, September 13, 1963: Lucky</u>
When beaming Lee picked me up at 9 PM, the parents, at temple services, missed meeting their daughter's Negro date. In his parents' well-used, very clean sedan, Lee drove me downtown. At the corner of Beaver and Lodge, integrated Barker's Musical Bar was characteristic of Albany venues: old, dark, smoky, and nothing fancy. Male drinkers filled the bar stools. Like other couples, we occupied a brown, leatherette booth. Lee drank Miller's beer while I sipped a sloe gin fizz. "Angela, even two years ago, Barker's never requested age proof."

Better than my fantasies, dancing with Lee was heavenly, especially to a live trio playing a favorite song, *Blue Velvet*. Protected by strong arms, I adored touching his chest and shoulders, muscular from summer construction work.

"Angela, at Cobleskill State College, I was a rare Negro. Though less than fifty miles west of Albany, Cobleskill village, full of bigots, felt like Alabama. At school clubs and social events, I felt unwelcome so I mainly studied. If isolated this fall, I'll transfer to Albany State."

"You deserve the best! Life is unfair! Being the only Jewish kid at Mayfield School in Colonie got me beat up in third grade. Will bigots ever get their comeuppance?"

"Maybe heaven will reject them." Lee gently squeezed my hand before we left to visit his neat, red-brick row house on Ten Broeck Street. I'm frustrated that we can't slow dance at nearby AHS hangout, all-white Mike's Log Cabin at 23 North Swan.

We chatted amiably with his tall, friendly parents. Lee's good looks come from his railroad-employee dad.

At the Polynesian Room, a hundred cocktails, fizzes, sours, cordials, rickeys, ryes, wines, scotches, and long coolers filled the menu! Drinkers abound in Albany. The bargain, fifty-cent house cocktail with fruit juice and rum and Lee's magnetism left me a little high. I saved the tiny, pink umbrella.

I felt cherished as Lee displayed the best manners, including opening all doors. Kissing his luscious lips goodnight, I imagined his powerful arms easily lifting and carrying me off. Fortunately, he's a respectful gentleman who stopped and thanked me for a great evening! This perfect Friday, the Thirteenth, broke the mold of prior bad luck!

<u>Saturday, September 14, 1963: Gloversville</u>
I dropped Dad at work before driving an hour to pick up my cousins. At Beacon Wholesale at 52 South Main Street, smiling, still trim, national high school basketball champion Uncle Peter, gave me size 12 navy wool slacks, size medium turquoise sweatshirt, size 34 striped blouse, and a blanket.

Lunch with my cousins preceded finding a size 11 yellow wool dress, nylon stockings, and size 6 narrow sneakers at their father's store (above), inherited from Grandpa, who died in 1946 before Lydia was born. My cousins, their parents, and I had a jolly, roast-chicken dinner at their spacious home.

Seated: Dad, Mother, fashionable Aunt Faith, athletic Uncle Peter, pretty Aunt Myrna with kind, affable husband Uncle Abner behind, others unknown

Elated from driving home on the Thruway, I picked up Dad at Montgomery Ward around 9 PM. "Angela, were you under the speed limit? A ticket will raise our insurance premiums.

"Angela, tomorrow at 2, we want you at the groundbreaking ceremony for Ohav Shalom synagogue (below). Mayor Corning, eight Rabbis, two cantors, four ministers, and two priests will speak. As a board trustee, I'm on the committee."

My eyes rolled about rude, late invites. "I've accepted another invitation. I'm less religious."

"What? You attended Sunday school and Hebrew school! This better be a temporary college thing. Get back on track soon!" I thought: *don't hold your breath*.

Later, I said, "Mother, I appreciate these clothes from my uncles."

Frown lines deepening, Mother looked vexed and sounded bitter. "They're compensating for my not getting shares of Father's business after working there for years." I lamented another example of unfair treatment of women.

I briefly replied to Carina's postcard, mentioning the marriage of our favorite singer, Barbra Streisand, age twenty-one, to actor Elliott Gould.

Sunday, September 15, 1963: Succulent

I skimmed the NY Times and packed for school until Lee escorted me to the Playdium. *Heat Wave,* on the juke box, made us want to jitterbug.

"Lee, your two bowling scores average 200! Your strength and athletic ability amaze me!"

His languid smile was irresistible! "Thank you! Did you hear that a Virginia state law, requiring segregated seating in publicly owned ballparks, has been ruled unconstitutional?"

"That's great! How do you stay positive after hundreds of years of inexcusably cruel treatment?"

"My parents and church leaders are role models. We follow King's guidance and look for progress, like my going to college!"

"We need his brilliant leadership and non-violent approach…. On another subject, has the AHS wrestling team co-captain gone out for sports in college?" "

Grades are more important. Can you help revive my rusty wrestling skills?" He looked me in the eye flirtatiously.

I giggled. "Cobleskill girls must beat down your door to volunteer for wrestling practice."

"My few dates there didn't inspire wrestling. The sweetest AHS girl makes others seem ordinary."

His soft, succulent goodnight kisses stirred me to breathlessness.

Blue Velvet lyrics repeat in my mind: *Warmer than May her tender sighs…. Feeling the rapture grow.* Refusing to pine away for long-distance men, I wish Lee were in NYC.

<u>Wednesday, September 18, 1963: Fun</u>
My reward for cleaning house was movies downtown at the Strand. *The Caretakers* about group therapy in a mental ward interested this future psychologist! I laughed at the British comedy, *Crooks Anonymous.* A criminal tries to go straight so his honest, pretty girlfriend will marry him.

After the NY State typing test for next summer's job and an optometrist exam, I picked up Yeats, home for the Jewish New Year, at the bus station.

"Angela, Albany's recent thirty-two-degree temperature made 1963's growing season the shortest on record, only 113 days starting May 24."

"I can't wait for warmer NYC." We dined at Howard Johnson's and bantered at The Boulevard with former classmates. I'm comfortable with Yeats who avoids romantic pressure.

My final paycheck is in my school bank account. My letter to Carina listed new wardrobe items from Ormond's and David's: white crepe choir boy blouse, size 34, $5.98; apricot-colored, V-neck, mohair sweater, size 38, $10.98; black stretch slacks, size 12, $8.90; two bras, size 34C; peds; and hair bows.

Thursday, September 19, 1963: Existentialism

This *good daughter* was at Jewish holiday services with her parents. At dinner, guest Yeats mentioned our plan to see Sophia Loren, Maximilian Schell, Fredric March, and Robert Wagner in *The Condemned of Altona*. The subtitled Italian movie is based on Sartre's existentialist play about post-Nazi-era Germans.

When the movie house lights came on, Yeats and I remained on the red-velvet theater seats. "Angela, what do you think about valuing freedom, authenticity, and individualism, as Sartre writes? How about the idea of the meaninglessness and absurdity of our existence explaining why life is often unfair?"

"I agree, based on my introductory philosophy readings. Bad things happening to good people, like most Negroes, bother me."

"Existentialists support individuals taking responsibility for their choices and lives."

"What if something is completely outside our control?"

"Like the movie characters dealing with Nazis?"

"What could most Germans have done instead of going along with Hitler? Though I don't understand every detail, these complicated, absorbing dramas stimulate scrutiny."

"Angela, this movie illustrates issues existentialists typically discuss. Existentialism seems better than other philosophies in dealing with modern dilemmas." I agreed.

Friday, September 20, 1963: Amusing

A real-life, romantic comedy began when the doorbell rang during Yeats' visit. Astounded to see Woodstock Bill, I invited him in and made introductions. Sheepishly, he said, "I should have called first. I apologize for interrupting. An all-day family errand brought me here. When it ended early, I impulsively dropped by, hoping for spontaneous time with you."

While we three chatted, I admired tolerant Yeats, who graciously said, "I'll run errands before stores close."

Over Moon Restaurant pizza, Bill seemed to turn on more charm. Our pleasurable goodnight kiss included my caressing his sexy arms and shoulders.

After I read Carina's letter, Yeats rang the doorbell, suggesting we watch Ibsen's marvelous drama, *Hedda Gabler*, on TV. "Angela, If only all TV programs were this superb!" We agreed that actors Ralph Richardson, Michael Redgrave, Trevor Howard, and Ingrid Bergman were superb.

Saturday, September 21, 1963: Fellini
Before dinner with Dad, Mother and I worked on paintings. My dark watercolor shows car headlights on the NY State Thruway.

Yeats and I enjoyed mint-chocolate-chip ice cream before an absorbing Italian movie *8½*. Leaving blue-velvet seats at opulent Hellman Theater, we visited Washington Tavern at 250 Western Avenue, a dated, commonplace drinking establishment. "Angela, movie flashbacks to director Fellini's childhood imaginatively illustrated the cause of his creative block about finishing his current science fiction movie. Marcello Mastroianni was effective as Fellini's alter ego. Did you like actress Anouk Aimee?"

"Yes! She, Jackie Kennedy, and I are brunettes in a world of blondes." We laughed. "Yeats, does movie directing or acting interest you?"

"No, thanks! If I'm at Columbia Law in two years, we can enjoy NYC together. Tomorrow, I'll call before returning to Boston." Did yesterday's competition motivate Yeats to step up his pursuit?

Monday, September 23, 1963: Final Albany Day
Grateful for passing the typing test to earn more next summer, I bought an eight-dollar, size 40, fur-blend, blue sweater. Ignoring menstrual cramps and Kevin sorrow, I'm thankful for summer highlights: driving freedom and dating special Yeats, Lee, Bill, and Dominic.

1963 NYC Sophomore

Many difficulties which nature throws in our way may be smoothed away by the exercise of intelligence.

Livy (Latin)

Tuesday, September 24, 1963: Hoot and Reid

Before I registered for classes, Woodstock Bill's brief visit and Yeats' letter buoyed my spirits. I'm relieved to be past summer tears about Kevin's betrayal, Negro suffering, and antisemitism against Doreen.

Enjoying *If I Had a Hammer* and other folk songs at a Columbia hootenanny, I met grinning, medium-sized Ray, who bought me a drink.

Carina and I reunited in modern Reid Hall. "Angela, will panty raids elude us, again facing the Barnard quad? I miss the 1907 Brooks' fireplace with mantle."

"Yes, but this real closet with sliding doors beats that wobbly wardrobe."

"Off-white walls are duller than Brooks' blue," she lamented.

"True, but these blond wood dressers and desks remind me of my beloved Heywood Wakefield desk at home. Later curfews excite me: 1:30 AM plus an extra hour Saturday!"

Wednesday, September 25, 1963: A Treat

Eileen, Barnard Class of 1962 star and Cousin Hal's wife (below), bused by Greyhound from San Francisco to see her NYC family. Strolling around Barnard, I said, "Eileen, your terrific book, *Questions Freshmen Ask, A Guide for College Girls,* helped me adjust to college." At Milbank Hall, I half-joked, "The facade's dancing bear makes this my favorite building."

"Angela, we enjoy this Nineteenth-Century architecture and Honeybear mascot from Columbia President Frederick Barnard's coat of arms because he couldn't persuade Columbia to admit women." Her blue eyes were bright above a wry grin.

We sauntered by the sparse trees of the misnamed *Jungle*. "Angela, sharing even an unfurnished 116 Street apartment beat missing parts of Barnard life while commuting. When I met Hal, I had my own 120 Street place near Columbia Teachers' College. Do Honeybears still *meet on Jake*?"

I shrugged. "I'm in the library stacks."

In the Barnard Hall lobby, Eileen mentioned, "About 50 years ago, Jacob Schiff, honored by this Jake statue, funded this building." Living in California seems to have made her NYC accent less perceptible.

In awe of Eileen as a role model, I asked, "How's University of California at Berkeley?"

"Different! After majoring in English and studying French at Barnard, I'm enjoying Proust, Moliere, and other comparative literature. Barnard psychology and philosophy courses sparked my current interest in Freud, Marx, and Reich." Her tone was ardent; her light eyes sparkled.

"Hoping to be a psychologist, I favor those subjects. What do you do for fun?"

"Recovered from *culture shock*, we dress more casually for classes, birdwatch, hike, and support CORE's (Congress on Racial Equality) non-violent, civil rights activities. The 1963 Berkeley Folk Music Festival with Pete Seeger and the spring Janis Joplin/Beach Boys concert were exciting! Our San Francisco digs free Hal from a grueling Bay Bridge commute. We fled summer fog with Napa Valley wine tasting. Hal described our overnight stay at Lassen National Park with a volcano as *wilder than NYC's Central Park*." I giggled.

At midnight, I said, "Carina, at the Columbia sundial, Ray, Spanky, and the Japanese-American engineering student from Denver stopped to chat. Wearing this required skirt (red denim), I unconsciously tapped my foot while answering Yeats' letter. Feeling a tap in the same rhythm on my shoulder, I looked up to see Gary's cute pal, Max, whose wide, green-eyed face looked elated. Savoring his long hug, I closed my eyes.

"Accompanied by the clatter of glasses at the Gold Rail, new guy Joel, also on scholarships, said, 'Not fixing up this place keeps these drinks more affordable than at West End Café.' Bill's message capped my fun before the academic axe falls."

"*Cheyah!*" She grinned. "Will Max be a keeper?" Smiling, I shrugged.

Thursday, September 26, 1963: Max
At the Gold Rail for a drink with senior Max, my raised eyebrows expressed curiosity about his parents living only forty miles southwest of Albany. His wry sense of humor, fair complexion, and dark blond hair attract me. An English major, he too loves classic novels.

Before our dorm floor meeting, Carina handed me pink phone slips from Bill's and Yeats' calls. Hearing about their unexpected Albany encounter at my house made her laugh. "Carina, how was French class?"

"Fun, but challenging!" Her expression was calm.

"Carina, I enjoyed the small mythology class and developmental psychology lab before book-buying and hours in the library."

Friday, September 27, 1963: Billiards
After ping pong at Barnard, Bill and a brown-haired pal escorted me to Columbia's Ferris Booth Hall. I complimented them. "You play billiards like pros!" Despite his beard, big, manly Bill attracts me!

I read absorbing history and sociology textbooks before answering Yeats' letter:

> In my small Latin class, Livy and Vergil's eclogues
> (brief pastoral poems) should be good reading.
> Only thirty girls are in introduction to sociology
> and developmental psychology, which both
> interest me! Unfortunately, over a hundred
> students are in required European history (1400
> to the present) lectures.

Saturday, September 28, 1963: Lions
Doubling with NY University juniors from his Connecticut high school, extravert Ray and I subwayed to Times Square for *My Son, the Hero,* an Italian comedy. In a Gold Rail booth, I joked, "Watching Zeus and Titans as movie characters should earn extra credit in mythology class." We celebrated our football team trouncing Brown at Brown, 41-14! I had fun, despite sniffles from a cold.

Sunday, September 29, 1963: Paper
"Carina, any thoughts about my sociology paper: *Barnard as an Agent of Socialization into Women's Roles*?"

"Mom's my model for having a big family with time for artistic pursuits. Last year's cynical date ridiculed my seeking a knight on a white horse for my parents' kind of marriage."

"Thanks for thought-provoking input! A nagging mother bossing a father who throws childish tantrums maximizes Barnard's influence on me." Her smile seemed caring.

Struggling for words all day in the library made me yearn for fluency. After autobiographical details about Albany, parents, and schooling, I wrote:

> Graduate school is unlikely if I marry and have children; I prefer a wife-mother career, unless financial hardship requires a job, preferably working with people.
>
> Unmarried President Park, advocating greater intellectual endeavor, has altered Barnard's administration. She has yet to model or encourage combining marriage and career, as did her predecessor, a mother of five. Dr. Park's labeling dorm open-house Sundays as in poor taste irks Honeybears who value dating.

She belongs in a convent! Though waiting to marry to make love, I adore privacy to exchange affection.

I lauded Barnard class advisors for balancing social and personal student concerns with academic subjects. I wrote:

> Three professors rued my dropping the career goal of a clinical psychology Ph.D.: a young, married mother; a young, single woman; and a middle-aged, married woman without children. Do they see homemaking as a waste of Barnard's superior education?
>
> Honeybears often say about being single: *she has her Ph.D., but what else does she have*? Marriage with work at least before and after raising children seems popular. Many want

careers, like physician, while parenting. Such
Honeybears may be speedier than I. Getting this
far in the paper helped me relax!

Monday, September 30, 1963: Attention

Bill's message, Max's date invites, and Yeats' letter about
school activities invigorated me!

The parents called. "Mother, thanks for your letter. I
reached Uncle Bert in the hospital Friday."

"Did you go to Yom Kippur (Day of Atonement) services
Saturday with your aunts?" Her accusatory tone made my eyes
roll!

"Do you want them to catch my cold?"

"Get more sleep and be at Sukkot (Harvest Festival)
services this week. You needn't stay overnight."

Silently counting to ten, I feared more low grades.
"Remember that keeping up on Latin translation and reading
for four classes require all day Saturday and Sunday. My long
sociology paper is due before Thanksgiving."

Long, judgmental silence. "At least, wish Aunt Lila a
happy birthday."

"I did when I called the hospital." I silently growled.

Dad talked on the extension phone. "Angela, the
Rabbi's *Kol Nidre* sermon about the new synagogue's steelwork
pointing to heaven raked in record donations: ten thousand
dollars." Where's the sacred in this materialism?

Mother said, "Dad's bridge has improved during games
with the Levines. Librarian Dr. Millard teaches our enjoyable
Tuesday folklore class. The NY State Museum's thirty-six
majestic, Corinthian-marble columns sparkle after whitening!"

"I love the museum's life-sized Iroquois long house and
models of Mohawk and Algonquin families."

"Without nursery school money, I took you there and to
the library weekly."

"Is the sweet librarian still at Harmanus Bleecker?"

"She retired. Remember Normans Kill Dairy?"

"Who can forget the long row of machines milking huge brown-and-white Guernsey cows?"

"Did these activities help in school?"

"Library visits made me love reading. The day trips were fun. Thank you, Mother!"

Tuesday, October 1, 1963: Prexy's

A sophomore class meeting preceded hours of burial in the library. Bill found me and asked me out for Saturday! Later, Carina handed me five MCNMs (man called no message).

With affable Ray at Prexy's on Broadway, I grinned at the cute logo, a hamburger with feet wearing a mortarboard hat with the tassel dangling in food. The slogan is *The Hamburger with a College Education*. "Angela, I heard about Prexy's on Jean Shepherd's entertaining radio show." While hazel-eyed Ray eagerly gobbled down the post-graduate, quarter-pound hamburger for sixty-five cents, his date enjoyed twenty-five-cent, soft vanilla ice cream.

Wednesday, October 2, 1963: Sensational

I gave Carina a Shanghai Café business card. "Near 125 Street at 3217 Broadway, Max and I had delicious hot-and-sour soup, shrimp with lobster sauce, and dumplings, far superior to Chinese *chow mein* dinners. Though off a dingy hall, his 122 Street apartment near Broadway, was clean and neat. Classical music expert Max made it a marvelous evening with Mahler, Schubert, Beethoven, and Mozart recordings!"

"Are you exulting?" Carina's expression said: *Angela has fallen again.* "Auburn-haired Bill was looking for you."

Picturing Max's hair, I asked, "Is this year for blondes?"

Thursday, October 3, 1963: Rivals

"Carina, Bill saw Max holding my hand on Broadway after an evening drink at the Gold Rail. Will Bill give up, like sensitive Hy after seeing me play ping pong with another guy?"

"If rugged Bill thrives on competition, he may chase harder to win you."

"I hope! A letter from our sweet AHS exchange student, Mista, in Norway, made my day! Yeats and Mother also wrote."

Friday, October 4, 1963: Bliss
"Max, thanks for taking me to the romantic 1939 *Wuthering Heights* movie, as good as the exceptional novel! Laurence Olivier as Heathcliff, Merle Oberon as Cathy, and David Niven as Linton were superb." We split a Serendipity concoction of ice cream, whipped cream, cherries, chocolate shavings, colorful sprinkles, chocolate-chip cookies, ribbons, paper flowers, and umbrellas! A nearby couple shared a giant banana split with similar trimmings! A waiter carried a gold-decorated ice-cream extravaganza to another couple.

In Max's darkened living room, slow dancing on the brown rug led to heavenly kissing on the comfy beige couch!

Saturday, October 5, 1963: Double Fun
At Columbia's homecoming football game, Bill, four engineering pals, and I bantered with Bill's Princeton friend, elated about edging us out, 7-6.

Planning to study all evening, I couldn't resist the fabulous Moscow Circus at Madison Square Garden with easy-going Ray, spiffy in a white button-down shirt, soft-blue, V-neck pullover, and charcoal-gray tweed jacket. Subwaying to Greenwich Village, we joked about getting lost.

"Carina, my favorite circus performers were Cossacks doing acrobatic tricks on horses galloping around a ring and three bear acts! Two bears in shorts boxing and a bear on hind legs running around a ring carrying a dog amused me! On top of a center tower, a hefty bear sat watching two smaller bears clinging to opposite, quickly revolving ends of two horizontal metal arms. Their precarious perches reminded me of my insecure economic situation at Barnard. Was the big bear a mother worrying about her cubs?"

"How was Ray?"

"Over drinks at Tom's on Broadway and 112 Street, he continued to be amiable, but less amusing and stimulating than Max."

Sunday, October 6, 1963: Women's Roles
Uninterrupted library hours produced sociology paper progress about my most important socialization agent, Columbia Lions, like Gary, Bill, Max, Ray, their buddies, and others met here:

> Men consulted avoided disapproval of women with careers. Viewing married women more favorably than singles, males sounded less liberal about women they want to marry. Though many preferred that their wives not work unless money is needed before children arrive, few objected to wives putting husbands through school! For their wives, men approved of traditional teaching, while sounding hesitant about professions, like medicine. All concurred that wives' careers must never inconvenience husbands and children.
>
> For instance, a friend said that he wants his wife to be happy. If a career makes her happy, he approves if it doesn't interfere with running the house and relating to him and the children.
>
> I asked, "How can a career not have some effect?"
>
> He responded that the career probably would interfere, so it would have to go.

"Carina, unrealistic males, like Gary, expect a working wife to manage her domestic role as efficiently as a full-time homemaker. Why can't the selfish bums share household tasks? Will men ever support wives' professional careers?"

"Only if parents raise boys differently. My parents expect my sister and me to do more chores than my brothers, who get to play more."

"Am I the only female wanting an enlightened husband to thwart being short-changed about career, marriage, or kids?"

"Angela, I want a family man, rather than a workaholic on a mad quest for money and status." I agreed.

Monday, October 7, 1963: Loss

After a history quiz, I ran into Gary's pint-sized roommate. This *Columbia Spectator* sportswriter was melancholy about yesterday's Los Angeles Dodgers win in the fourth and final World Series game. "Angela, the Series' most valuable player was Jewish NY Yankee pitcher Sandy Koufax, who studied at Columbia School of General Studies. Sandy outshined Mickey Mantle, who broke his foot this year."

"This Yankee and Mickey fan feels glum! Best to Gary!"

Tuesday, October 8, 1963: Interesting Father

"Carina, tantalizing dancing and kissing at Max's rewarded me for library hours yesterday. Today, after schoolwork, Max and I browsed in a bookstore before a Gold Rail drink. His face lit up and voice was energized, describing his robust retired, age 70+ father: former Russian revolutionary, current homemade winemaker, colorful raconteur. Max's admired half-brother, a NYC lawyer, enjoys considerable success."

Thursday, October 10, 1963: Children

Carina said, "French assignments are done! What's new?"

"Yesterday's developmental psychology class observed boring nursery school students (below). Is motherhood tedious?"

"My brothers have been more impertinently annoying than dull." She grinned.

I giggled. "Adults like Max interest me! Hiking south on Broadway about fifteen blocks, we shared a yummy bagel with lox and cream cheese and a potato knish at Rosenblum's. We studied, danced, and kissed at his drab, but comfy apartment."

Friday, October 11, 1963: Visitor

Yeats, here from Boston, and I strolled with Carina and date Dennis Alexis. She asked, "Yeats, are you enjoying NYC?"

His voice sounded hearty. "Yes. Angela kindly picked me up at the bus terminal before we visited my NYC pal. Later, meandering around Columbia, we chatted with Marcus, who's involved with today's Columbia rally for Louisiana Negro voter registration."

I added, "Marcus planned interesting AHS current events club programs when Yeats was president."

Yeats continued. "At Chock Full o' Nuts coffee shop, I appreciated *that heavenly coffee* and whole wheat raisin bread with cream cheese and walnuts. Angela had ice cream on a brownie."

I grinned. "Translation: cream cheese on yummy date-nut bread."

Later, Yeats and I subwayed to and wandered around Greenwich Village. At O. Henry's (menu below), Yeats asked, "How about splurging on a champagne cocktail?"

Noticing the $1.25 price, compared to a dollar for over thirty other cocktails (no Singapore sling), I smiled. "Thank you, Yeats!" He drank a dark Wurzburger beer on tap for seventy-five cents. At Barnard, a warm kiss capped a delightful date with a true gentleman, who's always interesting company!

<u>Saturday, October 12, 1963: Jail</u>
Yeats led me around Columbia's campus. Small flying birds watched over our Riverside Park romp and sandwich lunch. Handing me a copy of Martin Luther King, Jr.'s August letter from jail in Birmingham, Yeats said, "The Southern Christian Leadership Conference is fortunate that Dr. King is president. His detailed facts persuasively justify the current non-violent demonstrations as reasonable and necessary. How about these brilliant words?"

> Injustice anywhere is a threat to justice everywhere…. Nonviolent direct action seeks to…establish such creative tension that a community that has consistently refused to negotiate is forced to confront the issue…. History is the long and tragic story of the fact that privileged groups seldom give up their privileges voluntarily…. Freedom is never voluntarily given by the oppressor; it must be demanded by the oppressed…. Justice too long delayed is justice denied. We have waited for more than three hundred and forty years for our God-given and constitutional rights.

"Yeats, what great lines! I like his distinction between just and unjust laws and his St. Augustine quote: *An unjust law is no law at all.*"

Yeats' tone was fervent. "I wish that the Martin Buber reference to segregation, which substitutes an *I-it* relationship for an *I-thou* relationship and relegates persons to the status of things, would persuade people to improve. King is correct about laws being unjust, if inflicted only on a minority lacking the *unhampered* right to vote. I'm shocked that some Alabama counties lack any Negro voters despite their being most of the population."

"Yeats, I hope King inspires actions to end Southern bigots' cruel behavior." A tear escaped from my eye. "Angela, student-of-history King taught that today's academic freedom stems from Socrates practicing civil disobedience. King's right that everything Hitler did in Germany was legal and everything 1956 Hungarian freedom fighters did was illegal." I admire Yeats' passion about justice and courage to act on his convictions.

"Yeats, King is right: white moderates more devoted to order than justice block Negro freedom more than the Ku Klux Klan. Discouraging Negroes from actions for basic constitutional rights just because the quest precipitates violence by bigots *is* immoral. I agree with King: *Society must protect the robbed and punish the robber*."

Vigorously nodding, Yeats paced back and forth near our park bench as he spoke. "King, the cynosure we need, criticizes the *appalling silence of the good people* and notes that, without diligence, *time itself becomes an ally of the forces of social stagnation*. He's convincing that his way of *love and nonviolent protest* is the better middle road between the violence and *despair of the black nationalist* and the *do-nothingism* of cowed Negroes and the complacent white middle-class."

I replied, "King wisely warns about Negro *pent-up resentments and latent frustrations* being better channeled into marches, prayer pilgrimages, sit-ins, and freedom rides than a violent *frightening racial nightmare*."

Yeats agreed with King that the *contemporary church is so often... an arch supporter of the status quo.*

I laughed. "Down on organized religion, I'm like young people King meets *every day whose disappointment with the church has risen to outright disgust*."

Yeats sat down next to me. "Angela, I like his taking the high road of consistently preaching that nonviolence demands that means used must be as pure as ends sought."

King's eloquent final words, praising heroes like James Meredith for courageously facing jeering, hostile mobs at the University of Mississippi while in pursuit of the *best of the American dream*, made tears overflow my eyes. Yeats kindly produced a disposable tissue and put his arm around me.

<u>Sunday, October 13, 1963: With Carina</u>
At Takome, Yeats, Carina, and I chose roast beef with lettuce and Russian dressing baguette sandwiches. In Riverside Park, she asked, "Yeats, what do you think of Columbia?"

"After Campus Corner coffee woke me up, Angela and I visited the tennis courts and the *Jungle*, which needs more trees or a new name. At all-male New Hall dorm at 114 Street and Broadway, temptress Angela had to wait in the lounge, evocative of a dingy bus terminal. The rooms off endless, dreary corridors made me thankful for my Boston apartment."

"How was last evening?" Carina inquired.

"French onion soup, roast duckling, French fried potatoes, and French pastry at Paris-Brest at 50 Street and Ninth Avenue were delish!" My voice conveyed my excitement.

Yeats continued. "At the Paris Theater on 58 Street near Fifth Avenue, Godard's *My Life to Live* was gloomy. We learned that Parisians suffer from American materialism." His grin was wry. "My NYC pal and his date took us to a get-together with two other couples at 104 Street and West End Avenue!"

I added, "My Gold Rail nightcap, a grasshopper, was as good as mint-chocolate-chip ice cream!" They chortled.

Yeats sounded determined. "It's time for more diligent study to get into Columbia Law in 1965."

Carina's blue eyes twinkled. "Do you need a winning football team?"

Yeats replied, "Condolences about yesterday's 7-19 loss to Yale at New Haven."

Carina's friends, husky-voiced musician Dennis and bespectacled, free-lance writer Everett, joined us for chitchat before Yeats left on the Boston bus. Despite my fondness for Yeats, Kevin's crushing deceit rules out long-distance attachments. Studying in the library, I missed amusing Max, ideal for frequent, local companionship.

Monday, October 14, 1963: Concern
"Carina, for lunch Max and I shared a delicious Caravan Restaurant cheeseburger at Broadway and 111 Street before a sunny Riverside Park ramble. Small brown birds guided us.

"I hope Max thrives on competition. Tonight, his pre-med housemates spied me with Bill at the new Brick Floor Coffee House on Amsterdam Avenue north of 120 Street."

Tuesday, October 15, 1963: Albany News
Carina asked about my grimace.

"Mother's seriously ill close friend is having hospital tests... Mother's trying to tone down Dad's angry reply to his sister Lila, who's 'ashamed to tell friends' that I rode on the holidays. Religions have too many disapproving busy-bodies minding other people's business, even that of strangers!"

"Spot, I'm sorry you're in the doghouse again! Such guilt trips must stop!"

Valuing Carina's support, I barked a playful thank you. "The letter mentions their enjoying the delightful musical, *The Fantasticks*, which I like, especially the song *Try to Remember*. Though Beth, my red-haired, Albany cousin, was out when Mother dropped by, her affable husband and cute kids, ages three, five, and eight, were fun. On the Albany Medical College tour, the parents saw a removed heart beat with the help of oxygen. At the VA Hospital, Mother and her friend cheered a

Jewish vet, suffering from severe allergies and without family or friends. A ski instructor who emigrated from Nazi Austria, he regaled them with fascinating stories. Mother will borrow from her retirement fund to pay the father and uncle of Tad, my husband at age five, to repair and paint the house exterior. Mother sends regards to you and her crush, Bill."

Carina looked pleased. "Please send regards! Her letters are interesting."
At Max's, his studious housemates were out. Romantic, slow dancing is the way to my heart!

Thursday, October 17, 1963: Uh-Oh
"Carina, over Gold Rail drinks, Max asked what mischief I've gotten into. Did he mean my date with Bill? I irrelevantly replied, 'Yesterday, the nursery school youngsters were less boring.' Shock: he finds kids less than fascinating. When I yawned, I blamed this morning's dorm fire drill with sleep deprivation."

"Angela, his mischief question seems better than Hy's disappearance."
"Agreed! Have a wonderful train trip to see your high school chum at Wellesley College! May your Boston blind date be better than Columbia frog dates!"

Friday, October 18, 1963: Finished
Good chats with my Latin prof and sociology prof about a major preceded additions to my paper.

As a socialization agent for women's roles, the Barnard catalog, covering only academic aspects, supports careers with eight pages about Columbia-affiliated graduate schools.

Barnard courses, which work well for either sex, imply encouragement of female careers. I wrote:

Only the worthwhile, mandatory hygiene course supports marriage. Physical and emotional life are discussed, including reproductive functions and relationships with the opposite sex.

Considering every Barnard agent of socialization, I conclude that the administration seems to favor unmarried career status; the advisers, marriage with careers; the faculty, careers with or without marriage; students, marriage with jobs; Columbia men, marriage without careers; and most of the curriculum, careers.

Such inconsistent influences inevitably cause uncertainty. I've realized that my values and abilities make marriage with a career after graduate school too much. Omitting my slow, thorough inclinations, I included:

Young children need parental time and attention. A demanding profession, like clinical psychologist, and a typical uncompromising husband, who shuns housework and childcare, may present too great a burden for me.

I noted that self-analysis will produce diverse outcomes for others. Will my final sentence, critical of Barnard, sound impertinent and lower my grade?

The conflicting preferences of the various agents of socialization may complicate the choice of women's roles for some Honeybears.

Expected to do all the boring chores at home, women have a raw deal! Dad, who only takes out the garbage, reads the paper and watches TV while Mother does hours of housework after full-time office work. Asking him to get something fixed leads to months of procrastination and temper tantrums after reminders. Glaring at my heavy textbook, I naughtily dropped it on the library floor to vent exasperation about unfairness to women!

<u>Saturday, October 19, 1963: Mother</u>
Wearing a navy wool dress, Mother joined me for dinner in our cafeteria. "Did you call your aunts?"

"Yes." Rather than roll eyes or retort angrily, I silently counted to ten while staring at her.

"Everyone on the bus to NYC was in a good mood. My friend, her daughter, and I kidded around and laughed loudly at everything. After visiting the top of the Empire State Building, we saw elegant sights from a Fifth Avenue bus, watched Rockefeller Center skaters, and toured the theater district. This trip has given me a boost!"

Before taking a taxi to catch the bus to Albany, Mother met Max. She seemed keener about Bill's six-foot height than Max's green eyes and sandy hair.

I

In Greenwich Village, *Color of Darkness* (above), based on James Purdy's eponymous short story volume, touched Max and me. In a family drama about an emotionally distant father (the opposite of Dad!) and lonely son, whose mother left years ago, actress Doris Roberts excelled as their housekeeper.

We had Max's dark living room to ourselves. One housemate was visiting his Smith College girlfriend; the other was with his Long Island family for the weekend. Slow dancing was sublime!

Sunday, October 20, 1963: Garth

After a Caravan milk shake with ruddy-faced, robust Bill, I welcomed back Carina, beaming from ear to ear. Her fair complexion was flushed with ardor. "I'm infatuated with Harvard senior Garth! From Belmont near Boston, he's gentlemanly, urbane, amusing, un-arrogant, and creative! For a Jewish guy, his German literature major is unusual. His mom assists their local rabbi and his dad is an electrician. He has two younger sisters. He directs and acts in college theater productions. He played Joxer Daly in O'Casey's *Juno and the Paycock* last spring!"

"Wow!"

"He's very attractive: taller than I, good body, blue eyes, handsome facial bone structure, charming smile, and sexy voice."

"I'm thrilled for you! How about a joint business offering German and French translations?" She laughed.

Hearing about the panty raid on the other side of Reid Hall when it was over, we sighed in unison. "Carina, will we ever know in time to throw down torn underwear?"

Monday, October 21, 1963: Raid and JFK

Without finding *Barnard Bulletin* or *Columbia Spectator* mention of yesterday's raid, Carina said, "So much for freedom of the press! Administrators must have suppressed coverage."

"Censorship is disillusioning!" I exclaimed.

During a Riverside Park stroll following a Caravan lunch, Max said, "Saturday, JFK, spoke about foreign policy at University of Maine. During the first half of our 3-3 tie football game in Boston, 1941 Harvard grad JFK impartially cheered both teams' good plays and stood for both alma maters. He chuckled at Columbia band's halftime show, *The Nomination of J. Barry Silverwater for President*, a parody of Arizona Republican Senator Barry Goldwater."

"Max, I adore JFK!"

"Over 500 supporters from Archie Roberts' nearby hometown cheered our star quarterback." Romantic Max handed me a print of Renoir's *The Skiff*. "This Saturday is one month after our first date!"

Touched, I smiled. "Max, thank you! I'll put this up in our room. I adore your living room copy!"

Yeats' letter praised the UN Resolution banning nuclear bombs in outer space. My reply agreed and added, "Catholics, now switching to local languages in sacraments, will make my beloved Latin even deader."

Late ping pong with outgoing Ray was relaxing.

Tuesday, October 22, 1963: Weddings

"Carina, as a bride, will you be Cinderella or a princess?"

"I'll wear an unfussy white dress, maybe ballerina length, at a small family ceremony."

"Mother's nagging and Dad's yelling make liberty more appealing than unpredictable marriage."

Wednesday, October 23, 1963: Truffaut

Lover Come Back to Me on *The Second Barbra Streisand Album* played on Carina's record player. "Carina, if you're daydreaming about Garth, I commiserate."

"How's local dating?"

"Today's fun coffee hour included chatting with Gary's friend Harris and new guy Gus. Yesterday, before sundaes at

Tom's Corner, Max and I saw the Ferris Booth Hall rerun of Truffaut's *400 Blows*. My parents might appreciate me if they had a law-breaking son in serious trouble, like the movie's main character." We exchanged grins.

<u>Friday, October 25, 1963: Max and Ray</u>
The silvery, tranquil Hudson River glistened as Max and I split a Takome roast beef sandwich in Riverside Park whose trees are changing colors. Though favorite Max makes me laugh more than any other guy, I'm grateful that his Friday sex dates with a secretary leave me free to date intriguing Gus, who left a message. Who left two anonymous messages?

At the Plaza Theater, history major Ray and I appreciated *The Leopard*, starring Burt Lancaster, Claudia Cardinale, and Alain Delon! We sauntered along the edge of Central Park before downing thick vanilla milkshakes at Carnegie Corner Coffee Shop. "Angela, how did the movie compare to di Lampedusa's novel?"

"Both were absorbing with more adventure than Barnard history lectures. Sicilian life during the Italian unification was eventful!"

<u>Saturday, October 26, 1963: More Truffaut</u>
Protective Max comforted me as tears flowed after the film *Jules and Jim* with handsome Oskar Werner and *femme fatale* Jeanne Moreau. "Max, their World-War-I-era love triangle moved me more than the gangsters in *Shoot the Piano Player*."

"Angela, as a Truffaut fan, I appreciated both. Let's celebrate today's rare Columbia football win: 42-21 against non-Ivy-League Lehigh." Regretting that mid-year prep made me miss the game, I enjoyed NY State champagne and romantic dancing in Max's apartment. Looking into his olive eyes and kissing his wide mouth, I heard Sam Cooke's beloved hit song, *You Send Me*, go through my mind.

Monday, October 28, 1963: Poem
Sandwiches in Max's small, white kitchen rewarded my surviving the psych exam. His evening call included, "Angela, in the library, do you think of me?"

"Are you telepathically distracting me? I jotted lines about you but lack the nerve to ever show amateur verse to an English major. It may have four unrhymed couplets, each with a line of iambic tetrameter, followed by one of iambic trimeter." He sounded curious before I switched subjects.

Great Boyfriend (undisclosed to Max)
I have so much to do these days
Yet you are on my mind.
I said that you should stay away
But now I want you near.
I long to see your deep green eyes
To have you hold my hand.
I thought that I was done with love
With you I'm not so sure.

Does Max have that *Intangible X,* needed for me to fall in love?

Wednesday, October 30, 1963: Home
Unwinding from sociology and Latin tests, I answered Yeats' and Mother's letters. When Carina wanted Albany news, I shared this from Mother:

New record: no precipitation for twenty-three days! A lesson about applying dark and light colors enhanced my still-life oil painting. Our weeknight synagogue class covers the prophets. Dad likes his Sunday *Talmud* class. Our Saturday dance class includes the Levines.

Carina's voice sounded animated. "Remarkable energy after working all day!"

"Mother is always occupied. Even watching television, she often mends clothes. I'm grateful for five dollars from selling my unneeded yellow wool dress and wool tweed Bermuda shorts to a Honeybear! I'd be rich if I were a nudist and could sell my other outfits." Carina grinned.

Thursday, October 31, 1963: Halloween
The mythology test and psych lab left no time to devise a disguise. Picturing bobbing for apples at Julia's 1956 Halloween party, I read Carina my silly ditty:

Are Men Like Apples?
Nothing's as good as a perfect apple.
Nothing's so bad as a spoiled one.
I can't tell the difference by looking
Though careful eyes may see soft spots.
With most apples, I must take a bite
To label juicy, crunchy fruit.

Did over glorifying Max make our Gold Rail date feel less exhilarating than usual?

Friday, November 1, 1963: Fast
At Columbia's Crown Room, evening dancing, sipping cola, and eating ice cream with a new guy with brown-and-brown, average-Lion looks were fun until he tried for a smooch. His personality was fine, but nothing extraordinary. A guy I hardly know introduced us. I'd rather like him better before kissing.

Before afternoon library study, a sociable, brunette Honeybear commuter from psych class lunched with me on tuna salad at the dorm cafeteria. Psychology fascinates us.

Saturday, November 2, 1963: Ninth
A late, lovely date at Max's included Beethoven's dramatic *Symphony No. 9*. Max, who buys different recordings of favorites, asked my preference. "Max,

Furtwangler, leading the Berlin Philharmonic during World War II, thrilled me more than Klemperer's Philharmonia Orchestra version! I love the chorus in German, 'Be embraced, millions! This kiss to the entire world.'"

"Schiller's *Ode to Joy* is a cure for Columbia's football loss to Cornell 17-18."

"Max, is winning away from home tough?"

"Or at home… for Columbia." We chuckled.

At Barnard, Max said, "Keep this Bruno Walter recording of Beethoven's *Symphony No. 6*, which I replaced. The scratch drove me crazy."

"Thank you!"

"Let's listen to Chopin over Sunday brunch. The housemates are gone all weekend." Our hug turned into a long, delectable kiss. Pressed against his broad chest, I felt weak-kneed.

Monday, November 4, 1963: Movie

Lively Carina's face lit up about turning nineteen soon! She asked what movie I saw with Max. "Carina, dating a Negro like Lee generates sympathy for women who defy convention to follow their hearts. The *Hiroshima, Mon Amour* French actress shooting an anti-war film in rebuilt Hiroshima, took a former enemy, a Japanese architect, as a lover. Before returning home, she revealed that a German enemy, a soldier in occupied France during World War II, was her first love! On another subject, with only 69 right out of 91, I'm thankful for a psych test *B* and elated about my Latin test *A*!"

Tuesday, November 5, 1963: Socializing

A New Moon Inn Chinese dinner was fun with charming Max and clowning housemates. Lunch tomorrow will be at their bare-bones, clean, two-bedroom apartment. Every three months, a different guy sleeps in the living room.

To avert snap-judging that fast guy, I agreed to Lion's Den ice cream. He seems too enthralled with himself for my taste.

Between phone chats with Yeats, Harris, Bill, and Cousin Ron, who shared happy Temple University dating anecdotes, I answered letters from Yeats and Mother.

<u>Friday, November 8, 1963: Sociology</u>
Hoping for a good grade, I submitted my paper about Barnard's socialization for women's roles. Renowned full Prof Mirra Komarovsky's (below) is an ideal role model. Her history fascinated our class! She fled Russia at sixteen before graduating from Barnard and marrying. Though mentor William Ogburn discouraged her, she overcame antisemitism and prejudice against females to earn a Columbia Ph.D. and teach here since the 1930s. Older than Mother, Dr. K looks more presentable.

Previously, she described research for her current book: *Blue-Collar Marriage*. Does her 1953 book *Women in the Modern World: Their Education and Their Dilemmas* include the role conflicts my paper mentions? Dad's job woes motivate me to read her book *The Unemployed Man*.

A Minus on my history exam left me happily speechless!

Saturday, November 9, 1963: Date

At our Baker Field football game with Dartmouth, Max's drooping mouth said it all: we lost 6-47. "Angela, we need other players as talented as quarterback Archie Roberts."

Rosenblum's mouthwatering roast duck dinner preceded student-acted plays under Columbia auspices. Max preferred Genet's *Death Watch* about quarrels between three prisoners in one cell to the humorous murder trial in Mortimer's *Dock Brief*. Dessert was feel-good kissing during dancing in his darkened living room.

Sunday, November 10, 1963: Albany

After library studying with Max, I answered letters from Craig and Yeats, who enclosed *The New Republic* magazine.

Carina looked at my Albany map before asking to hear Mother's letter:

A nice Jewish boy rented the spare bedroom. A graduate of Long Island's Adelphi University, tall, slim Burke, 24, is a financial analyst for the state university, where Evelyn Levine works. A ham radio operator, he agreed to smoke cigars and pipes only in his room with the door always closed. His father is a shoe buyer for NYC department store Gimbels.

For allergies to bacteria, mold, grass, etc., I'm starting shots, which cleared a friend's sinus condition.

Election Day: "Fern, part-timers like you cost me $1,000 a year." Hearing another sarcastic remark about my not producing, I told off my real estate broker boss, who's bigoted against Jews and Negroes. Despite the difficulty of selling while working full-time for NY State, I may try working for a pleasant woman.

Monday, November 11, 1963: Grade

My sociology paper earned a *B Plus/A Minus*! Dr. K wrote, "Nice summary and nice distinction," about my contrast of marriage with a job and marriage with a career. She wanted more about my giving up on grad school. Self-centered males, too lazy to do half the housework, are my main reason!

Lunch at the Caravan: "Max, thank you for these German stories translated into English! I'm glad we both love fiction." His smile warmed my heart whose beat quickened.

Wednesday, November 13, 1963: Shock

After four months of silence, Dominic, now a Navy seaman sailing out of NYC, sent three pages. His oiler, USS Caloosahatchee, refuels Navy ships in the Mediterranean. He visited Rota, Spain, and Augusta Bay and Palermo in Sicily on leave. Next are Genoa and Naples. Will he see relatives in Greece? Treasuring this part, I felt happy:

My dearest Angela, I cannot explain why I never called again after our beautiful summer date. After letting weeks slip by, I lacked the mental strength or serenity to express that my words of love aren't just a line. As the Platters sang: *Only you can thrill me like you do and fill my heart with love for only you.* If, my precious love, you still care, write to tell me if you will give me another chance. I want and need you so much. If your feelings have changed, please kindly let me know. Perhaps we could still be (that awful phrase) just good friends. I wouldn't spoil our friendship because you didn't want my love. Please don't take this as an insult to your character; it's just my self-doubts. Fears keep me from acting.

I can think of nothing but you. These will be the longest days of my life awaiting your reply. I am unquestionably, indisputably yours forever till *The Twelfth of Never*!

With all my love, D

Though my eyes were closing, I stayed up to answer:

I have adored you since my parents prohibited dating and we spent countless hours on the phone. After our wonderful July outing, I was eager for regular summer time together without school pressures. At demanding Barnard, I need freedom to date others, especially for laughs. Until your service ends and we live in the same city, can we stay close romantically? Love, A

Thursday, November 14, 1963: Birthday Dinner

Carina, in navy suit over white bowed blouse, and I dined at huge, popular Mama Leone's on West 48 Street. Jazzed by the red-checkered tablecloth, we split one enormous meal, which totaled less than my twenty dollars of saved allowance: delicious antipasto with capers and anchovies, minestrone soup, and yummy baked lasagna. Waiters sang *Happy Birthday*! Pink candles on cheesecake lit her flushed cheeks!

In our room, I lit a candle in the center of Carina's favorite: a *Chock Full o' Nuts* crispy, whole-wheat doughnut sprinkled with powdered sugar. After my off-key *Happy Birthday*, she clapped, likely in relief that ear pain had ended.

<u>Friday, November 15, 1963: Embers</u>
Carina wanted details about my exceptional date with blue-eyed Gus, age twenty-two, from nearby, affluent Scarsdale.

Roomie, we taxied to The Embers, a fancy jazz supper club on East 54 Street near Lexington Avenue. After cocktails, we ate the thickest, juiciest roast beef and baked potatoes with sour cream and chives. Suave, well-traveled Gus, wearing neat, quiet clothing, seems less materialistic than my *bourgeois* parents. He's refined and mature with well-thought-out ideas about people, relationships, psychology, business, and money. We never ran out of things to discuss.

Sipping light crème de menthe, we appreciated famous jazz trumpeter Jonah Jones' quartet. *On the Street Where You Live* from *My Fair Lady* was my favorite. Our show was broadcast live on CBS radio!

The exciting evening ended at small Menemsha Bar on East 57 Street where a cool window diorama periodically re-created Martha`s Vineyard harbor storms. I confessed that pomegranate grenadine, rather than alcohol, is why I favor Singapore slings.

<u>Saturday, November 16, 1963: Idyllic Day</u>
Seeing Columbia beat Penn, 33-8, left Max and me euphoric. Over won ton, delish beef and broccoli, and chicken with mushrooms at Shanghai Cafe, he energetically said, "Our hero Archie passed and ran for more yards than the entire Penn team! He won the Ivy League lifetime passing record: over 1700 yards! Our talented kicker overcame his psychological block for his first field goal in fourteen career tries."

"Why hasn't Coach Donelli replaced him?"

His grin was wry. "Other Lion kickers are probably worse or dedicated Donelli may value student development over career statistics. That touchdown after an unpredictable pass from punt formation thrilled me."

"It was electrifying, like the amazing catch carried over forty yards for another touchdown!"

Our eyes met about my fortune cookie message: *romance is coming.*

Ingmar Bergman's *The Seventh Seal*, set during Sweden's medieval plague, was a masterpiece. The black-and-white imagery of the chess game, which black-hooded-and-clad Death played with the Crusader knight, was striking. Max said, "Bergman invented a universal allegory relevant in historical and modern times. What a profound line: 'Faith is a torment… like loving someone who is out there in the darkness but never appears, no matter how loudly you call.'"

Sunday, November 17, 1963: Happy
A superlative weekend continued with a Caravan lunch with Udeh's brunette roommate, average in attire and appearance. "Angela, our New Hall room's monotonous hallway suggests a surreal or Kafka dream. Female guest rules require books to prop open doors on Sunday afternoons. Our brilliant neighbor resourcefully interprets *book* to include an open matchbook cover squeezed between the door jamb and closed door."

Laughing, I accepted his Friday invite. Conversing with amusing, well-read Lions like him, Gus, and Max is a treat.

When Yeats called from Boston, I thanked him for a letter, a clever editorial, an issue of liberal *Commentary* magazine, and Carson McCullers' book, *A Member of the Wedding*. When he asked for news, I said, "My mythology grade of *A minus/B Plus* is a relief." During Thanksgiving break, seeing him should warm up frigid Albany.

<u>Wednesday, November 20, 1963: Burke</u>
"Carina, Mother's letter suggests a crush on our boarder, whose room abuts my parents' bedroom. When Dad falls asleep, will she tiptoe away and climb into bed with 'polite, auburn-haired' Burke, who loves golf and other sports?" We chortled. I want to drive his yellow Toyota Celica convertible.

"Carina, previous plans made me turn down attractive Gus and Ray. I encouraged future invites without mention of early birds catching distasteful worms." She looked merry.

Cousin Ron wrote about continued social success.

Falling asleep, I imagined Max's chiseled profile during today's easygoing Riverside Park lunch and stroll before library jail time. Was it Poe's *Raven* who swooped down close to us?

<u>Thursday, November 21, 1963: Harvard</u>
Carina filled her suitcase for a weekend with exciting Harvard actor Garth! "Angela, a worldly, charismatic senior with an apartment and exceptional Radcliffe girls nearby may expect full physical intimacy. I need to know he's in love with me."

"Meeting an extraordinary guy, but having different ideas about how far to go is tough. I'm glad that Max has Friday sex and respects my virginity-until-marriage goal without pressure to shed clothing, etc."

When Carina asked, "Did you once allude to an upsetting experience?" In a low voice, I shared this:

> Roomie, you're the first to hear this secret, so please stay mum. As a naïve sixteen-year-old, I took summer speedreading with other AHS students at the center owned by two middle-aged, pot-bellied, balding teachers. Mr. B said, "Angela, I recognize you and remember your special aunt." This married cad tried to date Sara at Hackett Junior High parents' night!

After reading classes, we teens bantered with and confided in both teachers. We liked their irreverent humor.

One night, I suddenly realized that Mr. R had left his nearby office and that I was alone with Mr. B, who was aware of my crush on Luke and intention of staying a virgin. Mr. B must have hypnotized me. Feeling zero attraction to him, why did I let his deep voice brainwash me into letting him try to make me *feel good*? Was I in a trance? His inappropriate genital advances, like a doctor's exam, left me cold. When he asked whether I felt good, my *No* was adamant.

Fortunately, he stopped. I was lucky to evade disease and pregnancy. I'm ashamed to be a ninny, lulled into allowing unwanted touching.

"I'm sorry that this predator abused you. I'm honored to be trusted. Your secret is safe." Carina's eyes looked kind.

"How many other girls has he molested? I was sympathetic about his suffering racial discrimination growing up in the South. He confided about escaping to Philadelphia after killing someone in self-defense. I felt a little afraid of him. Did an infuriated father or husband attack him? On to a happier subject: have a wonderful time with Garth!"

"Thanks for packing help! I'm too giddy to remember everything."

Friday, November 22, 1963: Devastated

Emerging from the library, I was shocked to overhear, "Once we learned that Kennedy was assassinated in Dallas, our prof let us go. We couldn't concentrate on *Wings of the Dove*."

The Honeybear's halting speech and gray-tinged complexion prevented disbelief. Rooted to one spot, I felt my jaw drop. Clusters of students looking distressed poured out of buildings. Riverside Church or St. Paul's Chapel bells pealed mournfully.

On Max's sofa, I said, "I hope Carina's okay. I wish I had her phone number."

"Angela, Brahms, an unreligious humanist, grieving the deaths of his mother and composer friend Robert Schuman, wrote this German Requiem a century ago." After the glorious music with soaring baritone and soprano soloists, Max quoted, "Blessed are they that mourn, for they shall be comforted."

Breaking down, I sobbed on his shoulder for what seemed like ages as JFK's assassination became increasingly real. Despite concentration challenges, I had to leave to study at Barnard after one slow dance with kisses.

Trying to fall asleep on the most tragic day of my life, I felt lost In an upended world without beloved JFK! What will happen to civil rights progress? Poor Jackie, Caroline, and Jon!

Saturday, November 23, 1963: Dancing
In Max's cozy kitchen, he and I downed soup, steak broiled in the small electric oven, yam pudding, stewed tomatoes, and plum pudding. His nice friends drove us to an unremarkable, dark East Bronx nightclub for romantic dancing to a jukebox. Mourning JFK, we tried to have fun. Sipped slowly over hours, one Ward Eight cocktail with grenadine and maraschino cherry, a Seven and Seven with Seven Up over Seagram's Seven Crown whisky, and one rum and cola affected me only moderately.

Sunday, November 24, 1963: Indifferent
Having hoped to dodge running into Kevin at Columbia, I was mystified about the November 20 Albany postmark on his unexpected letter. He's unchallenged at Albany State after his father's lay off. Despite scholarships, Columbia was too costly.

Angela, I'm writing this on impulse after finding your graduation picture and two letters I couldn't bring myself to destroy in the back of my desk drawer. Feeling nostalgic, I realized it's been too long since we communicated. From the time we first met, I was determined to always have your love. Having failed, I'd be grateful for your friendship. I'd like to hear from you. If not, I have it coming to me. I'd also like to see you over Christmas vacation.

As ever (whatever I am or was), Kevin

No, thank you. Who needs an untrustworthy friend who views love as something to get from me, rather than give to me?

Yeats called for mutual JFK consolation before the switchboard interrupted.

Monday, November 25, 1963: National Day of Mourning
Columbia's middle-aged chaplain, Episcopal Reverend Dr. John Krumm, led the St. Paul's Chapel memorial service. An overflowing crowd heard Columbia president Kirk's eulogy. With hope lost for a fairer country with justice for underprivileged people, grief-stricken Max and I were atypically silent. I'm outraged that one evil killer destroyed JFK.

In our room, Carina's voice was slow and sad. "On the train, we heard. Harvard's game was canceled. I was mainly with my friend's distraught family. I hardly saw Garth."

"How disappointing!"

"Still a virgin, I hope one bird in the bush is better than no bird. Garth has yet to be a bird in hand." I giggled.

Tuesday, November 26, 1963: Healing Music
Max and his tall housemate introduced me to Lincoln Center's beautiful Philharmonic Hall. Witold Malcuzynski's Chopin, Beethoven, Bach, and Brahms piano recital uplifted me slightly. In Max's living room, records of the same pieces by other pianists played. "Max, Malcuzynski sounded more passionate!"

I thanked Max for a used album: Beethoven's *Piano Concerto No. 5* by the Vienna Orchestra with Clifford Curzon.

"You're welcome. Tomorrow, let's lunch at the Caravan and ramble in Riverside Park before parting for Thanksgiving."

"Thanks for getting me through such challenging days!"

Thursday, November 28, 1963: Thanksgiving
In Albany since yesterday's bus trip, I enjoyed a soothing drive to Thacher Park lookout. Returning, I sang patriotic songs, like *God Bless America* and *America the Beautiful.*

Seeing Gloversville family at our house for a huge turkey dinner warmed my heart. "Angela, where were you when you heard?" asked Lydia, looking troubled.

"Exiting the Barnard library, I couldn't believe it."

With a somber mien, Ella said, "I'll always remember how devastated I felt."

Eyebrows quizzically raised, Mother said, "You girls idolized Kennedy." Who can expect old people to understand?

Lydia explained, "We grew up hearing about equality and seeing Negroes treated terribly and rich people receiving unfair advantages! We were cynical about politicians' promises until our hero restored hope."

After our relatives left, Yeats and I bowled. He did better than my mediocre ninety-nine. I hope that Carina, taking bowling for her gym requirement, scores higher.

At Mike's Log Cabin, Yeats and I greeted AHS classmates, including cute former heartthrob Artie. In our living room, Yeats kissed and consoled me until the wee hours.

Friday, November 29, 1963: Catching Up
After returning Craig's call, I strolled to Doreen's house to talk for a couple of hours. After nine years of friendship, she is as sweet, understanding, and wise as ever! After we commiserated about JFK, she said, "I should have started college at Albany State. Classes are better! My remaining uncertainty is about missing some of college life living at home.

At least, my closet has room for all my clothes." We exchanged warm smiles. I'm grateful for Doreen and Carina!

Jake's call, including a Pope John XXIII joke, made me laugh. The humble, beloved late Pope mentioned awakening at night, concerned about serious world problems. The Pope tells himself to talk to the Pope about them. Rising the next day, he remembers: "I am the Pope." I'm glad that Jake is excelling, even in tough RPI engineering classes!

At classy Century House, Yeats and I enjoyed green crème de menthe drinks and shrimp salad before getting a kick out of *Under the Yum Yum Tree*, a lighthearted comedy at the Palace. "Yeats, I needed this movie's laughs. Jack Lemmon was good as the playboy. Carol Lynley is my favorite magazine model."

"Imogene Coco and Paul Lynde added to the fun." Switching to current events Yeats said, "It's tough to muster fervor for political hack Johnson after brilliant statesman JFK." We still feel shaken up.

Saturday, November 30, 1963: Aunts

To study all day tomorrow for tests, I bused to NYC today. At French restaurant Larre's, I said, "Aunt Rhoda, thank you for this lovely Hanukkah present! *Je Reviens* perfume is much better than my usual Chantilly cologne! You're so kind!"

"You're welcome, dear. Scent is fun! What's popular among Columbia men?"

"I prefer sniffing Canoe to Old Spice after-shave lotion."

"Do you see Gary from our synagogue?"

"We once dined here! Last spring, he stopped calling. One guy I now date, wonderful Max, is an acquaintance of Gary." I wish I had time to see my romantic, widowed, lonely aunt more.

Seemingly ageless Aunt Sara is always in my heart and mind. Mourning JFK with exams looming, I must guard against upsets, which may lower grades.

<u>Tuesday, December 3, 1963: Max</u>
"Carina, Sunday evening, Max and I drank his father's tasty wine to celebrate Columbia's 35-28 Thanksgiving win at Rutgers! While listening to Beethoven's fifth and seventh symphonies, conducted by Fritz Reiner, I appreciated his senior class photo (below) signed *Love, Max*.

"At the Gold Rail tonight, Max sounded downhearted about the limited job market and low pay for English professors. Though his financially comfortable half-brother is happy as an attorney, Max prefers a Columbia Ph.D. To dodge the worst fate, the Army draft, he must be a full-time student.

"He looked happier when I touched his shoulder and said, 'Max, you are smart enough to succeed at whatever you do!'"

"He's fortunate to have a good listener."

"Carina, I'm lucky that *you* are a great listener!"

Wednesday, December 4, 1963: Guys

My flourishing social life elates me! I adore variety! At the recent Barnard coffee hour, I enjoyed listening to a witty piano player.

I regretted turning down enticing Gus because of prior plans. I wanted to say: *Be my second escort for the Dean's Drag!* Lions drag a date, unlike attending mixers solo. Flirting with Max on one side and Gus on the other would be heavenly. In my fantasy, dancing includes their cutting in and outdoing each other with fancy steps, breathtaking turns, and stirring dips.

Affable Spanky called from Brooklyn. "Angela, I'm trying to scrape up money for Columbia's School of General Studies part-time." Cut off by the switchboard, I pictured his appealing unkinky curly hair, which sticks out all over.

I was glad to accept a date with Ray and receive Bill's message before answering absorbing letters from Yeats in JFK's home area and Dominic, mourning JFK in the Mediterranean.

At a fun Caravan lunch, Max invited me to a Shanghai Restaurant dinner after tomorrow's psych exam.

Friday, December 6, 1963: Exquisite

I apologized to Ray for postponing our date to accompany Carina to Café Chevram for elegant French food with her charming, glamorous blue-eyed father and mother, the antithesis of my overweight, disagreeable parents. At thirty-nine, Carina's gorgeous, creative mother resembles an older sister. Easy to talk to, she puts me at ease, as Sara always did. Before bed, I finished a note, thanking them for treating me!

Mother wrote:

We enjoyed having you home. Hanukkah shopping included Frank Sinatra and Harry Belafonte records for Lydia and Ella, gray Whiting stationery with his name for Ron, toys for Beth's and Justine's kids, and a travel alarm clock for an upcoming Bat Mitzvah. Winter's here: four inches of snow and severe cold. Call your aunts!

Saturday, December 7, 1963: Party
Spiffily attired in a navy blazer, Max shared his recording of pianist Rudolph Serkin, playing Beethoven's *Appassionata* sonata, before his short housemate's lively birthday celebration. While dancing with me and joshing with twenty guests, jovial Max drank Scotch while I, unintentionally color-matched in my navy wool sheath, sipped sherry.

Eager to grow up, I am confused about feeling perturbed about turning nineteen in one month.

Tuesday, December 10, 1963: Rewards and Oration
Always aware of possible diary snoopers, I deliberately omit Carina's most personal sharing to protect her privacy. Today, she thanked me for listening before asking, "What's new?"

"Yesterday's history exam was challenging. I was grateful for *A Minus* on my Latin paper and celebratory drinks with Max at the Gold Rail. Tonight, we pinged and ponged. Yeats sent these moving excerpts from JFK's October Amherst College address." I handed the page to Carina.

Our national strength matters, but the spirit which informs and controls our strength matters just as much.... Robert Frost coupled poetry and power, for he saw poetry as the means of saving power from itself. When power leads men towards arrogance, poetry reminds him of his limitations. When power narrows the areas of man's concern, poetry reminds him of the richness and diversity of his existence. When power corrupts, poetry cleanses…. The artist… becomes the last champion of the individual mind and sensibility against an intrusive society and an officious state. In pursuing his perceptions of reality, he must often sail against the currents of his time…. If sometimes our great artists have been the most critical of our society, it is because their sensitivity and their concern for justice, which must motivate any true artist, make them aware that our Nation falls short of its highest potential. I see little of more importance to the future of our country and our civilization than full recognition of the place of the artist…. If art is to nourish the roots of our culture, society must set the artist free to follow his vision wherever it takes him…. I look forward to a great future for America, a future in which our country will match its military strength with our moral restraint, its wealth with our wisdom, its power with our purpose. I look forward to an America which will not be afraid of grace and beauty, which will protect the beauty of our natural environment…. I look forward to an America which will reward achievement in the arts as we reward achievement in business or statecraft. I look forward to an America which will steadily raise the standards of artistic accomplishment and which will steadily enlarge cultural opportunities for all of our citizens. And I look forward to an America which commands respect throughout the world not only for its strength but for its civilization as well. And I look forward to a world

> which will be safe not only for democracy and
> diversity but also for personal distinction.

Tears stung my eyes as I wrote thanks to Yeats. Will we ever again have such a brilliant, eloquent, caring President?

<u>Wednesday, December 11, 1963: Musicians</u>
Disarming Max and I energetically applauded an exhilarating Rudolf Serkin Carnegie Hall piano performance! At Tom's Corner, Max looked pleased, swallowing the last bite of shared rice pudding. "Angela, have you heard the Carnegie Hall story?" I shook my head no. "A tourist near there on 57 Street stopped a musician with a violin case and asked, 'How do I get to Carnegie Hall?' The violinist stopped, looked him in the eye, and replied, 'Practice!'"

I laughed. "Max, is Gina Bachauer the only female pianist performing with orchestras? Where are the talented women playing other instruments?"

"Musicians must compete aggressively for few positions. Married musicians with families may shun travel."

"Did the challenge of being hired cause my brave aunt to travel around the country alone, performing her one-woman vocal/piano/accordion show? All conductors are males; do they favor and hire other men?"

"Probably." He eluded eye contact, suggesting discomfort with the subject, and switched to Serkin's performance. Would gallant Max consider his wife an equal and support her career or does chivalry contribute to discrimination against women? Does his father boss his housewife mother? If Dad earned enough without Mother's salary, would he approve of her working and still treat her as an equal? Yeats seems more positive about women's careers. Marriage with an insecure husband who is consciously or unconsciously threatened by a working wife would be a nightmare, especially with children. Being a mother is irrevocable and seems thankless. What a scary step!

<u>Thursday, December 12, 1963: *A*</u>
To celebrate my infrequent *A* (psych exam), dear Max made us juicy cheeseburgers on rye and played Mahler's *Symphony No. 1*, Bruno Walter conducting. "Max, are Beethoven and Mahler more emotional than earlier composers, who sound more self-controlled to me?"

"Good question. Suffering, deafness, and family issues may have inspired Beethoven's deeply passionate music. If Mozart had lived a score more years to Beethoven's fifty-six, his music might have transformed during three decades of political turmoil and revolution until 1827."

"You know so much!" Max's bearing reminded me of a proud peacock, showing off his spectacular tail. Does my preference for Beethoven and Romantic composers stem from taking after emotional Dad more than stoical Mother?

<u>Saturday, December 14, 1963: Semi-Formal Dance</u>
Max was the perfect escort to the Dean's Drag (below)! His corsage of six lovely white roses contrasted with my 1961 black crepe cocktail dress! Fueled by wine-spiked punch, we danced by other revelers, like attractive Bill, austerely handsome Gus, and sociable Gary, who all grinned and waved. I'm content, grateful for Max's attentive, protective, endearing company.

<u>Sunday, December 15, 1963: Hanukkah</u>
Clearing weather let the parents and Levines drive to NYC to join extraverted Aunt Lila, quieter Uncle Bert, sweet Cousin Justine with husband and father, and me in Aunt Rhoda's traditional living room. Justine's adorable, blue-eyed kids opened toys as I happily unwrapped a beautiful aqua robe, pink blouse, black purse, and five dollars.

<u>Monday, December 16, 1963: Vacation Coming</u>
To reward my history test *B*, Max treated me to a delicious Takome dill pickle at Broadway and 115 Street.

Yeats called and sent two pictures, a *Commentary* magazine, and a letter. I accepted his respectful advance invite for New Year's Eve in Albany!

Thursday, December 19, 1963: Holiday Cheer

Will Max's housemates stay mum about my Gold Rail date with Ray? At a light-hearted lunch in their kitchen, I thanked Max for a small, but obese wooden male fertility god.

During the dorm holiday turkey dinner, Carina joked, "If I eat more stuffing, I'll soon resemble your fertility statue."

The dorm Christmas party was jolly until someone mentioned an upsetting incident: a Puerto Rican gang, raping a young woman walking alone at the edge of Morningside Park. Distressed, I felt thankful about escaping Tommy's attack in high school. Doreen's letter and plan to meet soon in Albany calmed me.

Friday, December 20, 1963: Frozen

Max served steak, yam pudding, and plum pudding to me and his plump, sallow pal, Rina. Her voice was energetic. "Did you know that salutatorian Max was the high school BMOC (Big Man on Campus)? He headed the acting club, starred in the senior play, and was on the yearbook editorial board. A chess club leader, he played on and managed the baseball and basketball teams."

Max added, "I still own the county record for consecutive baseball games left with a concussion, three!"

Giggling, I joshed, "Did girls chase you?" Max looked a bit embarrassed. To shift subjects, he lifted a glass of homemade wine. "Here's to Angela's mythology paper completion."

Shivering in a movie theater line for Charlie Chaplin's *City Lights*, Max and I left for the warm subway to stay well.

Carina, covered by rumpled, tan bedding, was sketching Garth. She asked about my date. "Carina, I met Rina, Max's platonic friend. My intuition says that she has a crush on him. Frightened by her long, pointy, blood-red fingernails, I must stay on her good side to sidestep fatal stabbing."

<u>Saturday, December 21, 1963: Prince</u>
At the Port Authority, I thanked Max for carrying our suitcases. Large Trailways bus windows revealed distant Catskill peaks behind pristine snow blankets dotted with tall evergreens.

In Albany, Yeats and I appreciated *Viridiana*, a special Spanish movie at the Delaware, and visited his genial parents. He gave me Saint-Exupéry's beautifully illustrated 1943 book, *The Little Prince*. I'm touched by its imaginative, philosophical pages!

Cheered by Christmas cards from Ric and Craig, I reciprocated. I'm ignoring Kevin's letter and holiday card.

<u>Sunday, December 22, 1963: Loquacious Boarder</u>
Six feet tall with neat auburn hair and glasses, Burke returned from his usual Queens weekend with family and friends. Not bad looking, he's articulate and sophisticated with a sardonic sense of humor, like Hy. In his room, Burke reads history and serious periodicals, like *The New Republic*. His brothers are "a soph at Queens College and a creative redhead, age fifteen." I could hardly get in a word as Burke talked fast until 3 AM.

I missed Max, despite Yeats' companionable visit.

Starting my paper, *Social Stratification at Albany High School*, I sat at my beloved Heywood-Wakefield, satiny, blond maple desk. I mentioned Hollingshead's 1949 book *Elmtown's Youth* about the impact of family social class on adolescents' social behavior. As a budding sociologist, I noted my goal of maximizing objectivity, despite subjectivity as an AHS grad.

<u>Monday, December 23, 1963: Painting</u>
"Mother, thanks for this large canvas board." Finishing a colorful oil painting (below) of two males above a full-skirted female figure in the lower right lightened my mood. The white male figure seems trustworthy, like Yeats and Max. The devilish, red-caped man suggests cheating Kevin. I like the intense hues, e.g., reddish swirling fog, and symbolic simplicity of the figures.

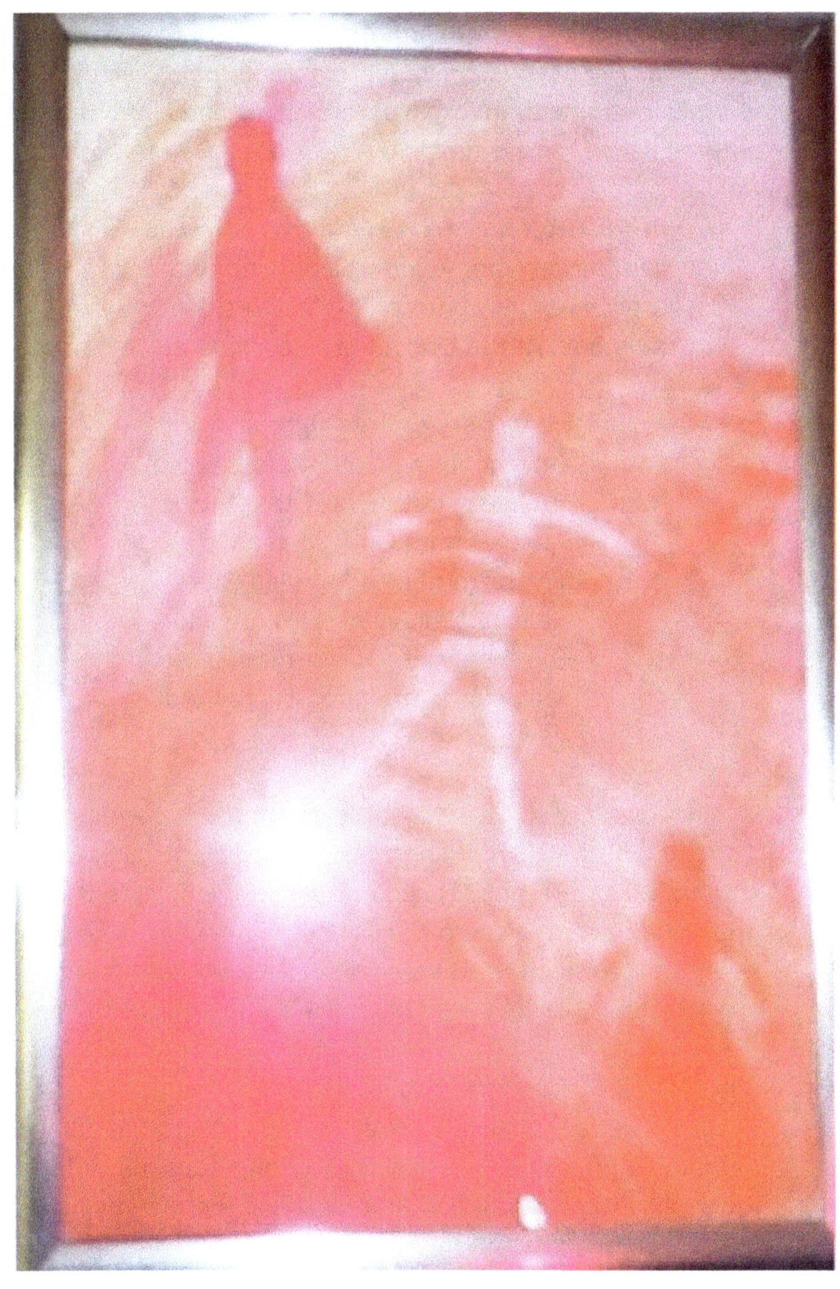

<u>Tuesday, December 24, 1963: Joe's</u>
Christmas Eve at the iconic, overcrowded Joe's Deli: dressed
warmly in red turtle-neck sweaters, Yeats and I imbibed sherry
and ate delish roast beef sandwiches. He gave me this clip:

> President Johnson presided over a candle-
> lighting ceremony marking the end of the
> official period of mourning for President
> Kennedy. At the Lincoln Memorial, Johnson said:

>> Let us here on this night
>> determine that John Kennedy did
>> not live or die in vain, that this
>> nation, under God, shall have a
>> new birth of freedom and that
>> we may achieve in our time and
>> for all time the ancient vision of
>> peace on earth, goodwill towards
>> all men.

Wiping away tears, I answered Yeats about my paper. "I
described both AHS buildings, three curriculums, and three
student levels. Recent AHS yearbooks showed student
population averaging two-thirds white Christians, one-quarter
Jews, and ten percent Negroes. Elmtown had five social
classes. Does Albany have only three?" Unsure, he shrugged.

<u>Thursday, December 26, 1963: Letters</u>
Dominic's letter about his travels and Ray's pretty holiday card
perked me up. With my left hand stroking the smooth top of
my desk in the bay window and with feet warmed by high
boots, I enjoyed the middle, stained-glass pane before writing:

Dear Carina, thanks for writing! Sociology excites me enough to share about my paper! In the 1960 Census, twenty-eight percent of Albany's 130,000 population was or had a parent who was foreign born; almost a quarter of this group was Italian. Does your smaller town have fewer immigrants?

I'm shocked that only a quarter of Albany's population over age twenty-five finished high school; eighteen percent have some college.

On a traced map, I marked social class neighborhoods. Is your town's median annual family income higher than Albany's unexpectedly low $5800? Even in this capital, government employs only one quarter of workers.

I described AHS's democratic homerooms, grading system, and student socioeconomic characteristics in each curriculum: college, general, and commercial. College-entrance seniors dominated leadership positions in thirty-six extracurricular activities.

At your school, are top students often from upper- and middle-class families and neighborhoods? Did top grades earn higher status than athletic prowess?

Did you have high-status, popular Negro academic achievers from lower-class neighborhoods? Glad that talented Negros usually attain high AHS status, I shunned bigoted classmates who denigrated other Negroes as lacking intelligence. Will things ever improve?

Do most high-achieving Catholics attend parochial schools, as in Albany?

Required NY State Regents' exams thwart Albany teacher bias in final course grades. Did college-educated teachers with different values than uneducated parents treat lower-class students less favorably? Were teachers less objective because clothing, speech, and hairstyles differed among socioeconomic classes, e.g., Ivy League attire having higher status?

Did influential parents exert pressure on teachers to favor offspring? Albany's greater anonymity may minimize parental influence.

Some AHS students griped about a disproportionate number of Jews in prestigious positions. Does Chicago's proximity give Jews in your town power?

Blustery, freezing weather makes daily work on a twenty-one-page paper bearable. I've enjoyed dates with Yeats and Max's calls and letters. Boarder Burke agreed to adoption as the brother I've wanted! Love and Cheyah!

Friday, December 27, 1963: Communicating

A long phone call with less-cynical-than-at-AHS Hank included his plans after Brandeis. "Hank, your debating expertise and high intelligence will make you a formidable attorney."

I was relieved when Kevin canceled our University Twist Palace date. I accepted only because typing my paper bored me. I answered Cousin Ron, happy on vacation in NYC.

Sunday, December 29, 1963: Job

Montgomery Ward laid-off salesman Dad! Apprehensive about sufficient money to finish Barnard, I appreciated sympathetic Yeats' treating me to Luigi's pizza and a later call from Craig. "Craig, have you danced at The Uptown?"

"Naughty temptress!" Feeling flattered, this goody-goody giggled. "I'm off to Hamilton to write papers."

"Empathy galore, Craig."

Burke's recording of Mozart's lively *Cosi Fan Tutte*, conducted by Herbert von Karajan, soothed anxiety about Dad's unemployment. "Burke, yesterday's humorous, suspenseful spy caper *Charade*, with Cary Grant and Audrey Hepburn, warmed this frigid vacation for Yeats and me!"

"Thanks for the review, Angela. I'll try to see it."

Monday, December 30, 1963: Worried
Mother's voice sounded concerned. "Herm, will a NY State desk job help your varicose veins?"

Dad's brow furrowed. "I could fail the test. I feel bad without money to celebrate our anniversary and your and Angela's birthdays." Sorry for Dad who enjoys meeting people, I realize his hearing loss makes a clerical job more suitable.

Badinage with political aficionados Burke and Yeats was a welcome distraction. The guys were all smiles about the Warren Commission investigating JFK's assassination.

Tuesday, December 31, 1963: New Year's Eve
Below-zero cold required bundling up. Under a bulky overcoat, Yeats wore a heavy, dark gray wool suit. My beige wool skirt, fur-blend pullover sweater, and matching cardigan were under a heavy cardigan and white dress coat with fur collar. Floridians miss the joys of clomping in knee-high, pile-lined boots while carrying bagged dance heels. Unsure where I want to live after college, I know that winters must be warmer than Albany's.

The enjoyable James Garner-Doris Day romantic comedy *Move Over, Darling* preceded dancing on DeWitt Clinton Hotel's marble floors, surrounded by dark wood paneling. The eleven-story, Classical Revival hotel is at the corner of Eagle and State. Kissing Yeats at midnight, I was tipsy from grenadine cocktails. A jazz trio played romantic standards, e.g., *That's All* and *Embraceable You*, until the wee hours.

After the temple's pre-paid Mr. and Mrs. Club New Year's Eve dance, my parents must have retired to their bedroom. In our living room, Yeats played his *Trini Lopez at PJs* album at low volume. Favoring renditions of *A-me-ri-ca* from *West Side Story* and folk songs *If I Had a Hammer* and *This Land Is Your Land*, we canoodled and talked until 5:30 AM. Gazing into his unique hazel eyes with long lashes is always a pleasure. I tried to stay in the fun present without apprehension about what 1964 may bring.

1964 NYC Sophomore

Life can only be understood backwards; but it must be lived forwards.

Soren Kierkegaard

Thursday, January 2, 1964: Friends

Winnie, the Pooh, was right: *a day without a friend is like a pot without honey*. Yesterday, warm phone talks with Max, Yeats, Jake, and Burke (en route in Kingston) helped me forget a scary dream about lack of money forcing me to leave Barnard. Indoors, I avoided snowfall, only nine hours of daylight, and ten-below-zero overnight cold. Shiver!

Today, dear Max visited for lunch. "Angela, your lettuce-and-tomato salad and bologna sandwich with mayonnaise on Jewish rye bread hit the spot."

"I've always favored this South Pearl Street Jewish bakery bread."

Returning from work, talkative Burke joined our repartee before I drove Max to the bus terminal. Is jealousy of Max why Yeats took Burke for drinks without me? I felt left out.

On the day before the parent's twenty-seventh anniversary, Dad showed his small, off-white teeth in a smile. "Thanks for the *Trini Lopez at PJs* record album. We can compare his *The Saints Go Marching In* to Louis Armstrong's."

Later, Burke described Northern Rhodesia, Southern Rhodesia, and Nyasaland becoming independent countries. Burke looked gratified when I said, "You'd be a good professor. To save my life, I couldn't name all African countries."

Friday, January 3, 1964: Two Males

I controlled a gasp when taut-bodied Kevin rang the doorbell. Barging into the living room before I could devise an excuse to end the visit, he glibly talked about his holidays before proposing a University Twist Palace birthday date with hm and Ric.

"Thank you, but I have plans until I leave. I must change now to go out."

"Where are you off to?"

"The Rensselaer Polytechnic Institute (RPI) hockey tournament."

"With an RPI engineer?"

"Why do you ask?"

"Just curious...maybe jealous." His laugh sounded uncomfortable.

"Please excuse me now." Though his two-timing has left me cold, I'd rather not be rude.

My dates with unreligious, but Jewish, Yeats and Max have spoiled Mother, whose facial expression soured, seeing personable Catholic Jake (below) whisk me off.

"Angela, RPI classes are so interesting that I can't choose a major. This week, it's mechanical engineering." I grinned. "I miss our late Pope's humility. Visiting a hospital, John XXIII asked a boy what he wanted to be when he grew up. The boy said, 'A policeman or a pope.' The Holy Father said, 'I'd choose the police if I were you. Anyone can become a pope. Look at me!" I giggled. Our energetic cheers probably helped RPI beat Loyola of Chicago, 5-3. Yale trounced Cornell, 5-1. Jake's easy company left me in a cheery frame of mind!

<u>Saturday, January 4, 1964: Early Birthday Dinner</u>
My pizza party at our house with Yeats and Burke (below with me) was enjoyable. I adore my gift of six pink carnations from Yeats, whose dark-olive-green suit made his eyes look greener.

Burke's tone was teasing. "Mrs. Weiss or, should I say, Dr. Pangloss, this London Broil is tasty."

"Thanks, Burke. Who's Dr. Pangloss?"

"His motto in Voltaire's *Candide* is *This is the best of all possible worlds*."

Yeats asked, "Are you an optimist, Mrs. Weiss?"

"For some reason, Burke dislikes Albany. I mention interesting activities, so he'll be happier." Mother's face and voice seemed resolute about making Burke like Albany.

"Like drinking during dreary winters?" Burke joked. Yeats and I snickered.

Mother frowned. "Why not write or create art? I love painting and ceramics!"

"I lack Dr. Pangloss' talent," Burke quipped.

I remarked, "Transplanted New Yorker Hank also views Albany as a backwater. Moving from Albany to NYC seems easier. Summer plays, operas, and concerts are fun here!"

"Sure!" Burke's facetious tone made me giggle. "Golfing and driving with the top down will help."

Yeats took me to Mike's Log Cabin and the Uptown for slow dancing crowned by a warm good night kiss!

Sunday, January 5, 1964: Barnard

My heart lifted seeing cute Max, with neck encircled by a new green-and-white Tartan muffler, meeting my Trailways bus! Our Caravan Restaurant baked chicken supper was tasty!

Warm family times made Carina sound bubbly. "Trying to perform a science experiment to learn about fire, my boldest brother used Hanukkah candles. With the best intentions, he almost burned down the house when nearby curtains caught fire. My poor parents!" We laughed.

"Carina, are you often assistant mother?"

"Yes! Even studying beats disciplining and controlling him. Thanks for your interesting letter about sociology! Immigrant families are rarer in Michigan City. Jews fit in less at my Midwestern high school, more like Elmtown. Athletes had top status. Negroes and Catholics had low status. Most smart students were middle-class or higher."

"Thanks for sharing." I appreciate AHS even more.

Monday, January 6, 1964: Party
Carina's midnight birthday celebration was unexpected! Candles in a Hanukkah menorah illuminated Yeats' carnations and dorm friends' large orange daisy with card. Dave Brubeck jazz and Barbra Streisand songs on Carina's portable record player accompanied Carina's readings from *The Pooh Perplex*. "Carina, thank you for the cards and three red, long-stemmed roses! These darling soft, stuffed bunnies are in my favorite pink and purple! I appreciate the delicious almond-filled olives, parfait birthday cake, and Pink Nectarosé Vin Rosé d'Anjou wine. This symbol of our gourmet cafeteria is especially meaningful: a stale roll!" We guffawed.

Tuesday, January 7, 1964: Grateful
Wearing a carnation in my hair on a lovely sunny birthday, I wore Yeats' silver birthday earrings and appreciated Spanky's *Happy Birthday* message.

"Max, we could be in Paris, thanks to these French travel posters, including the Eiffel Tower!" Champlain Restaurant on West 49 Street served delish roast beef, salad, baguette, cheesecake and rosé wine!

On Max's soft couch, we sipped homemade wine. "Max, thank you for this tasteful Art Deco pin and Trollope's novel *The Warden*!" His kisses seemed particularly amorous.

Cards from Doreen, the Levines, Cousin Justine, the parents, and Burke decorate my desk. Writing thank-you notes to everyone, including Cousin Ron and Aunt Rhoda who sent helpful cash, I felt grateful for a perfect birthday and beautiful life with many wonderful people!

Wednesday, January 8, 1964: Grenadine
Max's grin cheered me in the library. He was dressed in typical Columbia Ivy League garb: tan chinos, beige button-down shirt, brown tweed jacket, and tan trench coat with zipped-in pile lining.

At the Gold Rail, he bought me a Ward Eight. "Max, my sloe gin fizz and Singapore sling favorites also have grenadine."

"From pomegranates, it lacks alcohol. You're enjoying a red, sweeter whisky sour. The name Ward Eight is from Boston politics."

"Is there anything you don't know?"

"Plenty!" His smile suggested a Cheshire cat.

Sunday, January 12, 1964: Ward Eight
Yeats called. "Yeats, what's Boston's eighth ward like?"

"Interesting question! Urban renewal's high-rises have replaced a bustling, working-class area of old, brick apartments over shops at street level." The switchboard cut us off.

I waited for a pay phone to give Mother perfunctory birthday greetings.

At Tom's Corner, Max and I split a cheese Danish and a Ward Eight. "Angela, the upcoming Woodrow Wilson National Fellowship Foundation interview makes me jittery. The Wilson is America's Rhodes Scholarship."

"Max, being a finalist recommended by a distinguished prof is an honor!" He relaxed, releasing held breath.

He kissed me goodnight with gusto!

Monday, January 13, 1964: Engagement
Carina looked morose. "No more drawing and music with finals in a week! What's new?"

"In the library, Max mentioned his friends' engagement! Marriage seems like jail. Do you feel ready?"

"If Garth communicated and loved me…"

"He'd be lucky to have you!"

"I appreciate your loyalty. He's probably drowning in eager females." Her slowed voice sounded melancholy.

Wednesday, January 15, 1964: Twelve Plus Inches
Dad, still out of work, called about the fifth biggest January snowstorm in Albany's history, over fifteen inches. "The 1936

January record is almost eighteen inches. You lived through over seventeen inches in 1958 and 1953 and over fifteen inches as a newborn."

"Dad, a foot of Manhattan snow makes cramming in the warm library easier."

Wearing my knee-high, lined boots and sharing a Caravan cheeseburger, I sympathized with Max, impatient for Wilson results and distracted from finals prep. Signs of his ordeal, such as more facial pallor, are noticeable between wisecracks to lighten the atmosphere.

Thursday, January 16, 1964: Nuovo Anno

Dominic's beautiful card, with a painting of fox hunters and the Italian *Migliori Augur per Natale ed il Nuovo Anno*, included birthday wishes. Carina translated, "*Best Wishes for Christmas and the New Year.*"

"Thanks, Carina! He wrote: *Dearest Angela, buying this card in Rome, I hoped to write the most important, appropriate, perfect note, but lack illusions about my ability, so here follows the usual ordinary.*" Carina looked amused.

I enjoyed poetic Dominic's courtly words, including amusing equine images:

I cherish our summer date. Your thin sweater
vainly tried to protect you from chilly evening air
where your strapless summer dress failed,
mainly on the shoulders. I had the air of the
proudest, legendary stallion prancing around a
splendid band of broodmares, but I had the one
the stallion would choose if he forgot his
instincts and picked from the incomparable
band. I was overwhelmed that night. Being with
you was sheer ecstasy. I could hardly believe
that we were going out freely. I was so delighted
and thankful for just being with you that I feared
to show it in the *normal* way lest you think I was

after the usual thing, lest you think I needed
that more than you. I guess we both needed
that along with what we had.

Concerned that kissing would seem lustful, he held back. Since my last letter clarified that long-distance can't be serious, I understood his signing *With Deepest Affection Always,* rather than *Love.* Though I'll always love D, I need a guy like Max who takes the initiative to ensure we're together as much as possible. Dom, like Garth, seldom communicates.

Saturday, January 18, 1964: Basketball
Bundled-up Max and I rushed through frigid air to University Hall for the game. People arriving after we got two of the last seats had to stand. Coincidentally, Gary, our introducer, sat nearby and shared information. "Coach Rohan, who graduated from Columbia in history about ten years ago, played on the 1951 undefeated team, which won twenty-two games and the Ivy League championship. He coached freshmen here and at NYU before becoming head coach last year."

"Are our Lions good?" I asked.

"Fortunately, talented football quarterback Archie Roberts plays basketball and baseball! Ken McCullough, Ken Benoit, and Stanley Felsinger are strong guards. Forward Neil Farber shoots accurately. Power forward Mike Griffin is tall at six foot four. Luckily, Princeton's team lacks height. We must contain high-scoring forward Bill Bradley, who's six foot five."

A miracle occurred. Though Bradley got thirty-six points, McCullough sank six free throws in the last minute of the game! We won 69-66! At the Gold Rail, Max clicked his black Russian against my sloe gin fizz before his lion roar!

Sunday, January 19, 1964: Long Distance
Without time for newspapers, I appreciated Yeats' call. "Angela, for the Presidential race, conservative Senator Barry Goldwater is worse than our moderate Republican governor,

Nelson Rockefeller, who's worse than President Johnson. Though JFK is a hard act to follow, Johnson's a Democrat…. Did you hear that the U.S. Surgeon General reported that smoking may lead to lung cancer?"

"No. Skipping smoking was an uncommon instance of obeying my mother." We chortled.

Tuesday, January 21, 1964: Pithy
Imaginary australopithecine Pithy led our procession around the room, as we shouted *Cheyah*! Laughing while eating V and T pizza (Carina's treat), we unwound from a terror-ridden, wearying exam day (history for me). Uneasy dreams about Dad's unemployment didn't help.

Friday, January 24, 1964: Silly
Buried in the library, I surfaced for Wednesday lunch and an evening Campus Corner snack with Max.

Tonight, after my psych final, Max, housemates, and I got silly, laughing for no reason, while making dinner. Beating me at a comical chess game, Max kidded, "How about strip chess?" He started to pull off his navy, turtle-neck sweater.

I giggled. "I barely recall how the pieces move!"

He pretended to be upset. "Let's dance so I can get past your crushing rejection." Being dipped backwards thrilled me!

Tuesday, January 28, 1964: Exams
The only fun in days was Saturday dinner with Carina and her male pals at Takome, followed by milk shakes at Tom's Corner.

Letters from Dominic and Yeats helped this zombie revive after yesterday's Latin test and today's mythology final. A *B Plus* in history and *A* in psychology left me euphoric.

Wednesday, January 29, 1964: Departure
After the sociology final, I packed for Boston. Chatting with a cute, well-dressed, high-spirited guy on the bus was flattering!

Yeats brought me to his place on busy Commonwealth Avenue, a main street with small shops below aging apartments. By candlelight at midnight, I said, "Yeats, this onion soup, London broil, peas and onions, and salad with rosé wine are curing my exam trauma!" His lingering kiss felt whole-hearted at the Southern House hotel room he booked for me.

<u>Thursday, January 30, 1964: Boston</u>
Yeats showed me around his Boston University before we browsed at fashionable Newbury Street clothing shops in traditional townhouses with curved, triple bay windows.

At his place, we heard folk music records. Yeats' tall, genial housemate asked me, "What's new with the Harlem rent strike?"

I almost blurted: *what strike*?

Kind, well-informed Yeats rescued me. "Angela's been immersed in finals."

I recovered. "I've yet to notice anything different on occasional strolls to friends' apartments near Harlem."

In a taxi to Harvard Square, Yeats said, "Angela, you look elegant!" He touched the leopard collar of my white wool coat, worn over my 1962 yellow-and-white, fur-blend pullover and white wool straight skirt.

In a dark Wursthaus booth, my tasty shish-kebob and his popular sauerbraten, slices of spicy beef, arrived on antique pewter plates. "Angela, JFK ate here."

"I miss him!"

At the old-fashioned, brick Brattle Street Theater, endearing with a curved peaked roof, we saw a Greek art movie, *Antigone,* a family tragedy based on Sophocles' play. "Yeats, wasn't Irene Papas marvelous as Antigone?"

"The 1961 Berlin Film Festival gave her the best actress award. The Greeks were bold to write about Oedipus' four children with his mother."

"In mythology class, only Antigone was mentioned."

At the Brattle's Blue Parrot bar, I commented, "The name reminds me of my parakeet."

"In *Casablanca*, Blue Parrot was the rival bar to Rick's."

"I'd like to see that movie!"

Affectionate smooching on Yeats' couch preceded kissing goodnight at the hotel.

Friday, January 31, 1964: Thankful

Too polite to crack a joke about pregnancy, Yeats squelched a titter about my pickles-and-ice-cream lunch at his place. I was silent about mint-chocolate-chip ice cream forays at Barnard's cafeteria. "Yeats, I appreciate the comfortable hotel room and interesting activities, ideal for exam recovery!" He beamed when I complimented his stimulating city.

Conversing with a garrulous, strawberry blond Boston College alumnus, now a Rutgers political science grad student, made the bus trip to NYC fly by.

Exiting the bus, I happily accepted a fragrant pink rose from Max. Later, nestled against his soft, gray pullover, I closed my eyes during heavenly close dancing.

I told Carina, "I wish you and I could double date in Boston at Wursthaus and Brattle Street Theater!"

She agreed. Uttering *Cheyah,* toothy mascot Pithy joined us, lumbering around our cramped quarters.

Saturday, February 1, 1964: Disappointed

At fun bookstores around 14 Street near Union Square Park, Max bought seven used classic Victorian novels. For only two dollars, I bought Camus' *The Stranger,* Turgenev's *Fathers and Sons*, a Beethoven biography, history books, and, for Carina, *Our Hearts Were Young and Gay*, a comedy about the 1920s European graduation trip of two Seven Sisters college grads.

In Max's brightly lit kitchen, he beamed and bowed when I said, "This steak dinner with sweet potatoes and apple juice is delicious!" Deflated about his Woodrow Wilson rejection letter, he was bravely cheerful with his engaged friends in unfamiliar Bronx. In a dark club, we danced to a live quartet. During the Johnny Mathis favorite *That's All*, Max murmured, "You're irresistible in that black dress."

Transfixed by Max's green eyes, I felt carried away kissing his sensual mouth goodnight.

Tuesday, February 4, 1964: Answering
Jake's newsy letter with another Pope John XXIII joke delighted me. Soon after being elected, the Pope, walking in Rome, overheard a nearby woman say to her friend, "My God, he's so fat!" He turned and replied, "Madame, I trust you know that the papal conclave is not exactly a beauty contest." Chuckling, I replied while imagining future summer dates with Jake.

Cousin Lydia's amusing letter about her off-key high school glee club prompted a laugh. I replied:

> Intercession with Max has been a ball, including the Metropolitan and Guggenheim Museums! I adore the circular white galleries in Frank Lloyd Wright's fabulous building. Chagall and Kandinsky vibrant paintings were my favorites.
>
> Will I ever forget the carnal eating scene in the most entertaining movie I've seen in years, *Tom Jones*? Other good movies included *The Leopard*, *Sundays and Cybele*, and unique Russian films: *Chapaev* about a Russian communist civil war hero and Eisenstein's *Alexander Nevsky* with dramatic Prokofiev music!
>
> My upper-level Latin literature class with Columbia guys is exciting!

Wednesday, February 5, 1964: Classes
Interesting social psychology and social structure and personality classes helped me move past the marvelous interlude between semesters. Modern European history

continues along with introductory sociology, whose *B Plus* was fair after this comment on my paper: *pretty thorough, but the first half could have been more concise with less time on the merely descriptive.* Last semester's *A* in Latin and *A Minus* in mythology motivate continued diligence to keep my Barnard scholarship. Will Dad ever find a job?

After beating me at ping pong, Max returned later with chubby chum Rina, still sporting red-weapon fingernails. I complimented Max's blue, V-neck sweater. "Your eyes look bluer!"

"Rina's early birthday gift is appreciated." Uh oh! What will my ten dollars buy him?

"Rina, can you say more about Max's basketball career?"

She laughed. "Senior year, Max was the hero in the league title game. After poking the Hunter-Tannersville (HT) point guard, who scored 12 points in the first half, in the eye, Max outscored him in the 2nd half."

"Rina, you know that eye poke was a clumsy accident, though it held him to one point from then on. Angela, as a third-string guard, I played only after our star guard had foul trouble and his back-up got injured. I was lucky to score two points. I did excel as team manager!" We all grinned.

Rina said, "Thank God, our biggest player, Greg, saved your life when the three HT bullies attacked you."

Over a late Caravan soda, unattractive Malaysian Columbia medical student Keat prattled arrogantly. "As a Harvard pre-med, I got straight *As*." Uncharmed, I pictured puncturing a balloon symbolizing his insecure, bloated ego.

<u>Thursday, February 6, 1964: Men</u>
Floating into our room after dinner, study, talk, and canoodling at Max's place, I shared, "Carina, Max is a matchless boyfriend, always stimulating company and present almost daily. With similar interests to mine, he teaches me new things and communicates about feelings, but compatible Yeats seems

more egalitarian. To Max, I praised the thirteenth-century warrior, in a Russian movie, for marrying the courageous female warrior, who fought by his side and killed a traitor. Max's silence discouraged me. Expecting to be seen as equal, I may want a career. How are you?"

She sighed. "Discouraged without word from Garth."

I felt empathy. "Pithy just growled at Garth!"

Carina emitted an exasperated *Cheyaaaaaah!* Bent over with swinging arms, we shuffled around the cramped room.

Friday, February 7, 1964: Piano
On the subway to Carnegie Hall, Max looked pleased when I whispered in his ear, "The veal parmesan, sweet potatoes with sour cream, and fruit salad you made were yummy!"

After a brilliant Arthur Rubinstein piano concert, I was glad that critical Max described the Chopin and Rachmaninov pieces as, "Magnificently played."

On his old sofa, I answered his Valentine questionnaire, including: *would you ever marry yourself*? "Max, I want a male, not a female."

Question: *trip to outer space or bottom of the ocean*? "Outer space! Isn't drowning worse?" He grinned.

I replied affirmatively to these items: *Do you believe in love at first sight? Can you count to one trillion? Do you believe there's a perfect match for every person?*

"Soap and water on a paper towel," was my answer to, *Can you keep white shoes clean*?

If you're extremely quiet, what does it mean? "I'd rather listen to interesting Max." His long kiss rewarded me.

Saturday, February 8, 1964: Park Terrace Ballroom
My parents drove me to the lavish hotel wedding of Mother's cousin's daughter at 900 River Avenue at 161 Street, Bronx. About forty descendants of Grandpa's religious brother gathered. To Aunt Myrna, Lydia, and Ella, I said, "I wish more of

our branch of the family were here, like Uncle Peter's son." I longed to see perpetually youthful Sara (below age 23 in 1940).

I prefer Jackie Kennedy's less elaborate frocks to the bride's full-length, cream gown with floral-patterned seed pearls. As she glided down the aisle, was Mother in a trance, imagining my marrying tall, blond Marcus?

During the delish dinner, glutton Dad said, "Fern, your cousin does things right."

Dad read the menu aloud in his high school French accent. "*Hors d'Oeuvres Varies Chaud et Froid Smorgasbord, Caprice des Fruites, Celeri Amandes Noix, Consomme Vermicelli, Salade Verte*, Prime Rib, Derma Farci, Idaho Souffle, Stringbeans *Champignons, Parfait de Neige,* Wedding Cake, Dinner Mints, *Demitasse, Aperitifs*, Scotch, Rye."

When Mother asked, "How's Marcus?" I barely suppressed a laugh about her Jewish mother fantasies before escaping to dance with four male second cousins, ages 16 to 21.

Back from the ladies' room, I overheard *seduced,* as a cause of the feud between their grandpa and mine, before the guys clammed up. If Mother knows her idolized father's victim, she's unlikely to satisfy my curiosity. She has said that playboy Grandpa (below in 1945 with me) adored his *Chanalah's* baby talk on the phone. My never-used Jewish name is *Chana Rivka*.

Sunday, February 9, 1964: Angelina

At Cousin Justine's Queens apartment, my parents and I enjoyed Dad's relatives at the lovely, sixth-birthday dinner of adorable Angelina (above). I wore my blue-and-green paisley wool dress. I adore her and Herb, now ten!

Overweight Dad, Flirty Mother, Handsome Uncle Cal

When my parents left for Albany, kind but restless Burke, who spent a fun weekend with his Queens family, arrived to drop me at Barnard on his way to Albany.

In the dorm parlor, I flirted with two Alabama State University Negro exchange students. I'm thrilled to be free to date men of any race.

Yeats phone voice sounded concerned. "Angela, since the Russians trounced us at the Winter Olympics, their military could be stronger than ours." I tensed up with another worry.

Monday, February 10, 1964: Brits

During lunch in Max's compact kitchen, I said, "Dorm mates praise The Beatles, who sang on Ed Sullivan's TV show last night. Though I like their song *All My Loving*, I don't understand the fuss. Thanks to you, I enjoy classical music, especially the Beethoven symphonies, and composers, like Tchaikovsky, Mahler, Chopin, and Rachmaninoff."

Smiling, he handed me a romantic Valentine card and almost perfect record: Beethoven's *Symphony No. 2*, with Klemperer conducting London's Philharmonia Orchestra.

"Thank you! How do you detect scratches I can't hear and differences between various conductors' versions of music?" His mien suggested a peacock with gorgeous tail spread. He lovingly covered my smile with a kiss.

Wednesday, February 12, 1964: Haircuts

Carina laughed heartily at Mother's Sunday letter:

> Watching The Beatles on Ed Sullivan's TV show,
> Dad said, "What a weird name. Why can't they
> get haircuts before a big show? Nowadays, kids
> are so mixed up. We never looked slovenly." Do
> you actually like these Beatles?

Temperatures in the thirties kept Max and me indoors, batting around a ping-pong ball to unwind before study hours.

Barnard is ideal for meeting intriguing Lions! A fun coffee hour included raillery with four new men, two acquaintances, blandly dressed Gary, and energetic, pint-sized Udeh, who praised his contemporary civilization class.

Thursday, February 13, 1964: New Guys
"Carina, the six-foot-three veep of Columbia College Class of 1966 took me to Ferris Booth Hall for a drink and mild boasting about his WKCR radio station work, drafting college news items. With a slight stutter, he said, 'I'm excited to meet such an attractive Honeybear. Let's go to my apartment for privacy.' When I asked why we needed privacy, he massaged my hand. 'For intimacy.' Frowning with disbelief, I withdrew my hand and asked, 'Do you consider yourself a gentleman?' before striding off. What a waste of time!

"At the Caravan, tall, attractive Benson treated me to a sandwich for dinner. Though sharp, he seemed out for seduction, though less crude than the veep. Were both guys panicked without girlfriends on Valentine's Day?" We chortled. "Carina, such users make me treasure respectful Max and Yeats."

Friday, February 14, 1964: Valentines
I happily read Valentines from Yeats, Cousin Ron, and Max, who liked my Valentines and bought me a carnation and Caravan cherry float.

"Carina, Malaysian date Keat took me to a good violin concert at his Columbia College of Physicians and Surgeons on 168 Street. Showing zero interest in me, he bragged in his room and during ping pong at Barnard. Boredom made me decline another date."

"You're in a social whirl! Have you dated a dozen men since September?" She sounded curious.

I counted names in the back of this diary. "Fourteen, but I saw half only briefly." We giggled before I concluded, "Quality trumps quantity! One Garth, Max, or Yeats is better than the other dozen combined."

Monday, February 17, 1964: Lunch and Letters

Classes preceded lunch in Max's sunny kitchen. "Max, Saturday night was ideal: Charlie Chaplin's *City Lights*; your record of Bruno Walter conducting Mahler's dramatic, thrilling *Symphony No. 2*; your baby pictures; and romantic dancing." His kiss and hug inspired hours of library study.

In a peach-flowered-flannel granny nightgown, I curled up in my single bed to read letters from Dominic, Jake, and Yeats. On a Barnard postcard, I concurred with Yeats' praise of almost a half million students whose February 3 boycott protested segregation in their NYC public schools.

Tuesday, February 18, 1964: Lurid

The movie *Suddenly Last Summer*, based on Tennessee Williams' play, is complex enough to see twice. At Ferris Booth Hall, English major Max lauded actresses Elizabeth Taylor and Katherine Hepburn. "Angela, the symbolism of exploitation and predation, including the wildlife and garden, was striking. The shocking ends for mother and son seemed like poetic justice."

"Yes! The monster mother threatened and lobotomized her niece to protect her scary, messed-up son, who used his pretty cousin to prey on destitute boys. The mother-son bond was more pathological than D. H. Lawrence's in *Sons and Lovers*."

Wednesday, February 19, 1964: Quick Dates

A note to cousin Lydia included a question about whom Grandpa seduced, but I doubt she knows:

Lydia, when is your prom? May it and the rest of senior year be fabulous. You're lucky you can date non-Jews! Life here is endless study with copious note-taking. Brief dates maintain sanity, e.g., lunch and a funny card at Max's apartment, and late Seven-and-Seven drinks at West End Café with tall, lean, personable Henri. From impoverished Haiti, he can afford Columbia because his father is a doctor.

Thursday, February 20, 1964: Unique

I shared with Carina, curious about my date, "An oral surgery dental resident at Albert Einstein College of Medicine, manly Negro Benson is twenty-four. Undergraduate work was at University of Chicago and Northwestern. Sunday, when I initially refused to go to his apartment, he treated me to Chinese shrimp and rice, ice cream, and cookies. Making clear that sex was out, I enjoyed conversation, a glass of wine, and jazz records at his austerely furnished West End Avenue apartment off 98 Street. Tonight, can you believe that a call to perform surgery on an accident victim interrupted our date?"

"Angela, to keep Jewish mothers from pushing workaholic doctors on their daughters, someone should publicize such disruptions." We guffawed.
"Carina, I read about the boring Beatles in Newsweek magazine until Benson returned. After roast beef sandwiches and meatballs, he eluded answering my question: *Do dentists serve these Pepsis to dissolve teeth overnight and make money selling replacement teeth*?" Carina laughed. "I was eager to leave when he turned on a pro basketball TV game. I valued my late date with Max, who shuns TV."

Friday, February 21, 1964: Teeth

Psychologists write about teeth representing words in dreams; losing teeth symbolizes words spilled out or ways we've communicated. Did drinking a tooth-killing Pepsi trigger my nightmare, a re-creation of my 1959 reaction after Aunt Sara fled from near rape and asked if I believed her. My bewildered *I don't know* inadvertently hurt her.

Heartsick about years of no contact with my favorite adult, I called her on the pay phone. With no answer, I subwayed to 72 Street. Hearing from the burgundy-uniformed doorman that her niece wanted to visit, Sara replied that her student's music lesson couldn't be interrupted. Questioning whether I'll ever see my dearest aunt again, I felt too dispirited to cry or rehash the visit with Carina.

Saturday, February 22, 1964: Victories
Max and I doubled with his short housemate and a date at University Gymnasium. Columbia's win over Harvard elated us! At a coffee house over milk and lemon chiffon pie, Max said, "Yesterday, we defeated Dartmouth, 82-67, thanks to forward Mike Griffin's twenty-two points and twenty rebounds! Tonight's sixth Ivy League victory leaves us 11-9 overall!" We four celebrated this rare Columbia winning record with wine and dancing in their plain living room.

Monday, February 24, 1964: Birthday
A guy from my Columbia Latin class helped me select NY State Taylor champagne from Finger Lakes grapes at the liquor store.

On Max's comfortable sofa, he and I drank it at midnight to celebrate his twenty-first birthday! After reading his romantic, touching letter, I was glad to have fashioned a birthday card with artwork using Carina's purple, blue, and green colored pencils and a free verse I wrote about him, *Deep*:

> A brisk step, hurried, a trifle self-conscious,
> perhaps too eager to leave.
> Deep bottle-green eyes, never changing color
> but sparkling, alive, alight – for me?
> Invisible mind, visibly keen, always delving,
> Reading, perceptively probing beneath the

surface shell of this existence
To the submerged life deep below.

Max's perceptive comments about adored Victorian novels made me exclaim, "Max, you'll make a fascinating professor!"

Wednesday, February 26, 1964: Columbia's Library
For variety, imposing Butler was our study venue. "Max, images from yesterday's gripping Australian TV movie are in my mind."

"John Osborne's play about Martin Luther was riveting. Does it relate to your history class?"

"Yes. Eye-opening films should replace dry lectures to make sixteenth-century history come alive."

I answered Yeats' warm letter and Dominic's recent missive about Navy Mediterranean travels. Both are eager for the upcoming World's Fair in Queens.

Thursday, February 27, 1964: Anniversary
At the Gold Rail, I blushed with pleasure, hearing Max's manly voice. "Happy Five-Month Anniversary! It seems as if we just met. It also feels longer since we've grown close."
Beaming, I nodded. "I'm happy that you take the initiative for us to meet often!" His ardent goodnight kisses left me breathless! Ideal Max is always here for me while allowing freedom to date others, important after parent-caused AHS dating deprivation! Has Max become indispensable?

Friday, February 28, 1964: Loving
At noon, Max and I smooched on his much-used couch to celebrate acceptance at Stanford and Columbia grad schools! I sent a congratulatory note.

Arriving from Boston, Yeats took me to the V and T for pizza and Chianti wine and to the affordable Gold Rail for a Seven and Seven.

"Carina, what does it mean that I missed Max tonight?"

"What do you think?"

I grinned. "No fair answering a question with a question. Though Max has yet to say the 'L' word, he's very loving, making me feel happy and protected!"

Saturday, February 29, 1964: Every Four Years

Four-part dream: half involved distress about lack of money for Barnard. Rushing to get ready for Yeats prevented jotting down the happier half about Max before it faded.

Yeats and I visited his Boston housemate's girlfriend in Greenwich Village where we shopped. At Beck's, I got black leather heels, size 7 slim.

My 1961 classic black crepe cocktail dress worked for an elegant evening. Drinks at the Hotel Astor bar preceded the romantic Natalie Wood movie, *Love with a Proper Stranger*. Amidst the unaccustomed grandeur of Waldorf Astoria Hotel's Peacock Alley, Yeats joked, "Will I receive a marriage proposal tonight?"

My eyebrows lifted with the sudden realization that it's leap year day! "I didn't realize the date," I answered lamely.

Good-natured Yeats, attractive in a navy suit, grinned. "On the only day women can properly propose, let's dance."

"Yeats, I accept that proposal!" Appreciating his red diagonally striped tie, I hoped he wasn't hurt. He magnanimously splurged on a taxi to meet my 2:30 AM Saturday curfew.

Sunday, March 1, 1964: Carnations

"Carina, thanks for working at the library so Yeats could study here during open-house."

Asked how I feel about him, I replied, "I love that he's smart, communicative, gentlemanly, non-possessive, good at tennis and golf, and ironically humorous! Anything serious requires living in the same city. Giving me four pink carnations, he treated me to a Rosenblum's corned-beef-on-rye sandwich. I can't help but sizzle more with Max."

On the phone, Dad reported no job yet. Tonight, confiding worries about finishing Barnard to Max, I learned of his childhood poverty. "Angela, my father's dairy farm in Mount Upton, west of Oneonta, NY, went bankrupt when I was seven. Low income helped me win a special scholarship, covering college and living expenses, including our fun dates."

The scary movie, *Dr. Strangelove,* was a good diversion. Peter Sellers was hilarious in three roles. In 1959, Sellers also had multiple funny parts in *The Mouse That Roared.* I wonder if my date, creative Donald, is now a Queens College senior.

Tuesday, March 3, 1964: Naïve or Cynical

I'm broke after sending Dad a Columbia tie and homemade birthday card and buying a size 32C bra. "Carina, today is Ric's and Kevin's birthday. I hope Ric got my card. Last year, I was in love, ignorant about being two-timed. Is knowing better?"

"Ignorance is bliss until a glimpse of reality appears."

My answer to Yeats' letter included: *is being happily naïve and unaware better than cynicism after knowing the truth*?

Ping pong with affable Henri provided fun when dentist Benson stood me up. Thriving academically since junior high when our TV broke, I'm scornful of men, like Benson, who waste time on TV when with me.

Wednesday, March 4, 1964: Other Woman

Finding me in the library, Max introduced his pretty Friday lover, a friendly brunette. Did my Yeats weekend cause Max to introduce her? Max has said I'm the one he takes seriously, so I'm unjealous. After she left, he and I ping-ponged at Barnard.

Describing the charming secretary to Carina, I said, "Kevin needlessly ruined our relationship by dishonestly hiding sex with his original girlfriend."

Thursday, March 5, 1964: Lucy
A tall, dark, pouchy-eyed, gaunt Albany classmate from fourth through twelfth grade, now at Columbia, took me to Tom's Corner. Less eccentric and more confident now, this outsider poet amused me with an anecdote about President Johnson's teen daughter:

> Quite taken with The Beatles, Lucy Johnson
> wanted to meet the Liverpool lads at the British
> embassy and invite them to the White House.
> Imagine how unthrilled she was when her father
> sent her off to be queen of the Shenandoah
> Apple Blossom Festival, keeping Lucy from
> meeting her crushes.

Friday, March 13, 1964: Unlucky
On a break from mid-term cramming, I asked, "Carina, is Dominic afraid to see me? Yesterday's last-minute message said he's in NYC, eager to meet. Missing today's second call is disgruntling."

"He must underestimate the competition. Having struck out with Garth, I'm no expert." She laughed at herself. "Playing *hard to get* bores me, but some males seem to need to chase and overcome obstacles to fully appreciate us."

"Preferring sincerity without female wiles, I'm sorry that Dominic's delay may keep us apart. Staying here on Friday, the thirteenth, is probably safer." I giggled.

Saturday, March 14, 1964: Roses
Benson waylaid me, trying to patch things up after standing me up twice! Shaking my head, I moved away to greet Max. "Max, thank you for this corsage of two lovely pink roses, which will help me study for exams tonight. I wish the library were open Saturday evening. Thanks for your support all week, including the drink and dill pickle at the Gold Rail, Caravan lunch, and the Deli pastrami-on-rye sandwich."

He patted my arm. "You're welcome. Does the eagle-eyed Deli waiter get a bonus for swooping down on empty plates as if they're prey? I was still chewing the last mouthful." Holding his upper arm affectionately, I was relieved that Benson had disappeared.

<u>Sunday, March 15, 1964: Fight</u>
On the phone, I responded to Dad's thanks for my birthday gift, "You're welcome." He likely senses my coldness towards him.

Mother said, "Work was jumping Friday! In front of the NY State Employees' Retirement System offices across the street, a wife beat up her husband while yelling about his cheating with another woman when she was in England."

"Mother, I respect her standing up for herself!" I'm too cowardly and physically weak to ever fight a man. Does brilliant Eva, who works there, know that woman?

Yeats' call ended the parental chat. "Angela, heavyweight boxing champion Cassius Clay's new name is Muhammed Ali for distance from family slavery."

"Good for him!"

<u>Monday, March 16, 1964: Tests</u>
Recipe for a panicked zombie: European history, Livy in Latin, and introduction to sociology exams in one day!

Sharing a Tom Collins drink with Max at Tom's Corner, I controlled tears. "Max, Kazan's movie about his immigrant family, *America America*, reminded me of Eastern European poverty and pogroms, which made all four of my penniless grandparents emigrate in 1900."

Nodding, he mentioned his mother's Czech family arriving in Canada a few years later. Squeezing my shoulder supportively, he kissed me softly on the mouth. Relaxing, I sighed happily.

<u>Tuesday, March 17, 1964: Ghastly</u>
Sharing a roast beef sandwich at the Deli, I told sympathetic
Max, wearing a green, St. Patrick's Day shirt, "The grisly
Queens murder of young Kitty Genovese made me wear black.
If only neighbors had reached police after the initial knifing
before the assailant returned to rape and stab her to death." Is
my cousins' neighborhood safe? Hoping to avoid more
nightmares, I felt soothed when dear Max comforted me.

<u>Wednesday, March 18, 1964: Younger Man</u>
"Carina, at a coffee hour. Lowell, a White Plains freshman,
seemed mature. He beat me 21-10 at ping pong. Inviting me to
a Spanish-language movie, he vividly described his 1963
Mexican trip. A future lawyer, he has a green belt in karate. I
have a weakness for the few athletes at intellectual Columbia."
        "Is Max strong?"
        "Except for two years on the family farm, he lived in
Brooklyn and upper Manhattan until age 12. Since he's still in
one piece, he may be tougher than the average Lion." We
exchanged smiles.

<u>Friday, March 20, 1964: Israeli and RFK</u>
To satisfy the gym requirement without time-wasting showers
and clothing changes, I'm taking fun Israeli folk dance, first
learned at age 11 from Israeli Yaffa at our synagogue. The
direct manner of Barnard's Israeli piano accompanist, a City
College sophomore, reminds me of Yaffa's brother, a medical
student at Albany Hospital. As our Hebrew school teacher, tall,
darkly handsome, Amnon, sent us girls into a tizzy!
Yeats wrote about Attorney General Bobby Kennedy's
eloquent St. Patrick's Day oration. My answer lauded Bobby's
fighting for Negro rights. I quoted my favorite RFK speech
excerpts from a newspaper discarded in the dorm parlor:

        So much work of the Department of Justice
        today is devoted to securing...rights for all

Americans… There are Americans who, as the
Irish did, still face discrimination in employment,
sometimes open, sometimes hidden. There are
cities in America today that are torn with strife
over whether a Negro should be allowed to
drive a garbage truck, and their walls of silent
conspiracy block progress for others because of
race or creed without regard to ability….
Let us hold our hands out to those who struggle
for freedom today at home and abroad as
Ireland struggled for a thousand years.

Saturday, March 21, 1964: Jealousy

In the wee hours, Carina asked, "Did you and Max see Lorca's tragedy, *Blood Wedding*, at Minor Latham Playhouse?

I nodded. "Drinks at Top of the Sixes calmed me about the unfortunate bride going from two devoted men to none on her wedding day! Jealousy made them fight and kill each other!"

Earlier, Dominic, on leave from his ship, finally reached me, asking to meet. "Dominic, I'd love to see you, but I accepted a date for today over a week ago. Advance planning is needed, especially for weekends." I can't count on a passive guy, like him. A phone call for a dorm mate ended our brief chat.

Sunday, March 22, 1964: Snow

"Carina, we need to return bad weather, like clothing which doesn't fit."

"Yes! *Reason for return* for today's snow: too late, it's spring!

At the library, persistent Benson vamoosed when I mentioned my upcoming test. Barnard ping pong and studying with Henri preceded a call from Yeats in Albany for the weekend.

Before curfew, Max treated me to cheesecake and ice cream at the Deli. After we greeted Gary, I was happy to accept Max's invitation to an April concert! At the dorm entrance, I felt elated hearing, "Angela, kissing you is sublime!"

"Max, to raise my history test grade of *B Minus*, I need your wonderful kisses to transmit your superior knowledge."

He grinned. "Let's work on it!"

Monday, March 23, 1964: Prank
Carina said, "Though I like swimming for physical education, our basement pool is mildewed, overchlorinated, and overheated. On April Fool's Day, each Honeybear should drop a dozen grape fizzy tablets into the pool to fizz it into a purple oblivion." I guffawed!

Max rewarded my surviving the social structure and personality test with cheese pie a la mode at Tom's Corner. Why hasn't the misery of seven years of cramps taught me to skip eating on the first day of my period?

Tuesday, March 24, 1964: Dog
"Carina, Max gave me this darling carved wooden spaniel as we munched on a Caravan roast beef sandwich with French fries."

"Is Max still number one?"

"Definitely! Engineer Bill left a message. Though I like him, he has rarely appeared this year."

"Like Garth." Carina looked doleful. How can I get Garth to visit her without his phone number or address?

Wednesday, March 25, 1964: Aborted
I entered our room after midnight. "Angela, today's warm, sunny weather gave me spring fever! The attempted panty raid was exciting, though police intervened before the rogues could storm our citadel."

I giggled. "Another lost opportunity to donate ripped underwear! Across Broadway, Lowell and I saw the haphazard raid fizzle. A bomb threat added danger, as we drank Lion's

Den cokes after *Macaria*, a great old Mexican film at the Thalia Theater. I was surprised that he's Jewish culturally. Though I like him, he seemed to lose interest. *C'est la vie.*"

Thursday, March 26, 1964: Pink Carnation
"Max, thank you for this lovely flower!" An astoundingly violent rainstorm preceded a tasty shrimp tempura and chicken yakitori Japanese dinner at Aki's to celebrate six months of dating. The romantic *West Side Story* movie, a modern *Romeo and Juliet* tragedy, brought tears.

Wonderment! Max said, "I love you," for the first time! Though unready to say it back unless I'm sure that he's Mr. Forever, I'm supremely happy. Sensual slow dancing and fervent kissing in his dark living room were stimulating!

Friday, March 27, 1964: Passover
Subwaying to Aunt Rhoda's Eastside apartment, I said, "Max, I'm okay with *B* on the social structure and personality test."

The rollicking *seder* featured bantering with Uncle Cal, Cousin Ron, Aunt Lila, Uncle Bert, and my parents. Of Passover foods, Max and I preferred *charoset*: chopped apples and walnuts in wine.

Saturday, March 28, 1964: *Seder*
With Max at Aunt Lila's *seder* (below), I felt joyful to see Cousin Justine's family, plus everyone from yesterday and the Stowe family, including Ron's pal Johnny.

Does widowed, blond Aunt Rhoda go for fine-looking, charming brother-in-law Cal, widower of her sister Hannah since 1954? He's grandpa to Justine's adorable, bright Herbie and Angelina!"

Parting for vacation, Max and I appreciated Passover fun to distract us from gloom about a 9.2 Alaska earthquake with 100 deaths and more injured victims!

Front: Aunt Lila, Dad
Seated: Angela, Angelina, Herbie
Standing: Mrs. Stowe, Johnny Stowe, Mother, Johnny's
Brother, Cousin Justine, Uncle Cal, Justine's Husband, Aunt
Rhoda, Mr. Stowe, Uncle Bert

<u>Sunday, March 29, 1964: Vacation</u>
Dinner at Dad's sister Rhoda's apartment preceded returning to Albany in Burke's yellow Toyota Celica convertible with top up. Snagging the front passenger seat, Mother carried on a lively repartee about Burke's NYC weekend. Her crushes on tall, light-haired young men are rib-tickling! Wakening from a nap, I noticed that Dad had nodded off, too.

A whiff of fresh paint hit my nostrils when I entered my Albany room. I thanked Mother for robin-egg-blue walls, pretty after a decade of green ballerina wallpaper. I still love ballet!

<u>Monday, March 30, 1964: Grandpa</u>
Did fresh paint inspire a bizarre dream about Mother's dad, the rake, flirting with a Honeybear? Since the February family wedding, I've wondered whom Grandpa seduced. Hapless grandma, after five children and risky, back-room abortions, shared a locked bedroom with her daughters to keep poker-playing drinker Grandpa away and avert pregnancies. At least some women have easier lives nowadays.

Without sex at home, Grandpa went elsewhere. Years ago, Mother implied that he saw town floozies. The word *seduce* suggests unpaid sex. Today, when I asked whether he seduced anyone, Mother scowled without answering. Did he repulsively prey on teen virgins, like my teacher Dr. B? Shudder!

Mother's proud of his four rags-to-riches decades after emigrating from the Vilna area in 1900 with nothing. Peddling clothes and household goods to farm families from a cart, he toiled tirelessly through below-zero winters until starting a store and eventually buying a stately Gloversville house. Although illiterate, he achieved the American dream.

<u>Tuesday, March 31, 1964: Thankful</u>
If God existed or, better yet, Goddess, I'd express gratitude for wonderful friends. Dear Jake, cynical Hank, and adored Doreen called! Like me, she likes sociology and psychology. Letters

arrived from Max, who called, and Yeats, who called from Boston and sent eight attractive pink carnations!

Downtown shopping included fun chats with AHS girls, between buying a black, wrap-around skirt (size 10, $4.98) and pink and baby-blue Banlon shells (size 36, $3.98 each). I'm eager to wear my hot-pink, A-line dress from David's, size 9, $12.98.

Near the NY State Capitol, Kevin intercepted me. Though I agreed to coffee, he must notice my lack of vivacity.

Later, Dad, hearing about my dental checkups, was positive. "Good! No cavities."

Burke's presence seems to inhibit the usual parental fault-finding! At the bowling alley, I said, "Burke, your 200 score almost doubles mine!" He puffed up like a bird. In his cool convertible, we stopped at Third Place near Schenectady for drinks. "Burke, I've rarely gone to Schenectady and Troy."

"Exploring averts terminal boredom." I laughed.

Wednesday, April 1, 1964: Fools

Sitting between two mirrors to see the back of my long hair, I said, "Mother, please cut a little lower." As I trimmed the front and sides, my mouth turned upward at the memory of giving Frankie a haircut during eighth-grade art class.

Large Trailways bus windows framed a verdant vista before arrival in NYC for hours of library concentration.

A sharp-nosed, pretty dorm pal with straw-colored locks, shared, "Angela, I poured red nail polish on waxed paper, let it dry, peeled it off, and put it in my purse. While my boyfriend was in the men's room, I put the blob on his jacket. When he returned, I apologized. He ranted indignantly until I said, 'April Fool!'" She and I giggled delightedly! I must try this next year!

Thursday, April 2, 1964: Greenwich

Hurried hours in a library carrel preceded meeting Yeats at the Boston bus. We chatted at his genial friend's sunny West

Greenwich Village apartment. Across the street at cellar club
Ten Below, I said, "I dig this casual, artistic atmosphere!"

Yeats grinned. "This whiskey sour, salad with garlic
dressing, veal parmesan, and potatoes O'Brien are delectable

At Ninth Circle Steak House's brownstone on 10 Street
off Greenwich Avenue, we felt cool among beat and other
with-it types, eating peanuts from a barrel. The jukebox played
jazz by Miles Davis. Yeats joked, "Ninth Circle refers to part of
hell, which must explain such potent drinks." Tipsy, I tittered.

<u>Friday, April 3, 1964: Weird</u>
"Carina, what could this dream about Barnard's Greek Games
mean?"

> Watching my parents perform badly in a
> vaudeville-type song-and-dance, like Ethel and
> Fred Mertz on *I Love Lucy*, I felt self-conscious.
> Sitting next to me was an undersized, pudgy boy
> with a spotty complexion. He superciliously
> jeered at the Honeybear athletes.
>
> After a movie with grinning Max, I lost
> him on a subway platform when mazes of rolling
> garment racks with densely packed clothes
> sidetracked me. A beefy female officer was part
> of a police stake-out. Returning after curfew, I
> was dismayed to get my first demerit ever.

"Angela, it suggests fretful feelings."

"Do I fear losing Max because of dating Yeats?"

Later, at 1655 Broadway, I sat in a big restaurant with a
bar along one wall. "Yeats, Lindy's deserves its fame for this
luscious cheesecake!"

Anouilh's film *Becket* left us raving about superb acting:
Richard Burton, John Gielgud, and kissable-mouthed, blue-
eyed Peter O'Toole. Yeats and I snacked and imbibed at

stylish Top of the Sixes. Over-sized Tishman skyscraper windows revealed splendid Manhattan views, including the Empire State Building!

Yeats knew that Noguchi, designer of the lobby abstract sculpture and waterfall, attended Columbia. Since I had a festive evening, missing Max was startling. His Lion postcard about missing me warmed my heart.

<u>Saturday, April 4, 1964: Elegance</u>
Ornate, romantic Chateau Henry IV French Restaurant on East 64 Street was dressed to impress with stone walls, burgundy silk valances above arched doorways, elaborate crystal chandeliers, and candlelit, starched white tablecloths. Yeats looked pleased when I called the rich onion soup, fresh jumbo shrimp, and tender veal scrumptious!"

"Angela, the exceptional mother, age seventy-two, of Massachusetts Governor Peabody spent two days in a St. Augustine jail for demonstrating against segregation."

"Braver than I!"

Kind-hearted Yeats noted, "You're safer now with the vicious Queens killer of Kitty Genovese jailed after confessing."

"The electric chair's too good for him." I shuddered. To avert arousing male anxiety, I skipped asking if castration as mandatory punishment would decrease rapes, which tragically ruin or end too many female lives! Even Sara's near-rape has disrupted our family's lives.

When a foreign movie at a small art theater was sold out, dancing at the fashionable Waldorf Astoria was better!

Later, I said, "Carina, Yeats' considerate company contrasts with egotistical Hank from AHS, expecting me to be available for dinner tonight at the last minute."

<u>Tuesday, April 7, 1964: Nightmare</u>
Dream: stuck home married to a man who refused to do half of the endless diaper-changing and repetitive chores and meal-making, I was a miserable mom, longing for an interesting job.

At lunch with good-humored Max, I skipped mentioning the bad dream. We split antipasto, a roast beef sandwich, and French fries. "Angela, is it only my company which makes you look happy?" Hearing about my *A Minus* on the sociology test, *A* on the Latin exam, and okay Latin paper *B*, he commented, "Splendid!" and bussed me. "Here's a reward." I thanked him for an imperceptibly marred record: Vienna Festival Orchestra's Rachmaninoff *Piano Concerto No. 2* with woman soloist Vivian Rivkin!

Glad that my psych test was done, I eluded tenacious Benson before a late date with appealing Henri at the West End Café. Time rushed by. Wide-eyed, I learned about the *wave of the future*: computers. Henri smiled broadly, hearing about my Haitian doll, which Sara bought while living in his country, and my plan to visit his homeland.

Thursday, April 9, 1964: Hartley
Our Reid dorm party with Columbia Hartley Hall residents included dancing with well-coordinated Henri, whose even, white teeth are attractive.

Former date Gary bemoaned Columbia's baseball losses. "Even lowly CCNY shut us out, 5-0!"

At midnight at the Gold Rail bar, Max sipped a rum with cola. "Angela, my mouth still waters from Tom's Corner creamy cheese pie a la mode last evening." He looked serene.

"Our dates are tasty treats!" Kissing his bewitching mouth proved my point.

Friday, April 10, 1964: Bond
"Should I become a spy?" Max jested during slow dancing following the movie *From Russian with Love*. Sexy Sean Connery played British spy James Bond.

Arthur Rubinstein's brilliant recorded rendition of Liszt's Piano Concerto No. 1 accompanied rapturous kissing.

Carina was asleep when I quietly scribbled a soothing answer to Burke's political note, ruing Brazil's military ouster of democratically elected President Goulart.

<u>Saturday, April 11, 1964: Double Date</u>
At Serendipity, Max and Rina's husky-voiced, burly date intelligently discussed the spellbinding psychological play we saw at Actors Playhouse on Seventh Avenue in the Village: Ibsen's *Little Eyolf*. Listening intently, we gals downed decadent sundaes with mountains of whipped cream.

In the ladies' room, I asked about Rina's clear-polished, round-filed, shorter nails. "My date found long, red spears too scary." She sounded regretful. Relieved that the weapons were gone, I struggled to look sympathetic.

At Max's, my stomach protested the sweets. When I awoke from napping, he provided an aspirin and hot rum toddy. "Max, I appreciate your nursing me back to health!" Would he be as flawless a husband as he is a boyfriend?

<u>Sunday, April 12, 1964: Talent and Childrearing</u>
During open house, generous Carina let Max play his classical music on her record player while he studied with me. I thanked her for going to the library when she prefers our room.

Seeing her latest abstract landscape sketches, I exclaimed, "You're so talented! Did you consider art school?"

"Art and music as hobbies beat life as a starving artist."

"That's smart! Though charismatic performer Aunt Sara studied at Juilliard, her mother supplemented her insufficient income from music lessons, book royalties, and one-woman music shows around the country."

"Have you reached her?"

"I must stay calm for exams in this roller-coaster year of JFK's death, your meeting Garth, Dad's unemployment, my idyllic social life, civil rights triumphs and tragedies, Morningside Park rape, and two scary murders. Last year's swing between Kevin euphoria and withering parental hostility lowered my grades. Did jealousy of K fuel Dad's enraged letters? Unmotivated to be a mother, I commiserate with parents feeling abandoned after decades of investing time, energy, money, love, and attention. But how healthy are submissive offspring who let guilt keep them in the nest?"

Smiling, Carina nodded her understanding.

<u>Wednesday, April 15, 1964: SNCC</u>
Carina sounded animated. "The James Room featured field secretary Faith Holsaert's lecture about 1962-1963 Student Non-Violent Coordinating Committee (SNCC) work in Albany, Georgia! SNCC documented police brutality and voter registration abuses and canvassed tirelessly to develop *pockets of power* in the Negro community. Weekly meetings, announced in churches and through families, taught hundreds how to protest non-violently for jobs and justice. Faith lived with a valiant family whose heroic females participated in sit-ins and endured abuse in jail."

"Carina, I appreciate being inspired!"

I fell asleep, hoping to dodge another nightmare about insufficient money to receive my degree at beloved Barnard. Rotund Dad's heart disease and lack of work keep me insecure. I'm thankful to have overcome nervous habits, like nail-biting. My long nails look better!

<u>Friday, April 17, 1964: Flowers</u>
On a splintered bench near mature maple trees in Riverside Park, Max and I split a roast beef sandwich as dull-colored, tiny birds flew above. "Max, thanks for rewarding this week's marathon schoolwork sessions! I adore this white carnation and pink rose!"

"Last night at the Gold Rail, I meant to ask about your Latin prize exam."

"Difficult! Profs make Latin fun, I'm idiotic to major in a dead language. Max, finals start in a month! Yikes!"

Reading Lee's card signed *Love*, I felt happy about his planned transfer to Albany State.

Dear Lee, thanks for the warm note! Are you pleased that talented Sidney Poitier won the best actor Oscar? He's special, but you're more handsome!

Saturday, April 18 1964: Greek Games
Cute, quirky Spanky escorted me to the games (below). Our graceful sophomore athletes trounced the frosh by ten points!

Sauntering, Spanky and I ran into Henri who asked, "Did you hear that nuclear physics Professor Charles Gallagher was gruesomely killed in Central Park?"

Stunned and speechless, I clutched at my heart and shook my head no.

Spanky added, "A birdwatcher, he ignored police warnings and loitered in the park at night."

A shudder passed through me. Though I adore NYC, I'm leery about living in a high-crime, dangerous city after college.

An exceptional evening with Max in the Village kept the scary murder out of mind. O. Henry's delish *filet tips en brochette* (shish-kebob) with baked potato and mixed greens (menu below) were a bargain, Max noted, at $3.95.

"Max, thanks for enlightening me about the political movie, *The Best Man*. Resemblances to idealist Adlai Stevenson, despicable Joe McCarthy, and pragmatic Harry Truman went over my head. You're so perceptive!"

"Angela, I'm impressed with Henry Fonda's acting. Gore Vidal based the screenplay on his Broadway play."

Sunday, April 19, 1964: Progress

Carina sounded emphatic. "Congress on Racial Equality (CORE) is improving life for Negroes! The campus Democratic Club debate showed that CORE's work has upped Schaefer Brewing Company's previous token hires of Negroes and Puerto Ricans to half of the latest group! Schaefer's NY locations now employ fifty-seven minorities or two percent of the total workforce."
"Hats off to CORE Honeybears and Lions!

Monday, April 20, 1964: Substitute

Looking pale lying in bed, Carina said, "I'm too ill for my blind date. How about stand-in dating, like substitute teaching?"

"Haha! Did he request a replacement?"

"In the lobby after a subway ride from the Village, he'd rather drink with an attractive Honeybear than return home."

"If it helps you feel better..." Afterwards, I reported, "Age 25 and keen on psychology, he's a congenial stockbroker,

O. Henry's Special

DOUBLE CUT
Loin Lamb Chops
Mixed Green Salad
Baked Potato
4.50

ALL ENTREES, BOTH MEAT AND FISH,
ARE COOKED OVER LIVE CHARCOAL

APPETIZERS

Chilled Tomato Juice ... .30
Filet of Marinated Herring ... 1.00
Chopped Chicken Liver ... 1.00
Chilled Melon (in season) ... .75
Jumbo Shrimp Cocktail ... 1.50
Sauté Mushrooms ... 1.25
Barbecued Shrimp ... 1.50
Half Grapefruit ... .65

SOUP

French Onion Soup or Soup du Jour ... .75

ENTREES

MEATS:
O. Henry's Chopped Sirloin Steak ... 3.65
O. Henry's Thick Club Steak ... 4.50
O. Henry's Island Sirloin Steak ... 4.50
Prime Ribs of Beef au jus ... 4.95
Double Steak for Two ... 10.95
O. Henry's Filet Mignon (Mushroom cap) ... 5.75
O. Henry's Special-Cut Steak (Over One Pound) ... 9.75
Double Cut Loin Lamb Chops ... 4.50
Young Jersey Pork Chops ... 3.50
O. Henry's Famous Barbecued Spareribs ... 3.75
Virginia Ham Steak, Hawaiian ... 3.75
Barbecued Half Spring Chicken ... 3.25
Chicken Livers en Brochette ... 3.25
Filet Tips en Brochette ... 4.75

SEA FOOD:
Imported Rock Lobster Tail (drawn butter) ... 5.25
Barbecued Jumbo Shrimp ... 3.95
Broiled Swordfish Steak, Lemon Butter ... 3.25
O. Henry's Mountain Trout ... 3.50
Halibut Steak, Maître d'Hotel ... 3.00

ALL ENTREES INCLUDE
CHEF'S MIXED SALAD BOWL AND BAKED IDAHO POTATO

now available...

O. HENRY'S

Gift certificate
$5.00 each

O. Henry's Special

FILET TIPS
En BROCHETTE
Baked Potato
Mixed Green Salad
3.95

DESSERTS

Sherbert ... .60
Chocolate and Vanilla Ice Cream, Rum Raisin Ice Cream ... .60
  (with Black Cherries) ... .75
Hot Apple Pie (baked on premises) ... .60
  (with Cheese) ... .75
Cheese Cake ... .75
Nesselrode Pie ... .75

BEVERAGES

Coffee, Milk, Tea, Sanka ... .25
Iced Coffee, Tea ... .35

Special
IRISH
COFFEE
1.25

BEER ON TAP

Lowenbrau, Heineken, Wurzburger Light or Dark ... .75
Prior Double Dark, Half & Half, Michelob ... .60
Rheingold, Ballantine, Schaefer Beer ... .50

BEER IN BOTTLES

Carlsberg (Danish) ... .75
Miller's High Life ... .65
Ballantine Ale ... .65

Not Responsible for Personal Property Unless Checked

O. HENRY'S STEAK HOUSE, 4th St. and 6th Ave., GREENWICH VILLAGE, CH 2-5960

OPEN 7 DAYS FOR LUNCHEON and DINNER
DINNER and SUPPER SERVED DAILY UNTIL 1:30 A.M.
and UNTIL MIDNIGHT ON SUNDAY

finishing an MBA at night. Over Seven and Seven drinks, he mentioned his Purdue English major, Army service, and Columbia Law School studies."

Since Carina's menstrual cramps had eased, I accompanied Max to the Deli for a shared sandwich. In a worn wooden booth against a faded reddish Gold Rail wall, three of his pals noted spy overtones of brilliant, murdered Dr. Gallagher's Copenhagen collaboration with Russian physicists and February visit to Georgia in the USSR.

Knowledgeable Max countered, "His contract with the Atomic Energy Commission's NYC Pupin Lab was supposedly unclassified. His academic, pure science research reports appeared in regular physics journals. His supervisor at Columbia's Pegram Nuclear Lab mentioned Gallagher's study of nuclear structure through observation of inelastic protons and consequential gamma radiation, whatever that means." Marveling at the complexity of physics, I was too reticent to say that officials must routinely deny secret work. Whose 25-caliber automatic pistol shot the handsome 31-year-old?

Tuesday, April 21, 1964: With Max
Eating lunch in Max's snug kitchen, I asked, "Why do people eat turkey only on holidays? This white meat sandwich is better than chicken!"

"Bigger turkeys take longer to roast."

In the evening, we got engrossed in *The Trial,* a 1955 rerun movie on campus. At Tom's Corner, I said, "Mexican Americans seem as mistreated as Negroes."

Max nodded. "This legal drama was compelling. Capitalist injustices motivated the unethical Communist attorney to favor a guilty verdict for his innocent client."

Snuggling up, I complimented Max. "Professor, you're right and marvelously clever!" I visualized him as a peacock with iridescent tail feathers fanning out.

<u>Wednesday, April 22, 1964: New</u>
Despite a dreadful dream about the murder, I awoke wondering if spring has formed a more secure me with renewed faith in myself. Waving to but still done with undependable dentist Benson after Latin class, I felt sprightly. I ambled down Broadway south of 113 Street to meet Max at College Inn for a cherry coke.

"Angela, the World's Fair opened today in Flushing Meadows. Let's go after exams." Smiling widely, I nodded.

While Carina was on a date with the MBA student, I confidently flirted at a dorm floor gathering with a dark-haired Greek, studying international affairs. I beamed while imagining an international affair with this fine-looking, green-eyed grad student.

<u>Thursday, April 23, 1964: Dates</u>
Starting my annual tan on the dorm roof included reading Yeats' letter and studying for a few hours. In our compact, off-white, room, I enquired, "Carina, how was the MBA student?"

"Personable! I'd appreciate him more if I'd never met Garth. How was your date?"

"Henri and I saw Shakespeare's *As You Like It* and a Ferris Booth Hall *Happening* with student skits. At Campus Corner, he treated me to yummy cheese pie a la mode. During ping pong, I practiced my rusty, rudimentary Spanish with him. Well-read Henri is fluent in French, English, and Spanish."

<u>Friday, April 24, 1964: Lectures</u>
I laughed when Carina said, "This *Barnard Bulletin* motivates me to quit classes to hear lectures, like Louis Leakey, discussing *Homo Habitus*, his latest East African anthropological discovery."

I asked Pithy "Are you australopithecines related to *H Habitus*?" Silence.

Carina chuckled. "Surrealist artist Salvador Dali's recent outrageous lecture included five statements about his being a genius. Showing a slide of his famous *Persistence of Memory*, now in NYC's Museum of Modern Art, he labeled the melting clocks the body of Jesus, the closest thing to the *divine Camembert cheese.* Influenced by Freud and Einstein, Dali said the painting expresses *the anguish of space and time.*"

"Carina, he sounds hilariously brilliant!"

"A Raphael painting slide garnered his commendation. He deemed Abstract Expressionists so bad that they give him future opportunities. He said that they *paint nothing* because they *believe in nothing.*" Irreverence amuses us.

"His advice to upcoming artists: *study the academics of artistry and take the drug LSD.* Though he denied taking drugs, he admitted being *drunk constantly.*" We chortled.

Saturday, April 25, 1964: Fun

Carina treated me to a shared pizza. "At your French restaurant dinner date with the MBA guy, did you speak French?"

"A little. The waiter asked if I'm French.'"

"Your accent must be superb!"

"I'm working on it."

"You're too modest. I'm glad you had fun... Do you recognize this Honeybear model in this latest *Glamour* magazine?" Carina shook her head no.

Before dressing for my date with Max, I appreciated a brief phone chat with Dominic, on leave from his Navy ship.

Dirk Bogarde's powerful performance in *The Servant*, an absorbing psychological movie, impressed Max. Dirk and girlfriend gradually took control of his weak, upper-class employer, who became the servant!

At Max's niece's engagement party, Max mentioned recognizing stodgy Republican Senator Kenneth Keating on campus for a speech.

Making out on Max's couch left me jubilant.

Sunday, April 26, 1964: Sunbathing

On roof chaise lounges, thirty Honeybears in swim suits studied, including a familiar-looking girl. Later, I said, "Carina, I barely recognized the *Glamour* model. She looked so ordinary."

"Does she have good facial bone structure? Or family connections?" Carina sounded curious.

Grinning, I shrugged. "Always emulating models to enhance my appearance, I'm disillusioned."

On the phone, Yeats asked, "Do you know any Barnard and Columbia CORE demonstrators who non-violently sat in and got arrested at the World's Fair Schaefer Beer exhibit?"

"Do you have their names?"

"No. Pinkerton guards had them unfairly charged with disorderly conduct."

"I hope they're uninjured. Dr. Gallagher's unsolved murder haunts me while preparing for exams."

Late recorded music in Max's dimly-lit living room included Brahms *Symphony No. 2* with Pierre Monteux, conducting the Vienna Philharmonic, and Mendelssohn's *Symphony No. 4* with Sir Thomas Beecham, leading the Royal Philharmonic Orchestra. "Surprise, Angela! Scratches make them yours."

"They sounded flawless. Thank you, Max!" I gratefully surrendered to his captivating kisses.

Thursday, April 30, 1964: Future

Monday, sharing cheese pie a la mode at the Deli, solemn Max articulately explored his English prof and lawyer options. His jerkier-than-usual voice with varying pitch sounded anxious.

Tuesday, sharing a grasshopper at the Gold Rail, I preferred his gloomy visage when discussing his career to the inexpressiveness of most guys I've met.

Wednesday, over cheese pie a la mode at Tom's Corner, and today, lunching on corned-beef sandwiches at the

Fairmont, Max cracked self-deprecating jokes to keep from taking himself too seriously. I felt assured hearing, "Angela, I want us together next year."

At the coffee hour, dancing to a good jazz trio with Henri and Gary was a welcome change from library cubicles.

I smiled seeing personable Ray. "Angela, the physicist's murder is unsolved after two weeks without a gun or shells found. A pro assassin must have delivered the fatal chest shot. Did the CIA, aware of Gallagher's nocturnal forays, off him for selling nuclear secrets to Russians?"

"Ray, as a Nancy Drew mystery fan, I picture the assistant prof as a CIA spy who turns double agent to repay student loans and support two children. I'm sorry for his ill-fated English widow, a research assistant." My hands clenched with unease about the murder and exams.

Friday, May 1, 1964: Art

Playing hooky from the study grind, Carina and I viewed *avant-garde* art at Stable Gallery on East 74 Street. Her silky blue blouse with a bow at the neckline looked polished with a black A-line skirt. I wore my bright pink, linen-like dress.

A painted plywood Brillo soap pad box by artist Andy Warhol cracked us up! "Carina, shall I make giant Q-Tip boxes and colorful Polaroid instant camera film containers this summer to sell as great art to pay for Barnard?" Her grin was infectious. "In September, how will brown-brick Hewitt single dorm rooms compare to our Brooks and Reid doubles?"

Her shoulders lifted in a shrug. "I'm assigned to 552."

"My 554 is nearby! *Cheyah*!"

On the subway train back, nearby Columbia Lions mentioned a TGIF (Thank God It's Friday) campus gathering. We resisted temptation. I dropped a fifteenth-birthday card to Cousin Ella in the mail before exam cramming until after midnight.

Saturday, May 2, 1964: Romantic

"Carina, *Yesterday, Today, and Tomorrow* was a cute movie! Max and I liked Sophia Loren and Marcello Mastroianni in each of three short romantic comedies. Holding this lovely pink carnation from dear Max felt good."

"Sounds like fun! At dinner, a Honeybear described Columbia students, picketing the Soviet UN Mission yesterday to protest Russian persecution of Jews." Her tone was approving.

"So brave! With no easy classes here, how do they keep up grades? Are any on scholarships?

She shrugged. "Maybe they substitute politics for socializing." My hard-working childhood with insufficient play makes dating top priority for me.

Sunday, May 3, 1964: Spanky

On a breezy day in the high fifties, Spanky's cousin, who resembles him closely, drove us west over the George Washington Bridge in an ancient, rattling, blue Chevy coupe. In the back, I appreciated the ragged, but clean tan blanket covering upholstery rips and keeping my pink-and-orange plaid skirt unmarred. The guys raved about the new sporty Ford Mustang. In the wilds of New Jersey, I lost track of what towns we passed through. Getting out of NYC was a treat!

Spanky escorted me around campus and to the Deli for ice cream. Intelligent and artistic, he shared, "My white musician father disappeared after getting my Negro mom pregnant with me. A Brooklyn housecleaner, she's short of money. My delivery jobs pay for my City College (CCNY) night classes, cheaper than Columbia School of General Studies."

"In the 1930s, my father ran out of funds before CCNY graduation." I enjoyed Spanky's sweet good-bye kiss! Bright, interesting Negro gentlemen like him, Lee, and Henri make me hope that interracial romance and marriage become routine.

<u>Wednesday, May 6, 1964: Shanghai Restaurant</u>
At dinner, the blue eyes of Carina's lively, good-looking parents mesmerized me. I said, "Thank you for this yummy Chinese meal!"

Her mother, in a purple linen sheath, asked, "If you met the right man, would you marry at twenty, as I did?"
Carina replied, "With Garth, I'd be tempted, but he's probably fending off besotted females."

I commented, "Since junior high, I've been too boy crazy. A variety of romantic boyfriends seems like more fun than one husband, who might eventually take me for granted. Ducking long-distance trust issues, I appreciate local boyfriend Max and am free to enjoy meeting new men!"

In our room, I observed, "Carina, your parents are like lovebirds after twenty years and five kids!"

"They're inspiring. How's roof tanning?"

"The model's been absent. While sunning, I studied and answered letters from home and Yeats. He's excited about hundreds of students marching through NYC's Times Square to protest the war in Vietnam. He'll be disappointed that exam prep made me miss Michael Harrington's speech. His book, *The Other America*, shows how technology leads to more poverty."

<u>Thursday, May 7, 1964: Cornell</u>
Sipping a Tom Collins at a Gold Rail table for two, Max, in a navy pullover shirt, opened his new yearbook. "Angela, we're famous!" Seeing our Dean's Drag dance picture made me chuckle.

"Max, the V and T pizza and Tom's cheeseburger you fed me this week have fueled hours of Latin paper progress." We exchanged smiles.

He admitted, "For my English Ph.D., I'm leaning towards Cornell." I nodded. Since I'm too capricious for commitments, his career should come before our relationship.

Friday, May 8, 1964: Park and Brahms

On a Riverside Park faded green bench with carvings like *David loves Emily*, Max and I basked in the heat, shared a turkey sandwich, and watched his pals scamper around a tennis court. Perturbed about Dr. G's slaying, I tried to avoid being obvious while warily scanning the park as we romped in the grass under a cloud-dappled sky. I silently enquired of a bird flying by: *did gang members kill the physics prof*?

At Pamela, Ltd. at 2949 Broadway, I bought a scoop-neck yellow top for only two-dollars.

Serenaded by William Steinberg and the Pittsburgh Orchestra playing Brahms *Symphony No. 4*, Max and I studied, cuddled, and kissed on his bouncy sofa. At the Barnard dorm, he gallantly bowed before presenting the record! I wrote a typically enthusiastic thank-you. He's admirably giving!

Saturday, May 9, 1964: Spring Carnival

Roof study preceded Columbia's carnival. I adore the stuffed bear, gray donkey, and peach lamb Max won! We joked with friends and laughed at *Il Troubleshootore*, an original student musical comedy, spoofing Westerns and operas.

Max's engaged friends drove us to a nondescript cocktail lounge near La Guardia Airport for close dancing. Imbibing a Singapore sling, I agreed when Max suggested, "After you cram tomorrow, let's have cheesecake at the Deli at 10 PM."

I passionately returned his luscious goodnight kiss as he held my shoulders and slightly moved my chest against his. An image of Max, age six, milking a lucky cow on his father's farm popped into my mind, as I breathed more audibly and felt ripples down there. Grateful for a late curfew, I floated into the dorm, signing in at 3:29 AM.

Sunday, May 10, 1964: Answering Cousin Ron

My letter mentioned the horrifying Prof Gallagher murder, Kitty Genovese Queens rape/killing, and Morningside Park gang rape keeping me on edge.

> Ron, with our nervous parents, do you feel trained to worry, as I do? Dad's unemployment and heart condition may make Barnard unaffordable. Dreading finals, I must study! Good luck on yours! Love, Angela

Monday, May 11, 1964: Chase

My heart pounded and I panted, as if from sprinting, awakening from this petrifying nightmare:

> On a rainy Manhattan night, a teen gang intent on rape and murder chases me through empty streets! No matter how fast I run, pursuers gain on me. Barnard's gate is locked! Seconds before being grabbed, I wake myself.

Criminals getting away with ruining women's lives make life unfair.

Tuesday, May 12, 1964: Yearbooks and Bill

Carina and I tittered at *Jester*, Columbia's humor magazine, before scanning Barnard's *Mortarboard* yearbook. "Angela, these candid Honeybear shots need names."

"I agree. As AHS assistant editor, I prefer my high school yearbook. I wonder if Honeybears in activities have time to keep up grades and date."

Over pie a la mode, Woodstock Bill, handsome in blue jeans and blue-and-green-striped, button-down shirt, said, "Grueling engineering classes require studying every weekend.

Let's see another opera this summer." Aware of his low finances, I agreed. Nestled in his strong embrace, I felt stirrings during our good-night kiss!

Wednesday, May 13, 1964: Boyfriends

Touched to tears by Yeats' gift, *Of Poetry and Power*, I read to Carina Robert Frost, W H Auden, and Allen Ginsburg poems about beloved JFK. I sent thanks before answering Mother's letter. She's eager for the World's Fair.

"Carina, this summer, I can't count on Max or Yeats."

"Frustrating!"

"I love Max as a faultless boyfriend, but is he the ideal husband who considers women equals? Will he support my career by doing half the housework and childrearing? If we went steady, not that he's asked, I could miss meeting Mr. Right."

Carina nodded. To dissipate exam jitters, we followed Pithy in an australopithecine trudge, swinging arms vigorously and voicing *Cheyahs*.

Thursday, May 14, 1964: Choices

After Latin, my final semester class, and a study session with Max, he said, in a dark booth at the Gold Rail, "College has been the best. I'm sad it's ending." His voice alternated from a soft tenor to a loud baritone, as his dilemma unfolded: how to maintain self-respect and enjoy work as an English Ph.D. without starving. Tender-hearted Max sounded mocking while lambasting himself for being allured by a lawyer's income.

"Max, your qualms about low demand for and pay of English professors make sense." We both grew up without enough money.

His face scrunched up. "Angela, I'm undecided about starting fresh at Cornell in a small-town *versus* staying in exciting NYC with some supportive Columbia faculty." His usual smooth tone sounded raspy.

Sipping a Singapore sling, I squeezed his hand and tried to calm him with a subject change. "Carina said that our beloved *Barbra Streisand Album* won best album and best album cover at the Grammys at Waldorf Astoria Hotel! At twenty-two, Barbra's the youngest to win album of the year. She can't win too many awards for us!"

"When she sings opera, maybe I'll appreciate her." I giggled. "Max, you've helped make sophomore year my best!" His thrilling kisses, holding my hands behind my back, left me happily breathless!

<u>Friday, May 15, 1964: Joyful Tizzy</u>

Planning what to wear tomorrow with Garth, Carina had the glow of anticipation! On a warm, sunny day, Max photographed us on a Barnard building ledge (above).

In my red wraparound skirt, I passed muster at Butler Library. I studied with Max, whose new short-sleeved, white shirt and gray slacks I complimented during lunch at the Somerset.

When he left to see his other girlfriend, three *benign vultures* swooped down. A physics grad student mourned brilliant Professor Gallagher. "Friendly and passionate about physics, Gallagher was from my hometown, Norwalk, and earned a University of Connecticut B.A. before grad work at Berkeley and Cal Tech. A NATO-National Science Foundation fellowship sent him to Copenhagen Institute of Theoretical Physics. What a waste of brains!" He sounded distraught. I regretted having to decline a date to resume studying.

Saturday, May 16, 1964: Irresistible
Sauntering through Riverside Park with radiant Carina and blue-eyed Garth, I noticed his generous, kissable mouth, a pleasant distraction from my apprehension in parks. Unlike a peacock, he blended in with inconspicuous, standard Ivy League attire.

For hours, Max and I studied on his cushy davenport. Our reward was bantering over white wine with Carina, Garth, her outgoing cousin, and the cousin's reserved housemate in their nearby, sparsely-furnished apartment. Garth mentioned continuing at Harvard for a Ph.D. in German.

Max remarked, "I respect noble scholars. Considering law school, I'm like the worst money-grubber." His self-ridicule generated chuckles

Later, I said, "Carina, Garth is irresistibly good-looking, sexy, debonair, and witty with a modest demeanor, brains, and acting talent!"

"He's too popular." Without her usual grin, she sighed.

"A harem's no fun! Pithy and I understand long-distance challenges."

I joined her in squawking *Cheyah*. Imitating Pithy's deep voice, I growled about exams. Inanity soon had us snickering.

Sunday, May 17, 1964: Model

Studying on the dorm roof, I lost my illusion that models are beautiful, like Carol Lynley. With sun-streaked hair and good cheekbones, the Barnard model's figure is average, three inches taller than my five foot five. Makeup must cover her acne scars.

Max and I played dorm ping pong and studied in his living room, as Brahms *Symphony No. 1* played. Giggling, I felt titillated when he demonstrated wrestling holds on me.

I mailed a Honeybear picture postcard, thanking Max for slipping the marvelous, invisibly defective George Szell-Cleveland Orchestra record we heard into my green book bag to surprise me. This summer, I will miss his loving presence.

Tuesday, May 19, 1964: Puppy

Yesterday, Mother (above) phoned, insisting on dropping by after her group's World's Fair visit. "You have to eat!"

"I dined at noon. Every minute counts." Unwilling to let her affect my history grade, I politely but firmly declined, resisting temptation to rudely hang up on her strident voice.

Today after quick ping pong, I shared, "Max, I survived yesterday's social structure and personality test and Dr. Woodbridge's history final today."

"Here's your reward!" His broad smile was warm. "Thank you for this darling blue-and-white Columbia dog!" *Worry-Wart* on the collar made me chuckle. Max's enticing good-bye kiss spurred on more cramming.

Thursday, May 21, 1964: Shopping
Past yesterday's Latin exam and today's social psychology final, I exhaled after holding my breath, seemingly for days. Emitting giant sighs of liberation, I helped Max choose a gray suit, shorts, and sneakers. For the prom, I bought a two-dollar, white-beaded bag; one-dollar, plum-colored lipstick; and six-dollar white heels: size 7AA sling-backs.

At Paradise Oriental Greek Restaurant, our friendly waiter, long-nosed and compactly built, said, "That gentleman sent this red wine with his compliments." We gratefully lifted our goblets and smiled at the well-preserved, older man.

Savoring shish kebob, we split baklava before stopping at the gray-haired gentleman's table. Max said, "We appreciate the wine!"

His smile revealed a gold upper molar. "Romantic couples warm my heart. In the 1930s, I courted my wife before we lived happily ever after. She died last year." He thanked us for condolences before saying, "Run along and enjoy yourselves!"

At Barnard, ping pong and exhilarating kisses counteracted tension about one remaining exam. Max's sensual mouth was irresistible, as he clasped me tightly.

Sunday, May 24, 1964: Speculation
"How was your weekend?" Carina asked.

"Bad dreams about the dashing, dead physicist have made me wonder if he visited the secluded Ramble for secret sex with men."

"Columbia's *Spectator* wrote that homosexuals frequent that area, which has a history of violence. As a birdwatcher, maybe he was studying night owls." We giggled.

"Carina, the murder was the latest pick-up line yesterday at stately Butler and today at the crowded law library. Grad students started conversations by asking my opinion. I regretted that exams prevented my accepting coffee dates. Both evenings at Max's were study sessions."

"Silence from Garth kept me studying despite beautiful, warm weather." Wishing I could kidnap Garth to NYC, I shook my head helplessly.

I answered Yeats' note about the murder mystery. I'm thankful for *A Minus* on the social structure and personality final and *B Plus* for the course. Calling home, I felt my smile fade, hearing that Dad is still chubby and without work.

Monday, May 25, 1964: Statue

My sociology final preceded downtown shopping. With a big smile, Max thanked me for my graduation present: a satiny wood statue of lovers entwined. I breathed a sigh of relief that my dwindled allowance sufficed.

Seeing *Tom Jones* again, we relished the famous eating scene. A poster noted five *best film* awards, including the 1964 Oscar."

Tuesday, May 26, 1964: Busy

I hugged my roomie, off to a Midwest Jewish overnight camp. "Carina, you'll be a great counselor! I'll miss you! Love to your parents!"

Max cheerfully helped my parents and me load our jalopy. "Mother and Dad, thanks for taking my belongings home and bringing this envelope with *B* for the history final and the course!" The inquisitive folks lingered. Relentless Mother typically embarrassed me by interrogating Max about school and family. He barely answered one question before she doggedly fired another. Parental 1 PM departure to reach home before rush hour was a relief.

At an overflowing, used bookstore, Gide's *The Immoralist* for an autumn philosophy class and Mauriac's *Desert of Love* for fun were bargains at under a dollar for both.

Green Tree Hungarian Restaurant served Max and me tasty goulash before an excellent Italian movie, *The Organizer*, with charming Marcello Mastroianni. My skimpy summer top facilitated Max's stimulating shoulder and upper chest caresses. Trusting him to keep clothing in place and respectfully avoid private areas, I lost myself in disciplined pleasure before he dropped me at my friend's NYC apartment.

<u>Wednesday, May 27, 1964: Frankie</u>
Using a World's Fair postcard and stamp (above) from my parents, I thanked them again for driving to NYC and added:

> Viewing Medieval art at the monastic Cloisters
> in north Manhattan, Max and I ran into our
> rabbi's son on an arched, columned walkway.
> Though still a smoker, Frankie is past giving grief
> as an almost JD (juvenile delinquent), swearing
> and getting kicked out of seventh-grade classes.
> At Yeshiva University, he plans to be a rabbi. As
> at his Bar Mitzvah, a conservative crew cut has
> replaced his long, greasy DA (duck's ass) hairdo!

At the downtown branch of V and T, Max and I shared pizza and a delish *cannoli* pastry. In his nondescript living room, the three housemates chuckled while answering my *Glamour* magazine quiz, including: *would you rather have a mate who's much smarter than you or less smart*? I snickered when they shifted positions, uncomfortable about admitting wanting to be smarter. I answered, "I want a brainier mate."

Asked whether they follow their hearts or heads in choosing romantic partners, the ill-at-ease pre-meds hesitated and looked at each other for rescue before saying, "Both." I recalled jokes about the brain between their legs irrationally ruling males. I stifled titters at my mental image: a giant penis dragging its tiny attached owner away from his average brunette wife and towards a Marilyn Monroe type he ogled.

Thursday, May 28, 1964: Fair

Coincidentally both dressed in dark Bermuda shorts and white summer shirts, Max and I noshed on bagels before subwaying to Flushing Meadows. "Angela, *Peace through Understanding* is a commendable World's Fair theme. The giant, stainless-steel Unisphere globe of the earth near almost a hundred fountains is jaw-dropping (above behind Mother and on stamp)."

At Max's maternal Aunt Sylvia's nearby apartment, the old-fashioned mahogany dining room table and Hepplewhite chairs with plush burgundy seats resembled the furniture of Dad's sisters. Sylvia's matronly figure and conservative, brown-crepe dress contrasted with her upbeat, youthful voice. "Max, what did you like best at the Fair?"

Done chewing a bite of beef brisket, Max put down his fork and answered without hesitation. "A vacation resort underwater in the ocean, vehicle traffic on an exact replica of the moon's surface, an Antarctic weather station in a deep hole in the ice, and a completely mechanized desert farm, irrigated by desalinated ocean water! On a weekday, we were free of crowds. There for hours, we only scratched the surface. I wanted more time at the science and computer exhibits. Angela was keen on General Motors' *Futurama*."

His aunt's hazel eyes sparkled when I added, "I adored the sleek, sporty future cars. Our moving chairs glided past realistic miniatures of future life. Everything seemed extremely imaginative!"

On Max's beige couch, a whiff of his after-shave lotion made my eyes close. Arousing kisses and caresses of neck, arms, and shoulders capped a special day of novel sights and activities!

Friday, May 29, 1964: Shakespeare
Morning basketball with Max and housemates included paroxysms of laughter. Without practice since 1958, I was pleased to sink some baskets.

After lunch, I got up my nerve, buying three pink carnations and subwaying south with this letter:

> Dearest Sara, less than three miles away since 1962, I've missed you and longed for our heartwarming conversations. I wish I could redo my age-thirteen failure to back you after the attack. Though too confused to think straight

and understand such adult matters, I can't
excuse myself from hurting my favorite family
member, you, the only one who supported me
at family meetings and with hostile parents. I
will always love you and be grateful. Please
accept this early birthday gift (I'm returning to
Albany soon) and peace offering. Going through
life without you leaves an empty hole in my
heart. Love forever!

My heart leaped with hope after the doorman alerted Sara. I
rode the rickety elevator to her apartment where she waited at
the open door, looking youthful. When I handed her the letter
and flowers, she held up her palms. Her rough voice was
hostile. "I want no contact with you, your parents, or the rest
of the family. Don't bother me again." The door slammed in my
face. The wall stopped my keeling over in flabbergasted shock.
Leaning the flowers against the door and slipping the letter
under it, I stumbled off. More pessimistic than ever, I'm
frightened of never reconnecting with bitterly resentful Sara.

A Somerset dinner and Shakespeare's magnificent *King
Lear* at the NY State Theater with Max and another couple
provided diversion from today's ordeal and ongoing concern
about Dad's unemployment and survival. Over pastrami-on-rye
sandwiches at a Sixth Avenue delicatessen, the four of us joked
and guffawed until the wee hours, loving summer freedom
sans curfews.

Saturday, May 30, 1964: Decoration Day

On a cool but sunny holiday, Max and I joined two couples on
the university shuttle bus to the senior class picnic. Near the
Hudson River in Harriman, NY, Columbia's Arden Estate was
idyllic. While the guys played ball, we gals ambled, expressing
sorrow and trepidation about Dr. G's unsolved mid-April
murder. Dinner was routine: hamburgers and Orange Crush
soda, with a butter-pecan ice-cream stop on the way home.

Alone with Max, I noticed his jaw grinding a little while he voiced vacillating feelings about career options. "Angela, enough! How are you?"

"My parents called with good news: Latin: *B* on the final and *A Minus* for the course; social psychology: *B Plus* in both." I skipped the Sara trauma, which magical kisses and heavenly caresses displaced from mind as I touched his broad shoulders.

Sunday, May 31, 1964: Baseball
At new Shea Stadium in Flushing Meadows Park in Queens, Max and I relaxed outdoors. A sell-out crowd (55,000) saw the San Francisco Giants beat the Mets, 5-3.

Venezia Restaurant, painted green, white, and scarlet like the Italian tricolor, served delish veal parmigiana. "Max, I'll write Cousin Hal in San Francisco about seeing star Willie Mays play for the Giants! We were brainwashed to be Yankee fans."

Leaving his apartment for the last time, Max choked up. Two friends with cars full of his records, books, and clothes moved everything to his Aunt Sylvia's place. Max is lucky that his mother's ocean liner chief-bartender brother got Max summer work as a ship steward.

I admire his aunt for kindly sharing her Washington Heights NYC apartment with Max and his parents for years in the early 1950s when their upstate NY farm failed after two years. Never married, his aunt was already taking care of her crotchety mother. Does she have twinges of regret for staying single?

During an evening word association game with Max and his driver pals, one guy, hearing the word *woman*, blurted out, "Sex," before he could censor himself. His beet-red face produced irrepressible, prolonged laughter. Vacation is a blast!

Monday, June 1, 1964: Prom
Drizzle forced us indoors for Columbia College's class day at Uris Hall. In the shabby basement gymnasium, students received awards and an alumnus' speech was inspiring.

Rosenblum's turkey sandwiches with delish dill pickles and sour tomatoes, cookies, and ginger ale, fortified Max and me for clothes shopping.

The splendid prom (above) included Max's two gorgeous pink cymbidium orchids! He looked his best in rented formal wear. My old, silky dress over my new Lilyette size 32C strapless bra was comfy for care-free, starry-eyed dancing among scores of celebrants!

After the dance on a cool evening, clouds shrouded moonlight and stars during our romantic Central Park taxi ride. "Max, this is better than a buggy and horse needing a bath and deodorant!" He chuckled.

"Angela, after we left Shea yesterday, the second game began at 4PM. We missed the longest double-header and longest National League game in baseball history. Tied 6-6, the Giants took thirty-two innings to beat us, 8-6 at 11:30."

"Max, did thousands doze off and snore in the dark during those run-less hours?" Seeing him laugh was fun.

Remembering Jimmie Rodgers' 1950s hit song while sipping from a flask, I whispered, "Your kisses are sweeter than this wine."

"Thanks, but Dad's wine is dry." I giggled before yielding to delicious canoodling!

Tuesday, June 2, 1964: 210th Commencement

Wearing yesterday's wrist corsage and my A-line dress (above), I sat with Max's mother, dressed in medium blue, and his aunt, wearing eggplant purple, at Max's inspiring graduation. The petite sisters wore similar silky sheaths with matching jackets. Their short, teased auburn waves stayed in place despite a brisk afternoon breeze. Continually showing her pixie smile, Max's mom glowed with pride in her only child.

Over 6200 graduates in various university schools received diplomas; twice as many guests sat around us! The spiffed-up campus showed off newly planted flowers, trimmed hedges, and pretty bunting in Columbia blue.

I teared up when aristocratic Dean Truman aptly alluded to JFK's assassination as offering "a bitterly challenging opportunity to ask of yourself some questions of purpose and of value that otherwise would have lacked the insistence of reality and would have had the relevance of little more than conjecture." What a thrill it would have been if JFK were alive and gave an inspiring oration at this ceremony!

Was concern about Dr. G's unsolved murder on the mind of the Scarsdale, NY, physics-major valedictorian? Praising the liberal arts in a high-pitched voice, he wisely noted that technological advances "have not taught us how to make ethical considerations and how to organize our lives." I agreed with the diminutive Bronx, chemistry-major salutatorian's open-minded remark: "No man's way of living is the right way."

Seeing industrious Max in cap and gown receive his Columbia College diploma left us emotional.

Photos preceded dinner at Rosenblum's, where I heard more about Max's family. Extraverted Sylvia reminisced about speaking Quebec French during childhood!

When she mentioned three brothers, I shared, "My mother's immigrant family from Russian-occupied Lithuania also had two girls and three boys."

Max said, "My maternal grandma rejected me for resembling my flamboyant, green-eyed father, whom she disliked." Did an unpleasant mother make Max's mother quiet and restrained? Max and I both had daunting maternal grandmothers.

As we ate *kishke* (Yiddish for stuffed derma), Max asked, "Angela, do you like derma?"

"The spicy meat, grain, and fat filling is flavorful."

"You're okay with the wrapping?" Max looked mischievous. When I raised my brows, he added, "Eating intestines?"

Almost nauseated, I clutched my throat. Max, who could hardly keep a straight face, finished my derma. Ugh!

Later, I wrote to Carina, omitting the upsetting Sara visit:

> Calming baseball is less exciting than football. Even as the rare female who likes sports, I'm glad I attended only the first quick game. The typical wife, dragged to the second game and expecting three hours, must have suffered from terminal boredom for over seven hours. Even moving Max's belongings was better!

<u>Wednesday, June 3, 1964: Farewell</u>

After hugs, Max and I helped his sweetly smiling mom board the Port Authority bus to South Cairo. Max and I lunched at nearby Paradise Oriental Greek Restaurant before the film *Becket*. The phenomenal acting of Richard Burton and sexy Peter O'Toole made it equally absorbing the second time. I've rarely heard Max talk as glowingly about a movie.

Parting, I said, "Thank you for this unforgettable nine-day vacation with so many fabulous activities!"

"Angela, I'm sad that these halcyon days are over." Though perkier lately, I caught him moodily staring off into space. He admitted that his contemplations have left him ambivalent. "Angela, I hope that summer at home and sailing confirm Columbia for grad school."

Breaking off passionate kissing was wrenching. In my mind, Johnny Mathis sang the Erroll Garner/Johnny Burke hit *Misty*, from his *Heavenly* album.

Max's choosing Cornell would likely end our relationship. No more long distance! Poor Carina, pining away for Garth for months, as I longed for Kevin in 1963! I need a boyfriend I can count on to be present with me daily, as Max has been until now.

1964 Albany Summer

We are slow to believe that which if believed would hurt our feelings.

Metamorphoses by Ovid in Latin

Thursday, June 4, 1964: Tumba and Sara

Through the oversized Trailways bus window, the emerald Hudson River valley almost gleamed. Its tranquility failed to stop trickling tears, as my revered aunt's unforgiving words echoed in my head. I'm overwhelmed trying to reconcile the paradox of Sara's brutal response with thirteen years of loving behavior. I sympathize when bourgeois family conformity pressure drives away misunderstood artists, but Grandma and other relatives supported Sara financially. How do I manage without seeing her again? Can time soften her ire?

At home on a cool, windy day, I greeted Tumba (below).

"Pretty bird! At ten, you look as young as ever! Did you know this Barnard envelope revealed an *A Minus* in sociology?"

Sitting on my finger, my parakeet jabbered. Only an occasional word was comprehensible. "Tumba, I missed you." A gift from Sara, he's named after *Tumba La Laika*, a Yiddish song she performed.

"Mother, recent calls to Dad's sisters went well." Steeling myself, I described visiting Sara. "Her icy words may intimidate me from trying again."

Mother sighed deeply. Her mouth drooped. "My only sister must still be furious to reject all family for five years." Her usually energetic voice sounded listless.

Without ever hearing Mother apologize to anyone, I wished she felt remorse but diplomatically shunned reproaches. I wrote *Paradox*, a haiku:

> Big, brown teen eyes stare
> Into the mirror, looking
> Old and so weary

Before taking Burke to drive golf balls, Yeats, passionate about politics, praised the Supreme Court ruling that closing schools to elude desegregation is unconstitutional! He lifted my sagging spirits.

<u>Friday, June 5, 1964: Guest</u>
Wearing tan chinos and a blue striped shirt, Max arrived by bus from South Cairo. A cool, breezy Washington Park meander preceded a pleasant roast-chicken dinner with my parents.

At the Delaware Theater, *Family Diary,* a poignant psychological movie about two brothers, included Marcello Mastroianni's notable performance. At Aunt Jemima's, we split a waffle with apple slices a la mode. I drove our elderly sedan to the romantic Thacher Park lookout to gaze at distant Albany lights. Kisses of my mouth and bare shoulders were breathtaking. Back home, he slept on our lumpy, old couch.

<u>Saturday, June 6, 1964: Cascade</u>
I drove Max almost thirty miles southwest to the charming hamlet of Rensselaerville for a ramble in the woods. The narrow waterfall burbled happily, watching us kiss ardently in misty drizzle with bodies pressed together.

At home, I made a candlelit dinner for four. "Angela, this juicy, medium-rare steak hits the spot," said Max, as Bruno Walter's Beethoven *Symphonies No. 4 and No. 5* played.

"Max, thanks for the Columbia Symphony Orchestra record and your father's delish wine! Does he still create metal artworks?" This got the attention of my artistic mother.

"Yes! My favorite is a wall sculpture of three graceful ballerinas. Dad has mellowed since his revolutionary youth."

At Scrabble, English major Max easily trounced us three before he and I viewed a late showing of *Cleopatra* at the elegant Hellman Theater. "Angela, was Elizabeth Taylor regal enough?"

"She was convincing. Seeing ancient Romans I've read about in Latin classes, like Julius Caesar (Rex Harrison) and Marc Antony (talented Richard Burton), interact was fun."

<u>Sunday, June 7, 1964: Reply</u>
I thanked Carina for her camp update:

> Good luck with your dynamic guy! Have the fun you deserve! To cap a cheerful Albany weekend with amusing Max, my parents and I drove him home and lunched with his parents today.
>
> His robust father, who seems younger than seventy-seven, is a character. In the garden, he joked, "My vegetables are similar."
>
> With a straight face, Max explained, "He prefers cucumbers and zucchini squash."

Grinning, his dad responded, "I'd like to grow bananas." I controlled a titter until my parents got the joke and chuckled.

Carina, you'd love his dad's spectacular metal artworks! Without a high school diploma, he earned a tuition-free, metallurgy master's degree from impressive Cooper Union!

Max's reserved, petite mother grows roses with intoxicating fragrances. Our praise of her tasty chicken salad with garden greens and mixed vegetables elicited a shy smile. When asked, Max once disclosed that his reader mother is the more intellectual parent. Does she feel trapped with a domineering, old-fashioned mate, as I would? As a husband, will Max unconsciously mimic his dad's behavior? Will he always obnoxiously have to be right and have the last word?

In Albany, Dad commented, "Gentleman Max is smart, comes from a nice family, and seems to care about you. Most important: he's Jewish." My eyes rolled in disgust about religion outweighing personality, sense of humor, compatibility, intelligence, etc.

Mother's gaze seemed penetrating. "What does meeting his family mean?"

"Nothing. We aren't going steady."

"You're too young to settle down." Agreeing with Mother is rare! Haha! She added, "Max and Marcus have similar blond hair. Is Marcus home?" I suppressed a laugh about her unsubtle campaign for taller, unamusing Marcus as the perfect son-in-law.

Frowning, Dad exclaimed, "Fern, what difference does blond hair make?"

"Herm, you made me forget that I liked blue eyes." I snickered.

With the minimum wage at one dollar an hour, I'm grateful for $1.25 at the NY State Insurance Department. Henry Root Stern, a trial attorney, is the new commissioner. Love, Angela

Monday, June 8, 1964: Friends

At the synagogue mother-daughter dinner, we sat with Mother's friend Evelyn, accompanied by still-diffident daughter Robin, an AHS senior headed for college.

Sweet-faced, happier Doreen plans to major in sociology at Albany State. Mellow Tara, following in her social worker sister's footsteps, raved about Syracuse University. Despite bitterly cold winters, giggly future teacher Marsha sounded content at State University at Buffalo. All want jobs in traditional female fields and marriage with offspring, unlike trail-blazer Eva. I'm sad that her family killed her attorney career dream.

At Schade's, Yeats bowled smoothly: 124 and 176 vs. my 75 and 88! "Yeats, though I never practice, shouldn't my scores be better than my first games in junior high?" Smiling, he put his arm around me and kissed my cheek.

Over a drink at the Trailways bus terminal cocktail lounge, Yeats sounded optimistic. "Africa's future seems promising with Kenya now a republic with an elected president!" At beloved Mike's Log Cabin, we savored dancing, including the jitterbug *Heat Wave*.

Tuesday, June 9, 1964: Socializing

After seeing an Art Institute exhibit of local, contemporary paintings with Mother, I stamped my reply to an amusing letter from Max before Kevin rang the bell, startling me. "Kevin, I'm rushing to be ready for a date." His departure was a relief.

At Mike's, four of us shared antipasto. Yeats' Boston pal boomed, "What a cool hangout! Just call me Abe Lincoln!"

His date and I laughed as Yeats exaggerated a prideful puff-up. After a sip of dark beer, Yeats said, "At BU (Boston University), an administrator asked, 'How about visiting Europe for an experiment in international living? Philanthropist Margaret Scattergood, a Washington, DC senior citizen, will sponsor you if you mail weekly letters about your experiences.' Leaping at the opportunity for two months of free, mainly Scandinavian travel, I applied! Final approval arrived today!"

We congratulated Yeats. "Was the competition fierce?" I asked.

"Thank you! I have no idea who applied." When his friends left to drive to Boston, Yeats and I danced and shared a Singapore sling, a sixty-cent bargain if it weren't watery.

I was elated when Craig asked me to dance. "Craig, thanks for last night's message! I adore hearing from Fred

Astaire!" Happy at Hamilton College, he's on track to be a lawyer. We briefly bantered with pretty, blushing Tara and her crush since 1957. I'm glad they're finally dating!

Wednesday, June 10, 1964: Birthday
"Happy birthday to Yeats," my parents, Burke, and I sang before Yeats blew out twenty-two candles (one for good luck).

As we downed chocolate cake with orange sherbet, Yeats sounded sincere. "Angela, thanks for making juicy steak with mushroom sauce, salad, French fries, garlic bread, and cake! Burke, thank you for tasty champagne!"

During a cool, breezy ride around Albany's suburbs in Burke's yellow convertible, Yeats spoke excitedly. "Senate Minority Leader Everett Dirksen finally effected cloture to support civil rights legislation after 534 hours of filibuster over four months!"

Burke's tone was fervent. "I admire Dirksen's support of equal opportunity in government, employment, and education. Only 12,000 of three million Negro students in the South attend integrated schools. Negro life expectancy is seven years lower and infant mortality is twice as high. Author Victor Hugo wrote: *Stronger than all the armies is an idea whose time has come.*"

Burke and Yeats grinned at my jest: "Yeats, you must be well-known for Dirksen to stop filibustering for your birthday."

Thursday, June 11, 1964: Jag
My first ride in a Jaguar was for a Howard Johnson's cheeseburger and vanilla milkshake with lovable Jake. At Caffe Lena in Saratoga Springs, he said, "Unfortunately, folk singer Gil Robbins won't perform until tomorrow. Before he was in The Highwaymen folk band, I liked their hit record, *Michael, Row the Boat Ashore*. Robbins has written songs, sung baritone, and played the large, six-string guitarron."

I laughed at another Pope John joke: a cardinal complained that a Vatican usher earned as much as he. The Pope replied, "That usher has ten children; does the cardinal?"

Back from the ladies' room, I heard, "Your blue-and-white-dot dress is becoming!" Did his look convey longing?

"Thank you!" I pictured my other new size-9 dress.

"Angela, is that your worried, AHS pre-exam look?"

I couldn't help smiling. "Still overdoing desserts, Dad is ill with heart trouble. Though he's annoying, I don't want him to suffer or die at fifty-three."

"Following doctor's orders can keep him alive without a heart attack for years." I hope Jake's right.

Sunday, June 14, 1964: To Carina
Sitting on a chaise lounge in our sunny, warm backyard, I wrote:

> Kudos on your camp romance! Does he see
> women as equals? Will he share domestic tasks?
> Friday, Yeats, soon off to Europe, drove
> me to his Boston apartment. You and Pithy
> would have enjoyed our silly bubble-blowing
> before an art show. Garth likely enjoyed Joe
> Tecce's jovial café atmosphere and huge
> antipasti plate at 61 North Washington Street, in
> the North End. I stayed with Yeats' female pal.
> Saturday, a garage fixed a flat tire
> before we happily swam in the Atlantic. North of
> Boston, Crane Beach has beautiful sand dunes.
> In Cambridge, Wursthaus shrimp cocktails and
> sandwiches were yummy.
> Today, artworks in the park preceded
> delish scallops at English Room at 29 Newbury.
> In Albany, we dined at my house before
> award-winning *My Name Is Ivan*, a Russian
> subtitled movie about a World War II orphan.

Adolescent female antics in Peter Sellers'
comedy, *World of Henry Orient*, amused me.

<u>Wednesday, June 17, 1964: Busy</u>
At our U-shaped, red Formica breakfast bar, Mother handed
me a photo (below). "You look like Sara at your age." Sara was
prettier. Afraid to send her birthday greetings, I understand her
rejecting my parents because I feel the same! To be lumped
with them feels cruel. But I can't worm out of taking blame for
letting Sara down. Being a bemused teen is no excuse to her.
No one guarantees life will be easy or feel fair. At least, my job
and social life limit rumination.

When Max called, I thanked him for three letters and
reassurance about Dad. "Angela, my dad has lived for decades
with heart trouble."
Eating cheese pizza at the drive-in, Yeats and I watched
entrancing Paul Newman in a *Hud* rerun. My flood of tears
during Sidney Poitier's Oscar-best-actor role in *Lilies of the
Field* interfered with smooching.

<u>Thursday, June 18, 1964: Dad</u>
"Burke, Dad's a little better. Will he exercise and give up
Danish pastry and ice cream to lose weight?"

"My father with heart trouble cheats on his diet and is still overweight. Golfing's not enough exercise."

"Barnard counts on me to keep its supply of mint-chocolate-chip ice cream from going bad." Burke sniggered.

<u>Sunday, June 21, 1964: Answering Carina</u>
Enjoying heat topping ninety degrees, I wrote:

> Congrats on finding the uncommon boyfriend who treats women as equally smart and competent as men!
>
> Albany's too small. Hurting kind Yeats upsets me. Tuesday, he saw me playing pool while giggling at Jake's wit.
>
> Have the police found Gallagher's killer? Am I safe walking through Washington Park to work? Despite nightmares, I prefer NYC's anonymity. I'd have anxiety dreams about Dad's health and unemployment anywhere.
>
> On my favorite day of the year, I'm eager to date charming Lee and rugged Bill. Jake and Yeats have kept me from missing Max more.
>
> Fear of being taken for granted keeps me uninterested in marriage. If forced to wed, I'd accept romantic Max, who misses me, but may be long-distance at Cornell. Always amused, in awe of his knowledge and brilliance, adoring his protectiveness and generosity, I might be happy if he did half the housework. Haha!
>
> In a dream about our upcoming office picnic, a handsome co-worker's dynamite smile dazzled me! Is new romance coming? I cherish every boy-crazy minute of teen freedom and fun! Love, Angela

THE END

CHARACTERS
MOTHER'S FAMILY

1875-1946: Grandpa C born near Vilna (now Lithuania)
1880-1960: Grandma C born near Minsk (now Belarus)
1898: marriage
1900: emigration to NYC; later to Gloversville, NY
1903: Uncle Abner born
    Married Rosa, later divorced
        1932 red-haired Beth born
            1953 marriage
            1955 June born Long Island, NY
            1957 widowed; remarried in Albany
            1958 Jill born
            1960 son born
      1944 Gloversville marriage to Myrna
        1946 Lydia born
        1949 Ella born
1905: Uncle Peter born
    Gloversville marriage to Faith
        1927 Nick born
            1953 marriage Gloversville
            1954 & 1955 sons born
            1960 daughter born
1907-1946: Uncle Isaac, never married, no children
1912: Angela's Mom Fern born Gloversville
      1937 Albany marriage to Herm
        1940 Rowena stillborn Northville, NY
        1945 Angela born Albany
        7/3/54 pet parakeet Tumba arrived
1917: Aunt Sara born Gloversville
      1940-1947 Albany marriage & divorce George
      1948-1951 Spring Valley marriage & divorce Jules

FATHER'S FAMILY

1876-1947: Grandpa Weiss born Ukraine
1878-1954: Grandma born Ukraine
1898: marriage
1900: emigration to NYC
1901-1954: Aunt Hannah
    1925 NYC marriage to Cal
        1928 Justine born
            1950 marriage NYC
            1953 Herbie born
            1958 Angelina born
1903: Aunt Rhoda born
    1933 NYC marriage to Harvey 1900-1960
1908: Aunt Lila born
    1933 NYC marriage to Bert
        1938 Hal born
            1962: NYC marriage to Eileen
        1945 Ron born
1911: Angela's Dad Herm born
    1937 Albany marriage to Fern
        1940 Rowena stillborn Northville, NY
        1945 Angela born Albany
        7/3/54 pet parakeet Tumba arrived

MALES IN ANGELA'S LIFE

Name	First Mentioned	Description
Artie	2/2/57	Albany heartthrob
Barry	10/24/62	Columbia student
Benson	2/13/64	Columbia dental resident
Bill	5/22/63	Columbia engineering student
Burke	11/10/63	Parents' boarder in Albany
Craig	9/17/58	*Fred Astaire*, AHS class president
Cullin	2/4/63	Columbia College student
Den	1/13/63	Columbia engineering student
Dominic	9/29/59	AHS & beyond crush
Donald	7/20/58	Catskill romance & pen pal
Dr. K	10/8/62	English prof
Dr. W	5/9/64	History prof
Frankie	1/1/57	Rabbi's son
Garth	10/20/63	Carina's Harvard boyfriend
Gary	10/22/62	Cousin Ron's Columbia friend
Grady	2/4/63	Columbia student
Gus	10/23/63	Columbia sophisticated student
Hank	9/13/58	AHS brainy crush
Harris	10/23/63	Gary's former roommate
Henri	2/19/64	Columbia student from Haiti
Herbie	12/16/63	Columbia student
Hy	9/25/62	Columbia boyfriend
Jake	10/1/60	AHS and beyond crush
Jed	8/29/60	Albany date from Milne School
Jerry	6/24/61	1961 AHS prom date
Jim	9/9/63	1963 AHS graduate
Joe	8/17/58	Pen pal & NYC date
Karl	7/15/54	Dad's friend
Keat	2/5/64	Columbia medical student
Kevin	11/ 21/62	Albany boyfriend
Lee	3/25/61	AHS & beyond crush
Lowell	3/18/64	Columbia student
Luke	9/3/58	AHS boyfriend
Marcus	2/3/56	First date & classmate

Max	9/25/63	Columbia boyfriend
Mr. B	8/7/61	Albany speedreading teacher
Mr. R	8/7/61	Albany speedreading teacher
Oren	4/15/57	Son of parents' friends
Paul	11/9/53	Albany heartthrob since 4th grade
Pete	12/14/62	Columbia student
Pithy	11/11/62	Imaginary dorm room mascot
Ray	09/24/63	Columbia student
Ric	6/8/62	Albany friend & Kevin's pal
Spanky	12/19/62	Brooklyn date
Spike	9/22/62	Columbia student
Stu	1/10/59	Gloversville distant cousin
Tad	3/1950	Husband at age five
Triplets	9/23/62	Zed, Ted, Ned AEPi Columbia
Udeh	1/6/57	Classmate
Yeats	10/26/59	AHS & college boyfriend

FEMALES IN ANGELA'S LIFE

Name	**First Mentioned**	**Description**
Alice	12/26/60	Junior high classmate
Carina	9/19/62	Barnard roommate & close friend
Doreen	9/28/54	Albany close friend
Eva	12/13/58	Albany dear friend
Evelyn	4/16/57	Mom's friend, Karl's wife
Henrietta	5/29/61	AHS class secretary & friend
Dr. C	10/10/63	Psychology prof
Dr. E	10/4/62	Calculus prof
Dr. K	11/8/63	Sociology prof
Dr. L	9/22/62	Latin prof & mentor
Marsha	10/13/54	AHS friend
Mista	12/5/61	AHS Norway exchange student
Rina	2/6/64	Max's high school friend
Robin	4/16/57	Evelyn & Karl's daughter
Sylvia	5/28/64	Max's maternal aunt in Queens
Tara	10/14/51	AHS close friend

ACKNOWLEDGEMENTS

Boy Crazy at Barnard College: 1962-1964 is a work of coming-of-age, historical fiction, inspired by friends and cousins to whom the author is grateful for kindly approving use of photos, artwork, writings, and memories. Actions, dialogue, and qualities of the characters are products of the author's imagination.

The author holds the copyright to most of the photographs, including cover photos. Others are in the public domain, e.g., yearbook photos, or under Creative Commons Zero, which allows use and modification of photos for free, including commercial purposes, without permission from or attribution to the photographer.

Government officials' speeches quoted are in the public domain. A paid license provides permission to quote speeches of Dr. Martin Luther King, Jr.

As cover creator, the author is grateful for design assistance from talented architect/designer Kevin Canes.

The author thanks the Greater Los Angeles Area Mensa Writers' Group, especially Alan and Greg, for invaluable feedback and assistance.

Special appreciation goes to Alice, Barbra, Bela, Carina, Charm, Ginny, Max, Milt, Ric, Susan, Teresa, and Wayne!

Special thanks go to George V, for his father's photo.

AUTHOR

With a master's degree in psychology, Angela Weiss has enjoyed diverse careers, including writer.

Boy Crazy at Barnard College: 1962-1964, based on her college journals, is the final book in the *Boy Crazy* trilogy.

In 2015, *Boy Crazy: The Secret Life of a 1950s Girl* was published, followed by *Boy Crazy 1960-1962: The High School Diary* in 2018.

Still a bit boy crazy, Angela appreciates intellectual, outdoor, athletic, and cultural activities in Los Angeles.